Girl Wonder

Girl Wonder

ALEXA MARTIN

HYPERION
NEW YORK

First Edition
1 3 5 7 9 10 8 6 4 2
V567-9638-5-11046
Printed in the United States of America

ISBN 978-1-4231-2135-0

Reinforced binding

Visit www.hyperionteens.com

SUSTAINABLE FORESTRY INITIATIVE
Certified Fiber Sourcing
www.sfiprogram.org

THIS LABEL APPLIES TO TEXT STOCK

For Connie Martin, the best mother and cheerleader a girl could ever have. You taught me the importance of having dreams. Thanks for never letting me quit, and for carrying me through the hardest parts.

And for Larry Martin, my father, a brilliant story-teller who read to me often when I was a little girl. Your Oscar-worthy character voices helped me to internalize the rhythm of language, and when I started to read, the words became movies in my mind.

PROLOGUE

My best friend Kara and I were at the top of an old oak, scouting the land for intruders (intruders being our fellow classmates or teachers who would nail us for breaking the no-tree-climbing rule). We were playing our favorite game, Sarah and Jessie. Sarah and Jessie were two little orphan girls who lived out in the wilderness. They were tough and self-sufficient and knew the ways of the woods and the mountains. They could make fire from rocks and twigs. They knew which plants to eat and which ones had medicinal properties. They understood the language of animals.

Sarah and Jessie didn't need adults. They didn't need anyone because they had each other. Theirs was a friendship that could overcome any odds.

Kara and I had invented the game in the first grade, after our teacher had read us *The Boxcar Children*, a book about four kids who run away from an orphanage and end up living in an abandoned train car.

"We're getting too old for this," we told each other every time we played Sarah and Jessie. We were ten years old, after all. Make-believe was for babies. But it was simply too exhilarating to quit.

"Incoming!" Kara (Sarah) shouted. "Abandon ship!"

A teacher's aide was walking briskly toward us. We scrambled down quickly—we knew every branch of this tree by heart. Our feet touched the ground just in time.

"Your mother's here, Charlotte," the teacher's aide said to me (Jessie).

Kara frowned and brushed her bangs out of her face. "Where are you going?"

"Doctor's appointment," I muttered.

This wasn't exactly a lie. The school psychologist's name was Dr. Lattimer. My mom was waiting for me by the jungle gym. She told me my dad was on his way. Because of the lump in my throat, I could only nod.

The waiting room of the psychologist's office was cold and silent, save for the soft burble of a fish aquarium. The receptionist glanced up. "Have a seat. She'll be just a minute."

Mom and I sat down. Listlessly, I flipped through a *National Geographic*, looking at pictures of exotic moths. Mom patted my knee reassuringly. "You have nothing to be worried about."

"Then why am I here?" I blurted.

At that moment, the psychologist called us into her office. "Hello, Charlotte," she said, motioning for me to sit down. "It's nice to see you again."

I didn't return the compliment. The week before, because of some *inconsistencies* on my fourth grade standardized test scores, I'd had to spend an entire day with this woman. She'd run me through a bunch of tests, many of which seemed random and weird, most of which made my head spin—especially the math parts.

"Just answer as best you can," she told me repeatedly throughout the day. "This isn't something you're being graded on. We're using the tests to gather information so that we can better help you."

I needed *help?*

Today we were going to go over the psychologist's findings.

There was a knock on the door. It was my dad.

"Sorry I'm late," he said, taking a seat on the couch next to my mom. "What have I missed?"

"We were just getting started," the psychologist said, leafing through a stack of papers on her desk. She glanced up and smiled kindly at me. "Charlotte—let me start out by saying that you're a very bright girl. Your reading scores are very advanced. You have a lot of strength at writing."

"What's wrong with me?" I asked.

"Charlotte," my dad said. "Please don't interrupt."

"Have you ever heard of *dyscalculia?*" the psychologist asked my parents.

Their expressions grew tense. They shook their heads.

"Dyscalculia affects how a person sees and processes numbers. It's the reason Charlotte's math test scores have been so low."

My dad sat up straighter. "You're saying Charlotte has a learning disability?"

"I have a learning disability?"

"Look at me, Charlotte." The psychologist leaned over her desk. "You need to know this has nothing to do with how smart you are. Nothing. In most areas you score in a very high percentile. But yes," she continued, "I'm afraid dyscalculia *is* a type of learning disability."

Learning disability. The words broke over me like icy waves.

"What do we do now?" my mom asked quietly.

The psychologist glanced down at my chart. "I've spoken to Mrs. Sterling, the resource specialist. She has some ideas that I think might really help Charlotte see numbers in a different light. She's been a great help to a couple of other students in Charlotte's grade."

"Norman and Cassie?" I yelped. "You're saying I'm like *them*?"

Norman Wyatt and Cassie Mistros were in my class. Because of their problems, Mrs. Sterling was constantly pulling them out of class for extra help. We weren't supposed to tease them about their problems, but some of the meaner boys and girls called them *retards* behind their backs.

The psychologist folded her hands. "You're at a very different level than those two. You're fortunate that way. But you do need some extra help with numbers."

"Am I going to have to be pulled out of class?" I whispered.

"That's generally how the resource specialist works," the psychologist said matter-of-factly.

The following Monday, I started seeing Mrs. Sterling. On the bus ride home from school I asked Kara if anyone had called me a *retard*. The look she gave me told me everything I didn't want to know. "You just have to ignore those kids," Kara said. "They're the stupid ones."

We never played Sarah and Jessie again. We never even acknowledged that we quit. Overnight, it seemed, we left childhood behind, little guessing that the door into the great wide world only swung one way.

PART ONE
FALL

1

"You kids are lucky," my father said, putting on his blinker and turning down the lane to the Barclay School. "Moving isn't easy, but it sure gives you a real jump start on life."

Jump start?

Closing my eyes, I imagined those ski jumpers from the Olympics bulleting down an icy ramp, shoving upward to launch, the loud whack their skis made when they hit the ground.

As I recalled, a lot of them fell when they finally landed.

My dad rolled down his window. "You smell that?"

"The pine trees, you mean?" James Henry asked.

My father chuckled. "That's the smell of money, son. They don't cut corners at a place like this."

The Barclay School was spectacular. If you didn't know any better, you might think it was a resort. The buildings were made of wood and stone and had enormous glass windows. There were tennis courts. The lawns of the athletic fields were immaculately groomed and bordered by giant cedar trees. According to the glossy admissions catalog, the school's sports and academic teams were respected nationwide.

A pack of guys jogged by us, headed in the opposite direction. They wore silver and navy tracksuits and looked as sleek as thoroughbred racehorses.

One of them waved at us. He was tall and muscular, and looked like he might be cute. "That's Milton!" James Henry exclaimed.

I flipped around in my seat to look at my brother, lowering my sunglasses over my nose. "We've lived out here all of three days. How can you possibly know anyone yet? And what kind of name is Milton?"

"Why are you wearing sunglasses?" he asked. "It's not even sunny."

My dad pointed. "Hey. Check out that sign."

CAUTION: FUTURE LEADERS OF AMERICA AT PLAY!

Crossing my arms, I sank down in my seat. Unlike my brother—who'd been offered a scholarship to every private school in Seattle—I was not a future leader of America. Because of my math scores, the Barclay School had rejected me.

After dozens of arguments, I'd finally convinced my parents to let me go to a public school. I was ready for a change. I was ready for boys. And, quite frankly, I didn't want to deal with the anguish of another rejection letter.

"Know where you're going?" Dad asked my brother as we

pulled up to the main middle-school building.

James Henry grinned. "I memorized the map."

"Of course you did," I muttered.

"Good luck today, Charlotte," he said, scrambling out of the car.

"Yeah, yeah." Smiling weakly, I waved him away.

James Henry. Boy genius. At the tender age of almost twelve, he understood calculus. Teachers were always talking about what a *privilege* it was to teach him. I'd probably hate the kid if it weren't for the fact of his size. There were eight-year-olds who were bigger than my brother. To compensate for his smallness, he spiked his hair with gel, wore lug-soled hiking boots, rode a skateboard, and played the drums.

Still, in spite of his best efforts, I suspected James Henry was no stranger to bullying. Back in Florida, he'd get these texts sometimes that would make his face turn green. He never told us what they said, but you could tell they weren't of the warm-and-fuzzy variety. More than once in our old neighborhood I'd over-heard some kids calling my brother a fag.

A horn honked. My dad moved the car forward, then stopped.

"Are we waiting for something?" I asked.

"How about you drive?"

My stomach sank. "Or how about *not*?"

Ignoring me, he got out and walked around to the passenger side. Reluctantly, I traded places with him, convinced that every-one was staring. "You remember the basics, right?" He made this motion with his hands—the right representing the gas pedal, the left representing the clutch. "It's all about finding the sweet spot."

"Now's not really a good time," I mumbled.

"There's never going to be a perfect time, Charlotte," he said. "You've got to learn."

It was no use arguing with my dad. Now that he was a published author, he thought he was the authority on everything. Just being around him lately gave me an eye twitch. I swallowed a couple of times, cracked my neck to loosen up, and positioned my feet.

"You'll want to look at the road, not at your shoes," he said.

Letting off the clutch, I gave the car gas. The Audi—his new I'm-an-important-person-now-and-I-deserve-nice-things purchase —shot forward . . . and died.

"Jesus, Charlotte, you've got to be more careful. How many times have I told you—gas first, clutch second."

"I told you," I snapped. "I can't do this!"

Without speaking, we traded places again. A wad of bird crap splattered the windshield as we left the Barclay School. The day could only get better. Right?

A short while later, we turned into the entrance of Shady Grove High School. The building was gritty and its façade was crumbling. The students I saw walking around had angry looks on their faces. My stomach dropped. Instantly I felt like "other."

"Let me out here," I told my dad.

"Don't be ridiculous," he said. "We're almost to the front door."

I slid my sunglasses down over my eyes. On second thought, the day could get worse in a hurry.

* * *

"There must be some kind of mistake," I said, sliding my class schedule across the desk to the guidance counselor. "I'm supposed to be in the gifted and talented program."

The woman—one of those ageless types with dusty gray-brown hair—pursed her lips and plugged something into her computer. Then she shook her head. "I'm sorry, but there's no mistake. Your math scores didn't qualify—"

"Oh. That. I have a learning disability. It affects how I see numbers. I explained that in my application."

"You're a special-needs student?"

"No!" I took a deep breath to calm myself. "Look—I talked to this guy on the phone? He said it was fine about the math, that I could at least take gifted and talented English and History."

She seemed taken aback. "To whom did you talk to? Mike Burke?" When I nodded, she said, "He no longer works here. The gifted and talented educational program is a school within a school. Students are either in all of those classes or none of those classes."

"I'll take them all. I can get a math tutor," I said, trying to keep the panic out of my voice.

"There's a long waiting list for GATE."

"GATE?"

"That's short for gifted and talented education," she said, making me feel very ungifted and untalented for asking.

The guidance counselor beckoned suddenly to someone behind me. Turning around, I saw a girl about my age. She was rail thin with limp brown hair, braces, and clothes that looked downright cultish. "Hello, Mimi," the guidance counselor said. "I hope you had a nice summer."

"I had to work," the girl replied. "Welcome to Shady Grove," she said to me, her voice entirely too cheerful and bright.

"Charlotte—I'd like you to meet Mimi Zupinski. She's one of our student ambassadors. She'll be showing you around today." She rose from her seat. "You'll have to excuse me now—my next appointment is here. For the time being, I'd suggest you give your schedule a few days. And if the math feels too challenging, I'd be more than happy to arrange a meeting with our special-needs coordinator."

"That won't be necessary," I said quickly.

Mimi gave me a pitying look.

A bell rang. The meeting was over. I'd now, officially, missed the smart boat.

"Where are you from?" Mimi asked as we walked out of the office. "You have an accent."

"We just moved here from Tallahassee," I said, feeling like a lemming in the all-too-narrow hallway. "But I'm not really from the South. We lived in Boston before that."

"Are you a military brat?"

"My mom's a professor. She got this teaching job at Seattle University. We just found out a month ago."

Mimi made a sympathetic clucking sound. "Pretty sudden."

"Yeah. I kind of feel like I got kidnapped by my own two parents."

Right then we walked out into the main corridor.

The noise was deafening. Students scurried in every direction, like ants whose hill has just been kicked. It was impossible to see which way to go, but you'd be trampled if you stopped moving. Maybe I just wasn't used to going to school with boys, but the kids here seemed spectacularly enormous to me, like some mutant species of teen. Whether from body odor or some foul thing the cafeteria workers were preparing for lunch, the entire place reeked of raw onions.

"You okay?" Mimi shouted over her shoulder. "You look a little pale."

"Can we stop at the bathroom?" I asked.

She pointed across the hall and raised an eyebrow. "Want me to wait?"

I nodded. This place was a war zone. What had I done? Trying to think, I pushed my way into the girls' lavatory. As I stood in line, I studied the graffiti scribbled all over the plaster walls.

For a good time call Jonas Atkins.

Missy Valone sucks ASS.

Drugs, not hugs.

Some of the writing described sexual acts I'd never even heard of.

A toilet flushed. A girl burst out, reeking of cigarettes. "It's all yours," she said.

Covering the seat with toilet paper, I sat down and held my head in my hands. Soiled maxi-pads sprouted from an overflowing sanitary bin like bouquets straight from hell. There was some kind of syringe in the wastebasket.

Someone started pounding on the door. "This ain't free real estate!"

Too tense to pee, I flushed the toilet for show.

As I washed my hands, I studied the cluster of girls gathered around the sink. Everything about them was calloused, from the way they talked and laughed and teased one another, to the look of their tattooed and overly pierced bodies. One of them had a nasty bruise on her cheekbone.

She caught me staring, and her eyes narrowed. Then she backed me into a corner. "You got some problem?"

Rendered mute, I shook my head and tried not to stare at her boobs. Which was no easy feat since they were practically mashed into my face. The girl looked me up and down, checking out my dark jeans, red sandals, and sailor shirt. It was an outfit, I realized all too late, that was entirely too preppy for Shady Grove.

"Nice outfit." She laughed harshly. "Stupid bitch."

A moment later, she and her posse left in a cloud of hairspray and smoke.

Mimi was there when I emerged. Though it crossed my mind briefly that maybe she'd set me up, I glommed on to her like a stalker.

"What happened?" she asked.

"I pissed off some girls."

"I know the ones you're talking about," she said. "If I were you I'd try to stay out of their way."

Looking around, I saw that the halls were finally clearing out. Teachers stood at the doors yelling at students to sit their butts down.

Mimi sensed my discomfort. "Guess you're not in Tallahassee anymore, huh?"

"Yeah—well this place ain't exactly the Emerald City," I muttered, staring at a poster across the hall that said *STOP THE VIOLETS*. I really hoped it wasn't a misspelling.

"My old school," I began. "It was the all-girls parochial kind. Not that my parents are religious. And they're definitely not rich or anything. But the school was a bargain and way better than the public high school."

"Sounds unreal," she said.

I didn't tell Mimi that none of my old friends even drank. The only peer pressure I ever got in Florida was to "accept Jesus into my heart." I imagined Mimi would scoff at this.

"There's a nicer bathroom upstairs," Mimi said. "In the GATE wing. I'll show you later."

As the final bell rang, I stumbled into my first class, feeling as if I'd just been banished to the ninth circle of hell.

2

FIRST PERIOD: CHEMISTRY

Our teacher, Miss Gordon—"Call me Anita"—took an "experiential" approach to learning. She divided us into groups of four by lab table and handed us a copy of the periodic table along with a "fun" fact sheet about the elements. Then she walked around the room taping the name of a single element to each of our backs. "We're going to play a little icebreaker game," she said. "To figure out which element you are, you'll have to ask your classmates for clues. The first table to figure out all four elements wins the grand prize."

"What's the grand prize?" someone asked.

"Do we get cookies?"

Anita beamed. "Each member of the winning team will start out the semester with ten bonus points!" When everyone groaned, she waved her arms for silence. "One of the main reasons we have an obesity problem in this country is that we use food to reward our young people."

"Bring on the fat!" someone shouted.

This, apparently, was our cue to begin. I turned to the kid on my left. He was cute in a punk kind of way, with blue eyes and dyed black hair. More importantly, he was wearing a Radiohead T-shirt.

"What's your favorite album?" I asked.

The guy stared at me without blinking. "Um—what are you talking about?"

I bit my lip. "Your shirt? Radiohead? They're like my all-time favorite band."

He stared at me blankly. "Never heard of them."

Mimi, who was sitting across from me, passed me a quick note. *Don't mind Nick. He's an asshole. Is Radiohead a boy band?*

I didn't dignify this question with an answer.

The other guy at our table, a redhead with a short neck and a receding chin, showed us his back. "Am I a noble gas?"

"No," Nick said. "But that reminds me—I really have to fart."

Nick's element, as irony would have it, was sulfur. He wasn't kidding about the farting either. Suffice it to say, our table didn't win the game. So long, bonus points. So long.

When the bell rang, Mimi and I hightailed it out of the chemistry room.

"Yikes," she said, fanning the air with her hand. "Nick needs to lay off the beans."

13

"There's some bad chemistry going on inside that guy's gut," I joked.

She laughed, then glanced at her copy of my schedule. "Shit. None of our other classes are the same. How about we meet outside the cafeteria for lunch?"

To buy myself a minute to think, I pretended to search for something in my backpack. On the one hand, I didn't want to encourage Mimi. I had a feeling she might be something of an albatross—at least in the popularity department. But at the same time, I guessed that eating alone at Shady Grove would be akin to painting a giant bull's-eye on your back.

"Sure," I said. "Whatever."

She blinked a couple of times. "Are you going to be okay until then?"

"Of course," I said, bristling. Who was she to pity me?

She shot me a funny look, then said, "Hand me your map."

She drew on it, circling where we were currently standing (near a gym, where some kids were playing a game that involved lots of screaming), and circling where I needed to go. "It's kind of a haul from here. You better get going or you'll be late. Good luck."

As she walked away, I felt as alone as Orphan Annie.

I ran to make my Spanish class on time. But when I finally got there I discovered that I'd sweated for nothing, that half the kids weren't even there anyway, and that it didn't matter since the teacher was missing.

I would have laughed if I hadn't been so out of breath.

"Guess he's gone walkabout," I overhead this kid behind me say.

Another kid snorted. "Yeah. Right. If by *walkabout* you mean he had a nervous breakdown."

Nervous breakdown—the idea had some appeal. Not the actual breakdown part, of course. But maybe I'd get to go to one of those luxury retreats where they send the stars for "exhaustion." After what I'd been through this morning, I kind of liked the idea of lying in a sterile room with nice doctors and nurses checking in on me every few minutes. I sure as hell was exhausted.

Language Arts, my favorite and best subject, was down in the basement. After my first two "regular classes," I couldn't imagine what our teacher would have us read. *Winnie-the-Pooh*, maybe? *Walter the Farting Dog*? Or would we read abridged classics?

The room was very dungeonlike. Paint was peeling off the pipes and walls. There were no windows. The ventilation was terrible. The oniony smell was getting worse, only now there was a meat loaf aroma as well.

As I took a seat, a girl came up to me and asked my name. This was a plus. She was pretty and a snazzy dresser. She wore knee-high boots, a cute flared skirt, and a V-neck shirt that was just this side of daring.

"Are you excited about this class?" she asked.

I shrugged nonchalantly, having read somewhere that the fastest way to push people away is to seem overeager. "It's school."

She gave me this sad look that I had no idea how to interpret. A few minutes later she walked to the front of the room and cleared her throat. "Hello, class. I'm your teacher, Miss Mason."

It was all I could do not to bang my head on the desk.

At least I wasn't the only idiot in the room. Halfway through the period, Miss Mason made the mistake of telling us that this was her first year teaching. Even worse, she added, "You guys are lucky. You get to break me in."

"We'll break you in!" some guy shouted. "Pop!"

The class erupted with whoops and laughter. Miss Mason tried to regain control by steering the conversation to all the amazing books we'd be reading this quarter, starting with *Great Expectations*, a book I'd read in the eighth grade.

"It's a wonderful romance," Miss Mason said, completely missing the point of the novel.

The class, however, was not ready to learn about literature or romance. A couple of the guys started harassing Miss Mason about her V-neck top. One of them asked if she had a boyfriend, and without waiting for her to answer, he asked why her boyfriend hadn't broken her in yet. She ended up fleeing the room with her hands over her face. If even the teachers couldn't hack this place, what hope was there for me?

The vice-principal came in a short while later, yelled at us for causing a disruption, and threatened suspension.

The girl behind me woke up from her nap and tapped me on the shoulder. "Did someone just say something about suspension?" she asked. "I could use a little more vacation. Summer's never long enough."

Lunchtime. Finally. "I hope you don't mind biohazards," Mimi said when I met her outside the cafeteria.

"That bad?" I asked.

"Worse."

Mimi, I was noticing, tended to act very gleeful when delivering bad news. There was a word for that, right? *Schadenfreude?*

But she was right about the food. You could smell the preservatives on the salad bar vegetables. None of the toppings on the pizza resembled cheese or tomatoes or anything natural, for that matter. The spaghetti, on the other hand, looked all too natural—kind of like swollen earthworms.

"I usually just make a sandwich," Mimi said, leading me over to a counter where there were loaves of Wonder Bread and jars of generic peanut butter. "If you toast the bread you don't even notice that it's stale."

A fight erupted in the cafeteria line. A moment later a guy stumbled past me clutching a bloody nose. "Isn't someone going to do something?" I asked.

"Oh, someone will call security," Mimi said, sidestepping a mound of something that might have once been a hard-boiled egg. "You have to understand, though—fights are more or less white noise around here. Kind of like the morning announcements. If you stick close to me and give everyone else a wide berth, you'll be fine."

As we wove our way through the lunchroom, Mimi gestured around at the various tables, narrating their various idiosyncrasies. "We've got jocks, preps, goths, gangsters, ghetto babies, skaters, emos, losers, whatever."

"What are you?" I asked.

Was it my imagination or did Mimi stiffen at the question?

After a minute she said, "I get along with everybody. You could say I'm a floater."

Wasn't *floater* a police nickname for people who'd drowned?

Mimi eyed me speculatively. "We should hang out sometime after school. What's your number?" she asked, whipping out her phone.

"I'm getting a new cell," I lied. "I don't know what the number will be."

We sat down at an empty table near the back of the cafeteria. Surveying the room, I tried to figure out who the GATE kids were. If nothing else, Mimi was a decent mind reader. "They have their own cafeteria," she said.

I tensed. "What—are they spoon-fed catered gourmet as well?"

She giggled at this. "Now you're catching on."

We ate quickly, then took our trays over to the dishwasher. "C'mon," Mimi said, adjusting her backpack. "We still have some time. I want to show you something." She led me to the third floor. Topping the landing, she waved her hand before her as if showing me some great buffet.

"This is it," she said. "Home of the GATEs."

Now this was more like it. Though it wasn't the Barclay School or anything, the GATE wing was clean and bright and lit by skylights. There were couches and alcoves where students could hang out. Groups of kids sat around with textbooks and laptops—reading, typing, and quizzing one another. Apparently if you were a GATE, it was kosher to care about your grades. Teachers mingled with students, smiling benevolently and bantering in a fun way. The students up here looked a lot more like me. Had I made it into GATE, my preppy outfit would have been closer to okay.

Skimming my fingers along the freshly painted lockers, I tried to mask the yearning I felt. I was supposed to be here.

"Feels like an oasis, huh?"

I could only nod.

Suddenly, I heard this rhythmic clomping sound. Shuffling down the hall in wooden clogs was a girl with a mane of hot-pink hair. On anyone else it would have looked absurd or cheap. But for her it worked. Tremendously. It was like her hair was a reflection of some inner radiance.

"That's Amanda Munger," Mimi whispered. "Otherwise known as Girl Wonder. Last year she spray-painted a giant penis on the school gymnasium. The only reason she wasn't expelled was that her grandfather—some big-time executive for Microsoft—donated a bunch of money to the district. She's been kicked out of all the private schools."

Amanda was wearing this cool hobo hat and a vintage T-shirt that said LUCKY across the bust. It hit her curves in just the right places. Her green eyes glittered in a feline way—there was a lot of thought going on behind those eyes. Bossiness beamed from her like a blinding light. She looked neither to the left nor the right, but you knew that she knew that everyone was staring—and that this fact amused her. She was polished and cool. You knew she broke hearts, right and left. I wanted to be the kind of girl who could break hearts. I felt a tug of envy. I'd never seen anyone like her before, so instantly and flawlessly compelling.

"We should get going," Mimi said. "The warning bell's about to ring."

I was late to Precalculus—they'd put the wrong room number on my schedule—which meant that the only seat left by the time I got there was the one right in front of the podium. Most of my classmates were in a food coma—or poisoned.

If only our teacher had been too.

Mr. Johnson sputtered when he talked—and I was sitting dead center in the splash zone. I wasn't sure what was worse—this or the fact that his PowerPoint presentation on linear functions was as foreign to me as hieroglyphics. He was nothing like the teacher at my old school—a woman who explained math so well I didn't even need a tutor. It wasn't fair. My other classes at Shady Grove had been babyishly easy. How many ways could one stupid subject ruin my life?

Toward the end of the period, he announced that the current seating arrangement would be the permanent seating arrangement. Did this mean I was going to have to buy a wet suit?

When class was over, I waited until all the other students had left the room, then approached Mr. Johnson's desk. "Do you know of any good tutors?" I asked.

"This is a very basic curriculum," he said, straightening out his already immaculate desk. "If you need extra help, try the Special Ed lab."

By my last period—Political Science—I was all maxed out on mediocrity. I convinced my teacher—one of the football coaches—that I was in imminent danger of puking. Then I high-tailed it for the lavatory in the GATE wing. Whenever someone came into the restroom I pulled my feet onto the toilet seat. It was at once disgusting and oddly comforting to hear the sound of other people's bodies. At least in this regard, we were all the same.

I spent the final minutes of school texting my old friend Kara.

Even though my family had left Boston more than four years ago, Kara and I had remained friends. She'd remained loyal to me even after I'd been diagnosed with my learning disability, and had tutored me in math. I, in turn, helped her write papers. Kara was a terrible proofreader.

Kara: *How is life in the great Northwest?*

Me: *The inmates are running the asylum.*

Kara: *That bad?*

I thought carefully before answering. From her e-mails and texts I could tell Kara was getting to be quite popular. She wrote about football games, parties, and the stupid things boys did. I doubted she'd have time for me if she knew I was lost in loser-land.

Me: *Nah. Kidding.*

Kara: *Give em hell!*

For a long time I stared at the phone, rubbing it with my fingers like a talisman, hoping that Kara might buzz me back with something she'd forgotten to say.

3

In spite of her low-fat, mostly vegetarian diet, my mom had recently been diagnosed with high blood pressure. She was supposed to be working on "reducing stress" in her life. So when she picked me up after school, I tried to make light of getting shafted from GATE.

"Being a plebe is plenty educational."

"That's optimistic," my brother piped from the backseat.

"This is unacceptable," Mom said, putting the car into reverse. "I'm going to talk to that guidance counselor right now."

"Kick some ass!" James Henry shouted.

"Language," Mom warned. "Shit!" she exclaimed, nearly hitting a kid.

"I don't think you're supposed to park right here." I put my sunglasses on and brushed my hair down around my face. "People are staring at us."

She hopped out of the car. "Let them watch. I'll be back."

"Famous last words," I muttered, watching her stride away.

My brother pointed. "Those guys are checking Mom out."

He was right. Four cute guys were leering at my mother's ass. "Gross."

He shrugged. "Mom's a babe. Dad scored big-time."

"That's disgusting," I said distractedly, wondering if I was doomed forever because of my inability to grasp the language of numbers.

"It's the truth," he said matter-of-factly, climbing through the middle of the car to the driver's seat. He cranked the keys in the ignition to turn on the radio. Led Zeppelin—our mom's favorite band—came blasting out of the speakers a second later. James Henry banged on the steering wheel as if it were a drum, keeping time to "Communication Breakdown."

Halfway through the song he accidentally honked the horn—right as the gang of girls from the bathroom walked by. Hands on hips, they glared at me, mouthing what looked like death threats.

"Damn," James Henry said. "This place is scary."

"Don't look them in the eye," I said through clenched teeth. Finally, they ambled away. The car was starting to feel like a vault. Clawing at the door, I said, "I'm going to make sure Mom hasn't gotten arrested."

James Henry stopped the engine and came jogging after me. "Don't leave me alone!"

We walked into the school and headed up to the front office, which was just off the main corridor. A group of cheerleaders was sitting in the hall making posters for Friday's football game. They looked more like Hooters waitresses than cheerleaders, in their too-tight shirts and too-short shorts.

There was a DO NOT DISTURB sign on the guidance counselor's door. We sat down in the tiny reception area. On a coffee table there were pamphlets about STDs, teen pregnancy, drug addiction, and peer pressure. Our mom was definitely with the guidance counselor. Her voice rose audibly from the other side of the door.

"Charlotte's education is very important to us."

"Score one for Mom," James Henry whispered.

"That's called tracking!" she yelled.

"The tension mounts, folks!"

"Shh," I hissed. "By the way, that's only my life they're talking about in there."

"It's unrealistic to expect a student to be strong in every area," Mom said. "My daughter isn't going to be a mathematician. She has a learning disability with numbers. But she doesn't deserve to be limited in other academic areas where she actually has some exceptional strengths."

I chewed on my lip. She was starting to sound desperate. I couldn't listen anymore. "Stay here," I said, standing up.

James Henry rolled his eyes.

The school had cleared out fast, though the smell of onions lingered. A few teachers shuffled slowly down the halls, shoulders slumped, their eyes glazed with fatigue. The floors were scuffed with dusty imprints of thousands of shoes. I could hear a basketball game going on in the gym. The boys' sneakers squeaked across the floor. I stood at the entrance watching them. They were so at ease in their bodies. Standing there, I felt a pang of nostalgia, though I couldn't say for what. I didn't even like basketball.

After a minute I wandered aimlessly on, until I came to a large room where detention was being held. At least half the kids were sleeping. Some of the girls were painting their nails. One of the guys was drawing an elaborate tattoo on his arm.

Amanda Munger was in there too, sitting in the back row with her feet propped up on another desk. Though obviously out of place—the other kids were a hard-looking bunch—she didn't seem uncomfortable in the least. She seemed, in fact, to be relishing her role as delinquent.

She had her arms folded across her chest and was smirking at the teacher, who was trying his best to act like he wasn't noticing her. But you could tell she was making him squirm. The teacher glanced over at me and frowned, as if annoyed that I was witnessing his discomfort. Amanda blew an enormous bubble. It popped like a firecracker.

The teacher whirled around to face her, but it was too late. The gum had been sucked in.

Amanda smiled just as before, her pink hair framing her face like a halo.

"That woman!" my mom exclaimed as we drove away from the school. "Just what kind of show do they think they're running?"

"I'll make the best of it," I said, trying to hide my dismay.

"Dad's going to freak," James Henry said.

"That's not helpful," Mom said.

I turned my face toward the window so they wouldn't see the tears flooding my eyes. "It's true. You know it's true. Dad's going to be so disappointed."

None of us gave voice to the question that was most on our minds: Just how badly was the snafu with the GATE program going to hurt my chances of getting into a decent college? My SAT scores weren't going to win me any Brownie points or scholarships. Though I'd done okay in the critical reading and writing sections, my math results had brought me down to an "average" percentile overall. I planned to take the SAT one last time before I submitted my college applications, but I doubted I'd see much improvement.

Though Seattle was a pretty place, traffic was a royal nightmare. The jammed streets felt more like parking lots this time of day. Mom was gripping the steering wheel too hard. No doubt her blood pressure was nudging into the danger zone. She reached over and squeezed my elbow. "For now, let's not say anything to your father. I'll see about getting you transferred to another high school. This week is going to be manic, but I'll make some calls."

Gratitude surged through me. I glanced back at James Henry. "Can you keep your mouth shut for once and not tell Dad?"

He made a zipping motion with his fingers over his lips.

Mom took a deep breath and exhaled slowly, something she'd learned from a biofeedback DVD. "Oh, honey. I'm so sorry. We'll fix this. Don't let that stupid woman get you down. She has no idea how bright you are."

"Bright as a red light," I said. We were stuck again.

Changing the subject, I asked James Henry, "How was your

first day at the Barclay School?" I made *Barclay* sound extra snooty by drawing out the first *A* and dropping the *R*, the way they do in Boston.

"Do you really want to know?"

"Sure."

"It was heaven," he sighed dreamily. "The teachers are great. The food—no offense, Mom but it's better than what you make us. And they have all these after-school programs. They even have a snowboarding team."

"Snowboarding?" Mom's brow furrowed. "But you hate being cold."

James Henry shrugged. "Some of the kids were talking about it. It sounds pretty cool. And it's different enough that it would make me stand out when I apply to college."

I snorted. "Like you're going to have a problem with that!"

James Henry pointed at a sign for Northgate Mall. "Can we go? I need a TI-Nspire calculator."

"Why not?" Mom said, her mood brightening. "I think a little retail therapy might do us all some good!"

When we got to the mall, we dropped James Henry off at Best Buy and headed over to Nordstrom's. I was still wound taut as a violin string. Only now, Mom wasn't helping. She was a royal pain to shop with. Though she fancied herself a hip parent, she was clueless about teen fashion. Like a crow that snatches up shiny things, she was always drawn to the most outlandish outfits.

She thrust a pair of polka-dotted skinny pants into my arms. "These will look darling on you." To shut her up, I agreed to try them on.

"Those are perfect," a saleslady exclaimed when I walked out of the dressing room.

"They'd be perfect if I were a flamboyant leopard," I muttered.

Mom and the saleslady exchanged a look that said *Aren't teenagers fun?*

"Your daughter is very striking," the saleslady said.

Mom sighed. "I tell her that all the time. She just doesn't realize—"

"That can be a blessing. With girls."

Another patronizing look was exchanged. I retreated to the dressing room.

Squinting at the mirror, I frowned at my reflection. I was as pale as a vampire. Though I wasn't overweight, in the last year I'd gotten boobs. Oversized sweatshirts, baggy tops, and my running bras helped me to hide them. Of course, no one could really even tell if I had a figure. My lips I couldn't hide. They were, to put it nicely, "bee-stung." Adults were the only people who ever said I was pretty. I figured they were just being nice.

My mom knocked on the dressing room door. "If you don't want my help, that's fine." She handed me her credit card. "You have two hours. Get yourself a few things *within reason.* I'm going to check on James Henry."

Why oh why did figuring out what to wear have to be so freaking complicated? I was so not prepared for shopping. For the last four years I'd worn a uniform. Though I'd pretended to hate them, I'd secretly appreciated how much easier they made life. We all got to look hideous together. Before we'd left Florida, I'd tried to find some non-uniform things to wear. But everything was either too lightweight, too resort-y, too pastel, or too old lady. Nothing I'd seen in the mall had looked remotely "Seattle." Not that I knew what "Seattle" was—but I sure knew what it wasn't. And after today, no matter how trendy it became, I wouldn't be caught dead in sailor-wear.

Wandering out to the main section of the mall, I slid my sunglasses back on. Covertly, I studied the other kids to see what they were wearing.

Here's what I decided:

I lacked the guts to pull off a queen bee outfit.

I wasn't defiant enough for anything purposefully weird.

It was imperative that I not seem Goody-Two-shoes.

I didn't want my clothes to peg me into a specific social group.

After a frustrating hour, I went back to Nordstrom's and tried a different department. Finally I found a pair of jeans that made my butt look cute and some fitted black shirts that didn't show off too much cleavage. They were more expensive than they should have been, but they nevertheless had an edgy "city" look. Without calling attention to my body, these clothes had attitude.

Afterward, I bought mascara, lipstick, and smoky black eyeliner. To pull it all together, I got this cool chain choker that was both feminine and tough. It seemed like the kind of thing Amanda Munger might wear.

Before we left the mall, I went into the dressing room at Nordstrom's and modeled my new purchases for Mom.

"How do I look?" I asked, twirling around before the three-way mirror.

"You look like a teenager," she sighed.

I sighed back. Looking like a teenager guaranteed you nothing.

It was pouring when we pulled up to our new house—cold, thick, stinging drops. "This weather—" Mom shook her head. "It's just such a cliché."

I rolled my eyes. "Leave it to an English professor to find the rain trite."

"I like the rain," James Henry said. "It smells like the ocean."

I wrinkled my nose. "You mean it smells like fish."

We covered our heads with shopping bags and made a dash for the front door. Stepping into the foyer, we saw that the house had sprung several leaks.

"It's an old house," Mom said, a touch defiantly. "That's part of its charm."

The man who'd rented us the house had mentioned that it had a few "eccentricities." Because it was cute and historic—a 1913 Craftsman—and available on short notice, we hadn't pressed for details.

Our obese tabby cat, Steerforth—also historic—was howling at our ankles as if we'd contrived the dripping just to torture him. My mother had named Steerforth after the manipulative Dickens character in *David Copperfield*. She claimed there were some "parallels."

"Where's Dad?" my brother asked, dumping some food into the kitty bowl.

Mom was rooting around a moving box marked KITCHEN. "Oh, did I forget to tell you? He's on his way to New York."

"Really? And why is that?" I asked.

"Oh." She waved as if this trip were the very last thing on her mind. "He got a last minute invitation to do a reading at NYU." She stood up and thrust some pots into my arms. "Here. We can use these for the leaks."

I swallowed. "Is this trip something Meeghan set up?"

"Meeghan's very committed to promoting *Lily*." Mom's expression warned me not to say another word about my dad's book agent.

Lily at Dusk. Though my parents had asked me to hold off from reading the book—in a year or so, they'd assured me, I'd be more ready for some of its more "adult" themes—I'd read the thing cover to cover right before we left Florida. It was an experience I was now trying my damndest to forget.

In the book, the headmaster of an elite boarding school is seduced by one his teenaged students—Lily Bloom. *Lily was as ripe and succulent as her namesake blossom, at once coy and open, teasing and yearning, her nectar as moist and fresh as the morning dew.*

Maybe it wasn't quite that bad. But close. Really close.

What separated my father's book from all the other "middle-aged white man has an affair with young girl and gets caught with his pants down" stories was that although the protagonist *does* ultimately get caught (with his pants down), he and Lily end up walking blithely hand in hand into a Mexican sunset—after shooting a whole bunch of people first.

Ew.

Lily at Dusk hadn't gotten much of an advance, but it was now starting to gain some critical acclaim.

"Did you like it?" I asked Mom as she mopped up a big pool of water. "*Lily*, I mean."

She glanced at me sharply. "You read it, didn't you?"

"Um—" I bit my lip.

"Well, what did *you* think of it?"

I shrugged. "It's literary porn for middle-aged white guys."

"Charlotte!" Almost imperceptibly, I saw the corners of her mouth twitch. Then she got serious. "It does have some titillating content, and I'm sure that's the last thing you want to think about your parents thinking about. But ever since I've known your father he's dreamed of being a published author. He's definitely an inspiring example of what a person can accomplish with a lot of hard work and a little luck."

"I work hard," I said, glancing out the window at my brother, who was performing skateboard tricks in the rain. "Unlike some people I know around here."

"James Henry works very hard."

"Yeah? Well, he's also a natural at *everything*."

"There are plenty of things you're good at. You know that, right?"

"I'm an excellent kitty massager," I said, bending down to scratch Steerforth. He purred loudly as I stroked his chin. Then he swatted my hand.

"Cats," Mom muttered. "I'll get you some Neosporin."

"I'm fine," I said, wiping the blood off on my jeans. "It's my left hand anyway."

4

Someone was knocking at my door.

"Go away," I mumbled.

Sleep. I needed sleep. More sleep. Couldn't get enough sleep. I dragged my pillow over my head. Now, what had I been dreaming? Something about Robert Pattinson? Ah, yes. That was it. Robert Pattinson had been asked to star in a movie but had said he'd only do it if I could be his leading lady. Somehow in my dream I was a movie star too. Somehow in my dream Robert Pattinson and I were kissing.

Oh, no! Why was Robert Pattinson fading away? And why was I suddenly so cold?

Someone had removed all my covers. This was why. I sat up and blinked. My brother was sitting on the edge of my bed. "Why are you here?" I hissed. "It's the middle of the night."

He yawned. "It's morning. Time to get up."

I glanced at my alarm clock. "I still have half an hour, you idiot!"

"I found something cool. You have to come see." I lunged for my comforter. He snatched it out of my reach and grinned. "Wakey-wakey."

"Mom!"

He clapped his hand to my mouth. "Just come, okay? I'll do your math homework tonight."

The kid knew how to bargain.

Five minutes later, I was following him into the woods that bordered our new neighborhood. The rain had let up, but the air was foggy and moist. The temperature was lower than yesterday's. Luckily I'd thrown a sweater over my pajamas.

We headed down a narrow path in the predawn gloom. I sniffed the air. There was a bad smell. This wasn't reassuring. "You better not be taking me to see a body," I warned.

"It's not like that. You'll see."

This wasn't exactly reassuring either.

A few minutes later we came to the top of a steep embankment. A small creek flowed below. James Henry pointed. "Look."

I peered into the dark water. It took my eyes a moment to adjust. Then I saw.

"Omigod!" I gasped.

"Told you," my brother gloated.

There were dozens of fish in the pool below, their scales flashing silver in the pale light of dawn. Their bellies were pinkish-red. Most of them rested quietly in pairs. "Salmon," I whispered.

"We read about this in biology last year. This is so cool. They must be spawning."

Looking closer, I saw that the salmon didn't look so hot. Their breathing—or whatever it was that fish did—was fast and labored. Their mouths were bent back in snarls. Several of them were peeling flesh. It seemed too cruel that their life cycle was such an uphill battle. A lump caught in my throat as I said, "Guess the journey from the ocean isn't much fun."

James Henry gestured at a sandbar across the creek that was littered with rotting fish. "That explains the smell."

As I scrambled down the embankment to get a better look, I startled some of the fish. A couple of them took off upstream, their tails churning the water like torpedo propellers. For all they'd been through to get here, they still had some life left.

James Henry looked thoughtful. "It doesn't seem fair. You wait all your life to have sex, and then bam, just like that you die."

"Must be worth it," I sighed.

I certainly wouldn't know anything about it—sex, I mean. To date I'd only had one boyfriend—when I was eleven. His name was Aaron Brinkley. We'd gone to school together in Boston. The spring before we moved to Florida—I was in sixth grade then— we'd started hanging out. At Friday Night Skate, Aaron would glide by my side for the slow songs. When no one was watching, we'd sneak out behind the rink, skates still on, and kiss against the wall. A couple of times I let Aaron go up my shirt. One time he tried to touch my crotch, which scared me, and I'd backed away. The next week, we moved.

A branch snapped somewhere nearby. My neck hairs stood on end. There were, I remembered suddenly, all kinds of wild animals in the Pacific Northwest. Bears. Wolverines. Mountain lions. On the drive across the country, my brother had joked that we were moving to the land of Bigfoot.

Heart thumping, I grabbed a rock and peered into the trees.

"Milton!" my brother exclaimed.

I whirled around. There was a guy standing on the opposite side of the creek from us, just a short way downstream. He was holding some kind of basket. He hopped from boulder to boulder across the water, finally landing neatly in front of me. He was surprisingly graceful for someone so tall.

"You can put down your weapon," he said in a husky voice, gesturing at my hand. "I only attack when provoked." Unclenching my fingers, I let my rock fall to the sand. "You must be Charlotte," he continued. "I'm Milton Zacharias. I go to school with your brother. We're neighbors. I'm in the house with the red garage."

"Oh," I said stupidly. "I thought you were a bear."

Milton laughed. "Sorry to disappoint. But I played a bear once in the second grade. My school did this production of 'Goldilocks and the Three Bears'? I got to be Papa Bear. I sang a song about porridge."

"I think I know your house," I said. "Is it the one with the gnomes?"

"Uh—yeah." His face turned pink. He ran his fingers through his wavy hair. "My mom believes they're good luck. So you go to Shady Grove, huh?" he said quickly, giving me this look of pity.

"That place—" He shook his head.

I stiffened. "We can't all go to the Barclay School."

"That wasn't what I meant," he said, studying me with eyes as clear and gray as water.

Though my face was flushed with embarrassment, I held his gaze. "Explain yourself."

"Are those mushrooms in your basket?" James Henry asked abruptly.

"They are indeed," Milton said. "Chanterelles, if you must know. As the guidebooks like to say, they are 'edible and choice'!" He kissed his fingers the ways chefs do. "Mushroom hunting is a personal passion of mine."

Passion? Mushrooms? Yet he thought gnomes were embarrassing?

"Check it out," he said, waving a mushroom under my nose. "It smells—"

I took a step back. "No, thanks."

He cupped the mushroom in his hand, his expression indignant. "Do you have any idea how much we owe to mushrooms? Like modern medicine, for example?"

I glared at him. "Remember? I'm just a simple girl from Shady Grove."

"I never said—!"

"I figured it out!" James Henry interrupted. "Chanterelles smell like apricots!"

Milton snapped his fingers. "That's exactly right! Thank you!"

Shaking my head, I started climbing back up the bank.

"What's your hurry?" Milton asked.

"God forbid that I should miss a precious second of my third-rate education!"

"Don't worry about it," I heard James Henry say. "My sister's on crack."

5

On account of James Henry having an orthodontist appointment, my mom drove me to school early. She gave me a choice: I could either practice driving or I could ride in the backseat and James Henry could have the front. I chose the backseat. "You'd make my life a whole lot easier if you'd get an automatic," I said, fiddling with my new choker.

"I drive a manual on principle," she said, reversing the car down the driveway. "One day you'll understand."

"What—I'll understand why you're torturing me?"

She shook her head. "You're being melodramatic." Once we were down the driveway, she said, "The hard part's over. You sure you don't want to drive?"

"I need to finish my reading for Political Science," I muttered.

We were starting a unit on the executive branch of government. At the beginning of the chapter, there was a racy picture of Marilyn Monroe singing "Happy Birthday" to JFK.

Read this book, kids, and you too can have your own personal blonde bombshell!

While I read in the backseat, James Henry kept going on and on about Milton and his mushrooms and the fact that Milton was really into skateboarding and that he played the guitar and they might get together sometime and jam, and that Milton was on the snowboarding team and had won all these awards and . . .

I snapped my book shut. "You really think that guy wants to hang out with you? He's like my age, right?"

"For your information," James Henry began, overly enunciating each word as if I were a kindergartner, "the Barclay School has a mentoring program that pairs middle-school kids with upper-school kids. Normally you don't get to choose who you're paired with, but *because* we have similar interests, and *because* we're neighbors, and *because* his mom is a teacher there, Milton said he could pull some strings. "

"His mother teaches at Barclay?" Mom asked. "We'll have to invite them out sometime soon."

"Maybe they could come to my birthday," James Henry suggested. "It's Friday, remember?"

"Like you'd let us forget," I said.

"Have you decided what kind of food you want?" Mom asked. "Italian? Thai? Maybe Ethiopian?"

"Mexican. Duh." James Henry swiveled around to look at

me. "And since I know you're dying to know—Milton is a junior. So if you go out with him you'll be a cougar."

I snorted. "There's no danger of that. You can have Milton all to yourself."

"He sounds nice," Mom said. "Maybe you should give him a chance."

"Nice?" I rolled my eyes. "Whatever. He's a snob. And—he's weird."

"That's crazy," James Henry protested. "Milton is cool to everybody. You're the snob. And you totally misunderstood what he was saying to you this morning. He was just trying—"

"I understood perfectly," I said coldly. "He thinks I'm a loser."

My mom cut in. "Where in the world would you get an idea like that, Charlotte?"

"Never mind," I said sullenly.

A moment later we pulled up to Shady Grove.

"Be careful," my brother said as I climbed out of the car.

I found my locker in the labyrinth, grabbed what I needed for the morning, and headed to the library—the one place other than the gifted and talented wing where I might be able to relax. A group of students were sitting in a circle on the floor, surrounded by newspapers and magazines. They were clipping articles and sorting them into files.

Though I pretended to be absorbed in my political science reading, I couldn't help but eavesdrop. These kids were definitely not run-of-the-mill. They were talking about alternative energy, and they seemed to be experts on the subject. They sounded smart and sophisticated. They had huge vocabularies.

One guy in particular caught my eye. The other kids deferred to him a lot. He had piercing blue eyes, a movie-star jaw, and auburn hair that flopped down adorably over his brow. Even through his long-sleeved jersey you could tell he was muscular. He wasn't bulky, but strong and wiry like a soccer player. Whether he was talking or listening, he kept flipping his pen around his index finger.

I tried to concentrate on my political science chapter, but the words on the page—something about the Electoral College—began to congeal into one giant blob. Speaking of college . . . what was I going to do? I needed some kind of game plan. I knew my parents hoped I'd win a scholarship; though, as my dad was fond of pointing out, I was not Ivy League material. No sir. James Henry, on the other hand . . . My parents were the only members of their own families who'd gotten degrees, and they valued education over even health. Last year for Christmas, Dad had given me a copy of *Barron's Guide to the Most Competitive Colleges*. What I'd learned from reading it cover to cover was that I was screwed.

I wasn't a concert-level musician who'd composed her first symphony at the age of two. I didn't swallow fire or juggle knives. I'd never spent a summer vacation delivering medical supplies to Darfur. I'd never met the Dalai Lama or meditated in silence for a month. I'd never been arrested in a protest for the rights of hamsters. I certainly wasn't on the math bowl or the chess team. The most athletic thing I did each day was to make it to bed without injuring myself. There was nothing about me that would set me apart from the masses of the other applicants.

My parents insisted that an impassioned, well-written, and tightly focused personal statement could overcome a lot—even a learning disability. But how impassioned could you sound if you didn't know what you were passionate about? I didn't even know if I was good at anything, and because I was so afraid of looking stupid, it was hard for me to want to try new things.

This was not something the college books addressed.

Something landed on my foot.

A pen. A silver pen.

I bent down to pick it up. It was warm and heavy and felt good in my hand. Glancing up, I found myself looking directly at the face of Adorable Boy.

"Sorry about that," he said.

I wanted to say something funny and intelligent, something that would keep his hypnotic eyes focused on my face forever. Unfortunately, I had forgotten how to think or speak.

So I simply held out his pen.

His fingers grazed mine gently as he reached for it. An electric shiver ran up my spine. He smiled. Had he felt it too?

"Thanks," he said.

A moment later he went back to being engrossed in alternative energy, and I went back to covertly staring at him. He was gorgeous.

But it wasn't just his looks that struck me. Something about him reminded me of the movie *Dead Poets Society*—a flick about some guys at a New England boarding school. The boys in that movie were clean-cut without being dorky. They were eager to learn *and* eager to break the rules. You could tell my new crush had confidence in spades, not the arrogant kind, but a belief in his intelligence that he had never once doubted.

Who was he?

After that, the best I could say about my second morning at Shady Grove was that no one tried to kill me.

In Chemistry we colored in pictures of atoms. In Spanish, the substitute—our real teacher had yet to show—had us practice rolling our R's. In Language Arts, Miss Mason gave us a home-work assignment: we were to write a five-paragraph essay about the scariest thing that had ever happened to us (I refrained from asking if entering Shady Grove could count).

Due to a student ambassador meeting, Mimi had missed Chemistry. We met up at lunch—the special was reconstituted mashed potatoes with meat loaf gravy—and after assuring her she hadn't missed anything important, I told her all about the *chemistry* I'd felt with Adorable Boy.

"But I'll probably never see him again," I sighed.

"I've got just the thing." Mimi reached into her overly large orange backpack. "Voilà!" she said, holding up a yearbook.

Flipping through the glossy pages, I noticed that even the cool kids looked stupid in the pictures. You could tell the photogra-phers were trying to impose meaning onto moments that had only ever been trivial at best.

Amanda's picture was everywhere. Last year she'd won the Best Dressed Rebel Without a Cause award. She'd made herself up to look like a drunk Lindsay Lohan.

I found Adorable Boy on page ninety-three. He was a GATE, of course.

Mimi studied his picture. "I've seen him around."

"Neal Fitzpatrick. What a great name."

"Not to be a downer," Mimi said, "but I think he might be out of our league."

I stiffened at this. Mimi didn't know me. Who was she to assume that I was a misfit like her?

"Mind if I borrow this for the afternoon?" I asked, trying not to show my anger. When she said okay, I excused myself and headed upstairs to the restroom in the GATE wing. Hiding in a corner stall, I spent the rest of lunch hunting down every picture of Neal in the yearbook.

Here's what I learned:

Neal Fitzpatrick was editor-in-chief of the literary magazine.

Neal Fitzpatrick was a National Merit finalist.

Neal Fitzpatrick played lacrosse.

Neal Fitzpatrick was captain of the debate team.

Debate. This must have been what he was doing in the library.

I tried to guess what colleges he was going to apply to. Stanford? Yale? Columbia? He was classy. I could imagine him living in a place like New York City or Boston. I traced my fingers along the contours of his face, dreaming that I was touching his features for real. No one would ever mistake *him* for a misfit.

In Math, Mr. Johnson gave us a pop quiz on graphing parabolas. Luckily the quiz was easy ("This is a very basic curriculum"). I wasn't the last to finish either. Afterward, Mr. Johnson gave us some problems to work on so he could grade our quizzes in class.

At the end of the period he handed them back to us. So much for easy. I got a C. Well, this sucked.

On the way out of class, I stopped by Mr. Johnson's desk. "Is there anything I can do to get extra points?"

He looked confused. "But you passed."

"How was it today?" my mom asked when she picked me up from school.

"I don't know—maybe a little better?" Because of Neal I was loath to tell her how much the day had sucked. "We could give it another week before we make any rash decisions about me transferring. At least in the regular classes I can push myself extra hard. Maybe I'll get straight A's for once."

My brother was absorbed in doing homework—otherwise, I'm sure he would have scoffed at this.

Mom's cell phone beeped. It was Dad. He was at Smith College, where he'd just finished a reading of *Lily at Dusk*. Mom handed me the phone.

"How's it going?" he asked. "How do you like Shady Grove?"

"Okay." To change the subject from my education, I said, "It's really pretty out here. The air feels extra fresh."

He was not to be sidetracked. "You might want to consider adding an all-women's school to your list of prospective colleges. These girls are very articulate. Smith might be out of your league, but there are some less competitive women's colleges with similar prestige."

"I'm sure there are," I said. "But where are the boys?"

He laughed like he thought I was intentionally being hilarious. "You're not going to have time for boys next year."

I gave the phone back to Mom.

"Where are you staying tonight?" she asked Dad. There was a pause. Her mouth got tight. Then, "You're going to New York?" More pause. She was gripping the steering wheel like she wanted to break it. "I see," she finally said. "Well. We'll talk about this when you get home." She snapped the phone shut.

"Everything okay?" I asked. We were at a stop sign now.

"It's just that—" She studied me for a moment. I had this sense that she was seeing me in a new light, as someone more adult, someone she could maybe trust. Then, with a weak smile, she said, "It's just that your father's writing career is proving to be a big adjustment."

As I stayed up late working on my Language Arts essay—the one we were supposed to be writing about the scariest thing that had ever happened to us—my mind kept drifting off to what Mom had said about Dad. There was no denying the fact that success was changing him and also changing the dynamics of their relationship. I wondered if Mom was jealous of how well he was doing.

I also thought about my dad because the scariest thing that had ever happened to me had happened when I was with him. Back when we lived in Florida, back when Dad was simply a would-be author and had more time for us, he would occasionally take James Henry and me on these Sunday outings to give Mom a break. Though he wasn't a natural at it, he liked the idea of being an outdoorsman.

This one time he decided he wanted us to try crabbing.

I got carsick on the drive out to the Apalachicola Reserve, and when we finally got there I was too queasy to help set up the nets. "Why don't you go for a swim?" my dad suggested. "It might help."

The water, coffee brown and gathering dust, was not exactly inviting. The air was hot, though, at least ninety degrees, and it wasn't even noon. The sky was a glaring shade of white.

I dipped a toe in dubiously. "Is it safe?"

"Charlotte! You can't be so afraid of everything."

Just to prove that I wasn't a wimp, I jackknifed into the bay, making a huge splash—a fearless splash. The water was bathtub tepid and failed to cool me, but still it was wonderful to be buoyant. I kicked out a good ways, feeling more secure the deeper I went. It was the bottom I feared most—who knew what lurked in the mud?

Treading water, I watched my dad and brother set up the nets. Then, they too stripped down to their bathing suits and dove into the bay. Over and over, my father tossed James Henry backward off his shoulders. My brother shrieked with delight and flew through the air like a beach ball.

I remembered when Dad had done that kid stuff with me. I was pretty young—maybe five—when he'd shown me how to duck dive into the waves off Cape Cod. We used to camp there sometimes. Together we would swim out past the breakers, where my feet couldn't touch the bottom. Dad had said I must be part fish. No matter how cold it was, I would stay in the water for hours. Dad's admiration was worth a little hypothermia.

Now, after about an hour of swimming in the brackish water, we swam back in to check the crab nets. They came up empty, but the weird thing was that even the bait was gone. The last net, the one farthest out and closest to where I'd been swimming, was snagged. I yanked and yanked, but it wouldn't budge.

"Leave it," Dad said, gathering up the buckets. "It's fine if we lose one."

Whatever. We'd been studying pollution at school, and I was *not* going to be responsible for the death of the environment. Besides. I wanted to impress my father. I wanted to show him that I was strong.

The net finally gave. It was heavy, but rising.

And then—

Two beady eyes attached to a brown snout peered at me from the end of my tether. My net was ensnared in the jaws of an alligator. Its jaws weren't but two feet from my hands.

"Dad—"

My voice was just a squeak. I couldn't shout. I couldn't move. I was frozen. Paralyzed.

"I told you, Charlotte—"

Then he saw.

He was there in a flash, slicing the tether in two with the bait knife. The twine crackled when it broke. Bubbles arose from the gator's snout as it sank back into the murky depths. My knees buckled. Fear washed over me in waves.

This was by far and away the most afraid I'd ever been. It was the moment I realized my dad's judgment wasn't always sound. My dad's judgment could hurt me.

This was what I wrote about late into the night.

On Friday, Miss Mason called us one by one up to her desk to discuss our essays. I wasn't worried. The one thing I knew I was decent at was writing. The teachers at my school in Florida were always saying things to me like, "You are your father's daughter, Charlotte. Talent runs in families."

The guy behind me glanced over my shoulder on his way back to his seat. "What did you write about?" he asked.

I told him my alligator story. "How about you?"

"I wrote about this time in juvie when this guy held a knife to my throat."

"You've been to juvie?" I asked.

He shrugged. "No. But it makes a good story."

"Have a seat," Miss Mason said authoritatively, when it was my turn to talk to her. In a matter of days she'd gotten a whole lot meaner. "Your essay is certainly very *creative*," she said, making *creative* sound like a euphemism for *inappropriate*. "But I'm afraid it doesn't follow the five-paragraph format. I'm going to have to ask you to rewrite it."

I suddenly understood why the kids on the regular track were always sleeping. They weren't missing much. If anything, they were sparing themselves.

At lunch, I couldn't stop ranting about the stupidity of all my classes.

"No child left behind," Mimi said, making a face at the

cafeteria smell. Today's special: spaghetti with meat loaf balls. "It means the teachers have to teach to the lowest common denominator. What can you do?"

"Bitch about it?" I grabbed a bottle of lukewarm orange juice and set it on my tray. "Is it so wrong to want a good education? I want to get into a good college, and I don't want to be behind when I start."

"I guess I'm just more realistic than you," Mimi said.

"What do you mean?" I asked. My stomach felt suddenly cold.

She handed the cashier a crumpled five-dollar bill. "My grades aren't the best. But there's not too much I can do about it now. I'll probably live at home for a couple of years, get a job, and go to a community college. Then—who knows?"

"Don't you want to try to go to someplace good?" I asked, sitting down at the empty end of a long table.

She frowned at the expiration date on her milk carton. "What I want is to be able to eat lunch without getting sick."

We ate quickly before the cafeteria filled up. Then Mimi took me to the back of the school, to a courtyard that was surrounded on three sides by a brick wall. The overgrown hedges on the inside gave the place a private feeling.

"Welcome to the Maze," she said, moving quickly through various throngs of kids. "When the weather's nice, this is one of the few perks of being a regular-track student. The Maze is off-limits to GATEs."

My eyes widened. "That seems illegal. Can a school really do that?"

"Oh, it's not an official thing," she said, leading me over to a

51

sunny section of the wall. "In case you haven't noticed, GATEs are kind of hated by the rest of us. They know it too. The security guards don't monitor the Maze too much, so GATEs are afraid to hang out here." She threw her backpack to the top and climbed up. I hesitated for a minute. The wall was steep and crumbly. Mimi laughed and reached down to give me a hand. "You can do it. Promise."

Scrambling to the top, I took in the view. There were mountains everywhere, their summits as jagged and pointy as knives. The air smelled wonderful—like earth and pine trees. "This is more like it!"

"Those are the Cascades to the east," Mimi said, pointing. "The mountains to the west are called the Olympics. Have you heard of the Olympic Peninsula? It's where *Twilight* is set." She eyed me speculatively. "Jacob or Edward?"

"No-brainer. Edward."

"Hmm. I go back and forth."

I made a face. "Jacob's just too . . . werewolf."

"But Edward is so *mopey*. Plus, he's kind of snobby."

"He has good taste!" I protested. "What's wrong with having standards?"

A loud laugh echoed through the Maze. Looking down, I saw a flash of pink. Amanda Munger was immersed in a crowd of tough-looking skater guys. They were like puppies in her presence. She was flirting with them in that you-can't-have-me kind of way—which only made them want her more.

I turned to Mimi. "She's a GATE. Why does she get to be here?"

"She's Girl Wonder. The rules don't apply to her." Mimi's cell phone started ringing—the first evidence I'd seen that she maybe had a life. She pulled it out of her purse and glanced at the number. "Hold on. I'll just be a sec."

While Mimi talked—she seemed very irritated with whoever was on the other end of the line—I slid on my sunglasses and studied Amanda. She was laughing again. It was such a wonderful, joyous sound—uninhibited and completely natural. I wished I could laugh like that.

"Ugh!" Mimi said, tucking her phone back into her purse. "My mom is such a drunk. She's about to go in to work and she couldn't find her keys."

"Does Amanda have a boyfriend?" I asked, though I was sure she must. I imagined he would be a god. I wanted to know just how good she had it.

Mimi looked disappointed. She'd wanted me to take the bait about her apparently depressing home life. "Why are you so interested in Amanda all of a sudden?"

"She's a character," I said, trying to tone down my enthusiasm. "That's all."

Squinting into the sunlight, Mimi stared off at the Olympic Mountains. "The weather's supposed to be nice this weekend. Maybe we could go on a hike somewhere. I could probably borrow my mom's car. We could even go to Forks and do the *Twilight* tour."

I bit my lip, considering this. Mimi wasn't actually that bad. But was I really ready to commit to a friendship with her?

"I've got family plans," I finally said.

"No big deal," Mimi said, though it obviously was. She dug into her backpack, trying to hide the fact that I'd hurt her feelings. "You know, I think I'm going to head back in. I need to print something in the computer lab." She hopped down off the wall. "See you around."

I wanted to say something, but I didn't know what. How did you tell a person that they were *just a nobody*? How did you tell a person that you didn't want to be *just a nobody* by association? Was I wrong to want something better for myself? Was I wrong to want to swim with the big fish?

Hadn't I been raised to *aspire*?

I stayed where I was until the bell rang, watching Amanda hold court. Her smile permeated every aspect of her being, from her glittery green eyes, to the tilt of her head, to the laid-back stance of her body. She was, indeed, Girl Wonder.

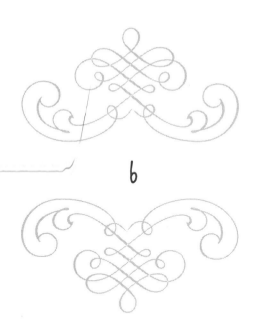

6

It was Friday night—James Henry's birthday. In just a few minutes we'd be leaving the house to meet Milton and his mother at a restaurant called Tres Amigos. Crazily, they'd accepted my brother's last-minute invitation. When I'd found this out, I'd tried to convince my mom that I had tons of homework to do. She'd informed me that staying home was not an option.

"Time's up, kiddo," she said, knocking on the bathroom door. "We need to leave pronto. I'm sure you look fine. This is Seattle. Anything goes."

"I'm ready," I said, stepping out into the hall.

"Oh dear," she said, staring at my face. "You look—"

"Scary?" James Henry suggested, coming up behind her.

"I think I look nice," I said defensively. "And you just said *anything goes.*"

"That's not exactly what I—"

"We're going to be late!" Dad shouted from the kitchen. "Let Charlotte make a fool of herself if she wants."

Gee, Dad—glad you've got my back.

I gave myself one last once-over, and frowned. So maybe I had gotten a little carried away with the black eyeliner and the bloodred lipstick. Maybe the new boots I'd picked up after school today were just a hair on the I'm-going-to-kick-the-shit-out-of-you side. I was trying out a new look, an I-go-to-a-scary-school-so-don't-mess-with-me look.

The horn honked. There was no time to wash off the makeup. I wiped my lips on the back of my hand. There. That was better. I slid on my sunglasses, popped a piece of gum into my mouth, and joined my impatient family in the car.

Tres Amigos sat on the shore of Lake Union. The lights of the boats glittered like phosphorous in the inky darkness. An energetic vibe permeated the restaurant. Everyone seemed to be in a jovial thank-God-it's-Friday mood.

Milton and his mom had already arrived. After introductions were made, Mrs. Zacharias said, "There's a half-hour wait. I put down our names on the list."

"I'm so sorry we're late," Mom said. "Traffic . . ."

"It's Charlotte's fault," James Henry chimed. "She took forever getting ready."

My face flushed. Milton raised an eyebrow. "It's dark out," he said. "You can probably take off your sunglasses now. Or are you trying out for the Secret Service?"

"Light sensitivity," I muttered. "Happens whenever I get migraines."

Mrs. Zacharias clucked her tongue. "You poor thing. You should be in bed."

I liked Mrs. Zacharias. She seemed kind and warm and wasn't stuffy in the least—unlike Milton, who was wearing khaki pants, a blue oxford shirt, and a blazer with the Barclay crest. What was he trying to prove, anyway?

Mom was looking at me like I was an alien species. "Since when do you get migraines, Charlotte?"

"Since always," I said, gritting my teeth.

"Bullshit," James Henry coughed into his hand.

"Here," Mrs. Zacharias said, holding out a bottle of aspirin. "I always carry it around with me in case of emergencies. Gas-X too."

Now it was Milton's turn to blush.

To hide my smirk, I tapped out a couple of aspirin and tossed them down without water. Wasn't aspirin supposed to be good for the heart? I just hoped it wouldn't upset my stomach. I was not about to ask Mrs. Zacharias for her Gas-X.

"Can I get anyone anything from the bar?" Dad asked. "A round of margaritas?"

"I'd like a martini," James Henry said in a British accent. "Shaken. Not stirred."

Everyone laughed. My brother. Wasn't he just a riot?

Right after Dad returned from the bar, the hostess approached with a stack of menus. "This way, please," she said, leading us back to a large circular booth by the window. Scooting in, I got sandwiched between my brother and Milton—who smelled like minty shampoo.

"So really," he whispered, "what's the deal with the shades?"

"So really," I whispered back, "what's the deal with the uniform?"

In a normal voice he said, "I'm in a service club. Every other Friday we visit a nursing home. We're required to wear our uniforms. Our faculty adviser says it makes old folks feel important if you dress up for them."

Mom beamed at Milton. "How wonderful that you volunteer."

Mrs. Zacharias smiled proudly. "The residents just love him. Barclay places a strong emphasis on giving back to the community."

"We've been impressed with the school so far," Mom said.

"How do you like Shady Grove, Charlotte?" Mrs. Zacharias asked. "I have to say—some of the kids that go there look pretty tough."

"Charlotte's in the gifted and talented program," Dad said, sliding into the booth with drinks.

Mom and James Henry exchanged glances.

"It's a school within a school," I mumbled, staring down at my hands. My nails were bitten to the quick.

Thankfully, our waiter swung by just then, sparing me further humiliation. He set down our chips and salsa, and then told us the specials. Mom and Mrs. Zacharias both ordered the taco salad. My brother asked for the fajita special. "It's my birthday," he told our waiter. "Just in case you do free desserts."

Milton ordered the chicken enchiladas. "Go extra heavy on the hot sauce."

Dad ordered the chile relleno and another round of margaritas, even though the ones he'd just gotten were still mostly full.

"I'll have a tostada à la carta," I said when it was my turn.

"That's all you're eating?" my mom asked.

"I'm not that hungry."

Mrs. Zacharias smiled sympathetically. "Headaches can do that."

"All this talk about headaches is *giving* me a headache," my brother said.

More laughter ensued.

The waiter left, promising to return shortly with the margaritas. The grown-ups became immersed in talking about a recent political scandal. Milton accidently bumped me with his arm. I wondered if he worked out a lot. His muscles, while not bulky, were solid. James Henry pulled out one of the protein packets that he carried with him everywhere like a security blanket.

Milton gave him a questioning look.

James Henry stirred the ingredients of the packet into his chocolate milk. "I'm sick of always being the shortest kid in my class."

"I get that," Milton said. "But being short can have its advantages. Take snowboarding, for instance. Having a low center of gravity will help you a ton, especially in the beginning, when you're falling a lot."

"What's this about snowboarding?" my dad asked.

"I'm thinking of joining the snowboarding team," James Henry said. "You said it was good to have athletic activities, that college admissions officers like to see that kind of stuff."

"I'm not sure we can afford snowboarding—" Mom began.

"Margot," Dad interrupted. "I'm sure we can come up with the funds."

Mrs. Zacharias turned to Milton. "Did you realize that you were having dinner with a famous author? Mr. Locke was called *the heir to Jonathan Franzen* in a recent book review."

Mom sniffed. "I think *famous* is a little bit of an overstatement."

"Who's Jonathan Franzen?" Milton asked.

"He won the National Book Award a few years ago," Dad said.

I dipped a chip into the salsa. "He's the guy who dissed Oprah, right?"

Dad frowned. "The media really manipulated that story—"

"Shit!" I exclaimed suddenly as a big glob of salsa slid down the front of my shirt. Everyone at the table went instantly mute. Dad glared at me. Mom shook her head. James Henry and Milton were trying not to laugh. "I meant to say *shoot* just then," I mumbled by way of an apology.

"I think swear words are warranted on occasion," Mrs. Zacharias said kindly. "And you do see a lot of swear words in poetry these days."

"I guess that means I'm very poetical," Milton said.

Everyone cracked up at this. Ha-ha, hilarious.

"Back to snowboarding . . ." James Henry started.

"Oh. Right." Milton glanced up from his cell phone. He'd been reading a text. Was he popular at Barclay? Weird as he was, it seemed like a stretch. But then, at private schools you could get away with being a little eccentric. "I meant to tell you—you don't have to pay for lift tickets if you're on the snowboarding team."

Dad nodded thoughtfully. "Snowboarding. I like that idea."

"Did you see the Olympics last year?" Mrs. Zacharias asked.

"Maybe I'll be the next Shaun White," James Henry exclaimed. "I could get sponsored!"

"Maybe you should actually try snowboarding first before you start signing autographs," I said, but nobody heard me because at that moment our food arrived. It came sizzling and in a cloud of smoke, thanks to James Henry's fajitas.

Coughing, I fanned the air. Milton asked for extra salsa. My dad ordered another round of margaritas. Too caught up in contemplating my parents' sudden descent into alcoholism, I failed to notice that our waiter had brought me the wrong dish.

"Is everything okay, Charlotte?" Mom asked, noticing my expression.

"Fine as wine," I said.

Seeing as how I'd already caused one scene tonight, and how I was causing a stir just by wearing my sunglasses, it seemed wise not to draw any more attention to myself. Even though the food before me smelled fishy and was puce. More for show than out of hunger, I picked at my rice and beans.

"Want some of mine?" Milton whispered.

To avoid answering him, I took a sip of my Cherry Coke.

"All you have to do is say 'Yes, Milton, I would love some of your big enchilada.'"

Coke came flying out of my nose and mouth. Again, everyone stared.

"I'm perfectly fine," I said. "I just swallowed wrong."

"No thanks," I hissed to Milton, when everyone had gone back to eating.

"C'mon." He bumped me with his shoulder. "You seem so serious tonight. I was just trying to get you to lighten up a little. Help yourself to anything you want off my plate. There's enough for a dinosaur here."

So now I was uptight?

"I'm fine," I said icily.

"Suit yourself. Char Char."

"I will," I said. "Mushroom boy."

He grinned. "Actually—it's mushroom *man*."

After dinner, our waiter brought James Henry a brownie sundae. The entire restaurant staff gathered around the table to sing a Mexican birthday song. Milton plugged away at his phone . . . probably making snide remarks about the embarrassing people he was with.

"Don't forget to make a wish!" Mom exclaimed.

Right as James Henry was blowing out the candle, my father's cell phone rang.

"It's New York," he said, rising from his seat. "I have to take this."

New York was code for *Meeghan.*

The bill had been settled and still my dad wasn't back. Mom was trying to act relaxed about it, but you could tell by the way her foot was jiggling that she was none too pleased. Feigning a yawn, she stood up. "I think it's my bedtime. But it's been so good getting to know you both." She squeezed Milton's shoulder. "I'm grateful that James Henry has such a nice guy to mentor him at Barclay."

"I'm sure he'll be mentoring *me*," Milton said.

"Whatever, dude." James Henry rolled his eyes, trying to hide his pleasure at the compliment.

"We'll have to do this again sometime," Mrs. Zacharias said as we reached the door. "I hope you feel better soon, Charlotte. Feel free to stop by the house sometime. We're neighbors, after all."

We watched them walk to their truck—a gray Toyota Tacoma. Milton got in the driver's seat. He waved at us as he drove out of the parking lot.

"He's a good egg, that one," Mom said thoughtfully.

"I don't like eggs," I remarked.

"Eggs have lots of nutritional value," James Henry said. "Give them a chance."

"I'm going to remind you of that when I crack an egg over your head," I said.

We finally found Dad wandering up and down a dock behind the restaurant, still deep in conversation. He got off the phone when he saw us approaching. Mom didn't even try to hide her anger.

"That was very rude of you to disappear like that."

"It's my *career*. I have to be available."

"Oh, you seem plenty *available*!" Mom said.

Dad rubbed his brow. "Margot—I can't do this right now."

"You're drunk!" Mom snapped.

"You're drunk!"

James Henry glanced at me. "Maybe Charlotte should drive us home," he said.

"Um," I stammered.

"I don't think—" my father began.

"Excellent idea," Mom said, tossing me the keys. "You'll be fine."

James Henry crossed himself. "May the Force be with us."

For about five minutes I handled myself like a Jedi, the Audi my X-wing starfighter, the lanes of downtown Seattle the canyons of the Death Star. Not even the Emperor himself could stop me.

Then we came to a hill.

"I'm not ready for this. It's too steep."

"Nonsense!" Dad said. "A lot of people climb mountains to get over their fear of heights."

Halfway up the nearly vertical incline, the inevitable happened. We came to a light.

As far as I was concerned, Darth Vader would have been a preferable nemesis. Sweat pooled under my arms. The seconds ticked by like blips on a life-support monitor. Suddenly a woman staggered out into the intersection. She was either drugged or crazy or both. She stopped briefly right in front of our car and shook her fist at us—as if in warning. When the light changed, I pressed down hard on the accelerator. The Audi—no longer an X-wing—shot forward. And died.

"Oh, dear," Mom said, as the cars behind us began to honk.

"I'm sorry," I said, tears of frustration pooling in my eyes. "I'm not much of a mountain climber, I guess."

"It would seem not," my father heartily agreed. "This is why you need to practice more often."

1

Monday morning in Chemistry, Mimi sat at a different table. I gave her a little nod, but she looked right through me. She'd been assigned a new student to lead around, a boy with glasses and a giant mole on his neck. You could tell by the way she was batting her eyelashes and twirling her limp mousy hair that she had a crush on her new charge.

Her face looked sunburned. I wondered if she'd gone hiking over the weekend. It had been nice on Saturday, but I'd spent most of the day inside helping Mom finish unpacking the house. My hands were dry and calloused from all the cardboard boxes I'd broken down.

Sadly, there would be no hiking this week—at least not in western Washington. The rain had set in on Sunday and showed no sign of letting up. Everything was glossy with water.

The loudspeaker crackled with the morning announcements. In a hokey disc jockey voice, our student body president said, "Fall is here with a vengeance. Due to the mud, the Maze will be closed indefinitely. Please do your best to keep our beloved building clean."

The class groaned.

When lunch period rolled around, I grabbed the cheese and tomato sandwich I'd made at home and headed up to the restroom in the GATE wing. With the Maze closed, this was my only good option. To my dismay, however, I found a security guard stationed by the door.

"New rule," he said. "Five minutes max. Any more and I give you detention."

I turned around and left.

Though I'd heard that the library was off-limits for lunch, I figured it couldn't hurt to try. Maybe if I sat at an out-of-the-way carrel, no one would notice I was there. Just as I was settling in to work, the librarian scurried over. "Which class are you here for?" she demanded.

"I'm not here for class. But I'm studying."

"General library hours are before and after school. If you forget the times, they're posted on the door. You can't be here right now." She was swatting me out like a mouse. Like it or not, I was going to have to brave the cafeteria.

When I got there, I stood at the periphery, scanning the tables for a friendly face. I tried to project calm and confidence. Spotting Mimi, I waved. Maybe she'd give me another chance. Once again, she blatantly ignored me. She and the new guy were certainly sitting very close together. Hope he likes braces, I thought unfairly, forgetting that it was I who'd rejected her and not the other way around.

Miraculously, I found an empty table. Even better, it was in the back corner of the cafeteria. This was a little strange, but I didn't think too much about it as I sat down. For something to do, I stared at my cell phone and contemplated sending Kara a text. But what was I going to say? *Hello—I'm a loser, how are you?*

Before I'd even swallowed the first bite of my sandwich, someone tapped my shoulder—someone with fake black nails as long as talons.

Turning around slowly, I discovered that I was surrounded by the girl gang.

"Excuse me," the leader said in a fake-nice voice. She sat down beside me and slung an arm around my shoulder. Her muscles were as large and meaty as a linebacker's. "Is there some reason you're here?"

I wriggled away from her and got to my feet. "Um—I was just leaving?"

"Right. Looks to me like you were settling in."

"You've got some nerve," another girl said. "Don't you know this table is reserved?"

"I'm new," I said. "I don't know anything."

"Not so fast," the leader said, blocking me as I tried to walk away. "Forgetting something?" Lifting my backpack from the floor, she gave me an evil smile.

Then, without warning, she rammed my backpack hard into my chest, and I stumbled backward in surprise. Thankfully, everyone in the vicinity was studiously ignoring me.

Devoid of dignity, I somehow managed not to cry as I left the cafeteria. When I made it to the main restroom I found that it too was guarded. "Five minutes."

In desperation, I returned to the library.

From behind her desk, the librarian glared at me with exasperation. "I told you—"

"Please," I interrupted. "Put me to work. I could shelve books. It's a matter of life and death."

"You girls are such drama queens. I'm sorry, but we don't need extra help."

"Fine. I'm going."

"Uh, hello!" a voice said from behind me. "Who says I don't need help?"

I spun around. And found myself face-to-face with Amanda Munger.

The librarian sighed at Amanda and turned to me. "You can stay. But no talking, texting, or eating, got it?" A phone rang from in the back. She stood up. "Excuse me."

Amanda blew a bubble at me with her neon orange gum. I pointed to the room where the librarian had disappeared, tapped a finger to my temple, and made a loopy motion with my fingers.

The bubble popped. The gum was sucked in. Amanda grinned. "Rough day?"

"Something like that," I muttered, too upset from everything that had just happened to appreciate the miracle that Amanda Munger had just saved my ass.

"Boy problems?"

"It's . . . complicated," I said vaguely, hoping she wouldn't press. How could I possibly explain my recent humiliation without humiliating myself? "Why are the bathrooms guarded right now?"

"It's all over YouTube," Amanda said. "Apparently on Friday, some guy filmed the principal's daughter making out with another girl in one of the school bathrooms."

"Guess that's one way to come out of the closet," I said.

"I know, right? It sucks for us, but I give her credit for being so ballsy. Wait—is it PC to call a lesbian *ballsy*?" Changing the subject, she gestured at the book cart. "It's pretty simple. All you have to know is how to read numbers."

"Got it," I said.

Amanda put on her iPod, and we worked together in silence, she pushing the cart, me putting the books back in place. Amanda shimmied her hips and bobbed her head to the beat of whatever band she was listening to. Today she was wearing a flouncy white skirt, combat boots, a black corset, and this cool lacy scarf. It was a brave outfit—very Madonna à la eighties—but she had the panache to pull it off.

Toward the end of the period, she removed her earplugs and studied me with a thoughtful expression. I could tell she was trying to decide something about me. Then, abruptly she asked, "Have you heard of Abney Park?"

Her question caught me off guard. It was just so . . . random. "Are you talking about that steampunk band?"

"My boyfriend's in an industrial band," she said. "They're opening for Abney Park later this month down in Portland."

"That's not a bad gig," I said. "Abney Park is huge in Europe."

"Do you like steampunk?"

Taking a gamble, I answered honestly. "Sometimes it's cool if I'm in a weird head space. But mostly I think it's a little over the top."

She nodded approvingly. "That's what I think too. Here," she said, handing me her earbuds. "Listen to Reptile—my boyfriend's band."

Reptile played the kind of songs the music industry would market to "disaffected youth." You could replace them with about a million other bands. I listened for about thirty seconds. "Love 'em," I said.

Amanda shrugged. "Boone—that's my boyfriend—he's the lead singer. He looks exactly like Adrian Grenier—you know, that guy from *Entourage*?"

"Sounds hot," I said, returning a book to its shelf. "Do you have pictures?"

"No. I slashed them up during our last fight." She smiled sheepishly, but you could tell she was proud of herself.

I laughed. "Must have been a bad fight."

"Not really. It's just that we're both such passionate people."

The librarian was back at her desk. She beckoned to Amanda with her finger. Amanda sighed. "Dragon lady calls. Be back in a flash. Hold down the fort."

I shook my head as she walked away. *Surreal.*

Amanda returned a minute later, rolling her eyes.

"Everything okay?" I asked, trying not to sound overly curious.

"Hold on," she whispered, pushing the book cart over to a more discreet location. Then she leaned against a wall and slid down into a sitting position. "God. I'm so sick of this shit. The bitch just took away my iPod to remind me that I'm here on her terms, that I'm 'serving time for a crime.'" She made quotation marks with her fingers when she said this last part.

"The graffiti incident? I heard about that."

"It was art!" she said tongue-in-cheek, holding her hand to her heart. "*My* art."

"I think what you did was awesome," I said. "Totally subversive."

"It was the stupidest thing I've ever done," she scoffed. "Now I'm supposed to do community service every weekend, I have detention every afternoon, and I'm grounded until like Christmas."

"Most artists don't get respect until after they're dead," I joked.

She seemed to like this. "What did you say your name was?" When I told her, she nodded but didn't introduce herself. I guessed she knew she didn't have to. When the bell rang she said, "See you tomorrow?"

"Probably," I said, trying to hide my excitement.

There was an assembly at the end of the day. Attendance was mandatory. I sat with my Political Science class smack dab in the middle of the auditorium. It was mostly a bunch of bullshit. The principal welcomed us to the new school year. The vice-principal went over disciplinary guidelines. The guidance counselor reminded us that her door was always open.

Ha.

I pulled out *Great Expectations*. I was at the part where Pip, the main character, first encounters Estella, the object of his obsession. Miss Mason, it turned out, didn't much like the book. She kept apologizing for Charles Dickens's "wordiness." She didn't see the comic brilliance of his sentences, the way he made everything seem so animated, be it a person or an animal or even a mere speck of dust.

I was just turning the page when a new voice, a student voice, started speaking from the stage. Something about the voice—some rare ineffable quality compelled me to look up. Neal Fitzpatrick was standing before the podium like he owned the auditorium. "I'm here to talk about the scintillating topic of the recycling bins," he said, his expression amused. It was as if he were silently acknowledging the pointlessness of our being here. "I know that saving the planet isn't always easy or fun. . . ."

I sat up straighter.

"I know that trash can be a little gross. . . ."

I LOVE trash!

"All I ask is that each of you do your part. . . ."

ANYTHING!

Neal wasn't an impassioned speaker. That wouldn't have worked at Shady Grove. But he was funny in a self-mocking way, and somehow, without taking himself too seriously, he managed to make the subject of trash feel relevant. I glanced around the room just to see who all was listening. It was amazing. Even the total deadbeats were paying attention.

He took a quick sip of water. (How I envied the glass for

getting to touch his beautiful, refined mouth!) "On a different note," he continued, "as some of you may know—I'm captain of the debate team." Some of the kids hooted. Neal bowed. "Yeah. I know—I can hardly believe it myself sometimes. My point is that we still have a few spots left to fill for the year. Debate is open to anyone who has a GPA of at least 3.0. If you're interested, we have some applications available in the office."

With impeccable timing, he finished speaking just as the bell rang.

Almost without knowing what I was doing, I stopped by the office on my way out of school. I was just reading over the questions on the debate application when this voice said, "Hey, Neal—looks like we have ourselves a live one."

I looked up and saw a Hispanic kid with a long ponytail giving me an amused smile. Neal Fitzpatrick was standing right behind him. My stomach dropped. My heart went into arrhythmia.

"You're interested in debate?" Neal asked. My face grew hot. I forgot how to speak. Neal shot his friend a dirty look. "You're scaring off the applicants, Diego." Then he gave me this soft smile like I was a timid animal he didn't want to frighten.

I gulped. "I liked your speech. About the recycling, I mean. Let me know if I can help."

Diego laughed. "There is something you can do. You can recycle."

Neal rolled his eyes. "Diego has a condition. It's called diarrhea of the mouth. It comes in handy with debate. The rest of the time . . ." He shook his head.

Diego clutched his chest and pretended to stagger.

I laughed nervously.

"Debate is the art of persuasion," Neal said. "Are you persuasive?"

"You should hear me at home," I said. Hadn't I, after all, talked my parents into letting me attend Shady Grove? Whatever that was worth . . .

"Good. That's very good." Neal rubbed his hands together like he couldn't wait to mold me into a speaker extraordinaire.

"I should probably get going," I said, terrified of the moronic things I might do or say if I stuck around any longer.

"Get that application in soon," Neal said. "Like tomorrow, if possible. Our first tournament is less than six weeks away. Oh, and you should give me your application directly. I'll put in a good word with the coach."

"Thanks," I said, stuffing the application into my backpack.

"What's your name?" he asked as I turned to leave.

"Charlotte. Charlotte Locke."

Like Amanda, he didn't introduce himself.

For dinner, Mom made steak and mashed potatoes. What was she thinking? This was not blood-pressure-friendly fare.

"These potatoes are great," Dad proclaimed after he'd taken his first bite. Then, "How was everyone's day?"

"There's a science fair next month," James Henry said. "I'm going to do my project on mushrooms. Milton said he'd help me."

Mom perked up. "Milton Zacharias?"

"Do we know any other Miltons?" I asked.

My brother took a big gulp of his protein drink and said,

"Milton told me this is the perfect time of year for mushrooms—especially with all the rain we've had."

"I think mushrooms are cool," Mom said.

Dad looked thoughtful. "Maybe I'll add a mushroom scene to my next book."

Annoyed, I asked, "Isn't anyone worried that Milton's going to teach James Henry about psychedelic mushrooms?"

My brother shook his head emphatically. "Milton had a friend who almost died doing 'shrooms. Besides, he's not like that."

I'd heard enough about Milton.

"How were your classes today?" I asked Mom.

"Great," she said. "A couple of my Victorian Literature students came up to tell me how much they're enjoying the class." She cleared her throat. "Actually—I've been thinking that I might want to turn this course into a book."

"That's a good thought," Dad said. "Seems like a perennial topic in academic circles."

"In *academic circles?*"

Dad laughed. "C'mon, Margot. A book on the Victorians is University Press material."

"I'd read it," I said.

Mom gave my arm a little squeeze.

"Any headway on your college applications?" Dad asked me.

Was he gearing up to give me a lecture on all the ways I wasn't cutting the mustard? Well, he was in for a surprise tonight. "They're not due for a while yet," I said. "But I have been thinking of some ways to make myself stand out."

"Oh, yeah?"

It was all I could do not to smirk. "I'm going out for the debate team. I talked to the captain today."

Dad nearly dropped his fork. "That's nice to hear, Charlotte."

Mom gave me a funny look. "Do you have an interest in public speaking?"

I shrugged. I had an interest in being eloquent. Wasn't that the same thing?

"Debate is an excellent foundation for a legal career," Dad said, shaking some A1 sauce onto his plate. "We'll need a lawyer in the family if James Henry is going to be a stockbroker."

"Dude." My brother took a big gulp of his protein drink. "I'm going to be a professional snowboarder, remember?"

"Dude. You can be both."

"Is there an application for debate?" Mom asked. "Or do you have to try out?"

"It's all written. There's a topic. We're supposed to write a three-page essay arguing either for or against it."

"What's the topic?"

"Juveniles charged with violent crimes should be tried and punished as adults."

My brother made a sizzling sound. "Let them fry."

"James Henry Locke!" Mom exclaimed.

"I'd be happy to look over your essay when you're done," Dad offered.

"We'll see."

Mom glared at me. I could practically hear what she was thinking: *He's trying, sweetie.* Though I could have used the help on the essay—I had no comprehension of the legal system, juvenile or otherwise—the last thing I needed was Dad pointing out any more of my mistakes.

After dinner, James Henry and I watched an old French film called *An Occurrence at Owl Creek Bridge*. It was about a Civil War soldier sentenced to hang, and it was a total mind trip. Right as the soldier's noose goes taut, the rope breaks. The soldier plummets to the river below and escapes his pursuers. Slowly, he works his way back home. Just when he finally sees his wife, there's a sickening sound and a flash of light—the entire movie up to this point had been the elaborate fantasy of a man on the gallows. The soldier hangs for real. The credits roll as his body twists in the wind.

I stayed up all night working on the debate essay. Before class the next morning, I trekked up to the GATE wing, where I spotted Neal right away. He was sitting on the floor in the lounge area, knees bent, his head resting against the wall. Eyes closed, he was flipping a silver pen around and around his thumb.

Was he practicing a speech? Contemplating the meaning of life? Dreaming of me, perhaps?

Fat chance.

I noticed I wasn't the only girl watching him.

Just when he opened his eyes, I lost my nerve and retreated back downstairs. Writing was such a personal thing. If not for my actual words, Neal would judge me for my thoughts. I took the coward's approach and handed in my application to the school secretary.

8

My second day and then my third day in the library, Amanda failed to show. "She has a legitimate excuse," the librarian said, sighing as if she wished it were otherwise. I couldn't tell if she missed Amanda or if she simply wanted to nail her for being delinquent.

On Thursday, about ten minutes after lunch began, Amanda waltzed into the library as if she owned it. "Love the scarf," she said, gesturing at the turquoise one I was wearing around my neck.

"It was my grandmother's," I said proudly. I'd spent a lot of time in front of the mirror this morning trying to decide if I had the guts to wear it. Unlike the rest of my outfit—dark jeans and black T-shirt—it was not subdued. "It's from the seventies," I added.

Amanda frowned. "You should wear it more off-center," she said, and retied it for me with fingers as smooth and cold as pearls. Then she stood back and admired her work. "So much better. It was too old-lady the way you had it."

Amanda reminded me of a French actress today. She was wearing skinny jeans, high-heeled boots, and a cool black raincoat. "I like your boots," I said.

"Aren't they amazing?" She glanced down and wiggled her toes. "I got these in Buenos Aires last month."

"You've been to Argentina?"

"I've been all over the world," she said matter-of-factly. "My dad's an infectious disease specialist. He specializes in tropical medicine and contracts with the CDC. He has a very high level of security clearance. Some of his research is . . . controversial. You know. With PETA people."

Flopping down in a chair, she tossed her enormous book bag onto the table, not in the least concerned that she'd just spilled half its contents. Noticing the book that was emerging from her bag, my eyes grew very wide.

No! It couldn't be!

"This?" Amanda caught me staring and picked it up. "You have to read it. It's the literary equivalent of a Tarantino film. You can totally borrow it when I'm finished." She flipped to the author photo on the back jacket. "Don't you think he looks like George Clooney? Yum. He writes the best sex scenes!" she exclaimed, fanning herself.

"Stop! Please!" I covered my ears.

"What—are you a prude or something?"

"Julian Locke is my father."

She snorted. "That's a good one."

I grabbed my cell phone and scrolled through some pictures. "There," I said, handing it to her. "That's him with my brother."

"Shut up!" Her mouth dropped. "That's only like the coolest thing ever!"

"I guess."

"Omigod!" she said, rocking back in her chair and staring at me as if seeing me in an entirely new light. "Were you the inspiration for Lily?"

"Me? Like Lily? Shit no!" I said, turning bright red.

"That must be awkward, huh?"

Glancing over at the librarian's office, Amanda said, "Dragon lady seems to be MIA for the moment. I'm *dying* for a smoke. You?" Without waiting for an answer, she dragged me back to the library restroom. "Stand guard," she ordered, clamoring up onto the sink in her boots. After opening the small skylight window, she pulled out a red and gold pack of cigarettes. "Do you like Dunhills?"

Though I'd never smoked before, I shrugged nonchalantly.

"They're all I ever smoke," she said, exhaling perfectly formed doughnut rings. "I'm on probation right now, so it's kind of a big deal if I get caught. Not that I'd miss this place."

I couldn't help but stare while Amanda smoked. She smoked in a way that made you forget that smoking was bad for you. She held her cigarette as if it were some natural extension of her body. When she exhaled, it was like she was breathing out her thoughts.

It looked artful and pretty, like dancing.

"How often do you see your boyfriend?" I asked, to fill the sudden silence.

She sighed loudly. "Not nearly enough. He goes to school in Portland. I talked to him last night, though. He says we're destined to be together."

"You say that like it's a bad thing. It sounds like he worships you."

"Maybe." She blew on the glass of the skylight and traced a heart. Then she rubbed it out. "But who wants to be committed at seventeen?"

"I wouldn't mind having a boyfriend," I said, leaning toward the mirror and dabbing a lash out of my eye. "I could use a little action."

"Too bad the guys at school all suck," she said.

"Yeah." I cleared my throat. "They're such tadpoles."

She hooted at this. "You're totally crushing on someone!"

"There's no one," I declared, feeling my face grow hot.

She wiggled her fingers at me in this witchy way. "No one keeps secrets from Madame Amanda."

I laughed nervously.

To my relief, she changed the subject. "I still can't get over who your dad is. You and I were so meant to be friends. It's fate."

"Fate," I agreed, trying to ignore the slightly queasy feeling I had in my gut. It's just the cigarette smoke, I told myself.

Climbing down from the sink, she offered me a Dunhill. "Go ahead."

I waved my hand in a blasé way. "I wish! But I'm just getting over a chest cold."

On Friday night, after I'd gone to bed, my parents had a huge fight. It sounded like my mom was grilling my dad about some credit card charge. Mom thought Dad was spending irresponsibly. Dad thought he was entitled to spend like a movie star now that his book was starting to receive critical attention.

Because of their shouting, I didn't fall asleep until very late. When I finally drifted off, I dreamed about Neal. In my dream I was in college, and he was my economics professor. He'd asked me to stop by his office to discuss my grade. I was failing his class because I couldn't grasp the concept of the law of supply and demand. "It's basic math!" he kept shouting. I was trying to tell him that this was the problem, but couldn't seem to make my mouth form words.

I awoke to a loud pounding on my door. Keys in hand, purse slung over her shoulder, my mother announced, "We're getting out of here."

"Huh?"

"Road trip," she said. "You. Me. James Henry. Now. Throw on some clothes."

"Are you and Dad okay?" I asked. "I heard you . . ."

"Your father—" She shook her head. "We're not getting along."

I didn't ask her to elaborate. I wasn't sure I wanted to hear what she might say.

By eleven a.m. we'd reached the outskirts of Aberdeen,

Washington, "the town that gave the world Kurt Cobain," James Henry reminded us for the third time.

"And possibly the bleakest place in all of North America," I proclaimed.

The town sat where two rivers converged, just before they emptied into the aptly named Grays Harbor. The nickel color of the sluggish water mimicked the color of the sky. A layer of grit coated every surface in town, from the burned-out neon signs to the paint peeling away from the fishing boats. Houses that in other places you might call fixer-uppers just looked plain hopeless in Aberdeen. Locals shuffled listlessly down the streets, apparently unaware of the rain beating down upon their backs.

"I'm hungry," James Henry said.

"We can fix that," Mom said, pulling into the parking lot of a dubious-looking restaurant/lounge called the Sawmill.

"Today's special is gizzards," the hostess said, plopping down our menus.

"'Spotted owl tastes like fried chicken,'" James Henry said, reading a dusty poster on the wall. "Since when do people eat owls?"

"It's a relic," Mom said, slipping on her reading glasses to look at the menu. "Back in the nineties, when the spotted owl was put on the endangered species list, this area of the country was a political hotspot." She looked up. "The Olympic Peninsula is prime timber country. The spotted owl lives in old-growth forests. Suddenly these people who'd been logging for generations were facing massive restrictions as to where and how they could do their work."

"Wow," I said. "That's sad for everyone."

Mom took a sip of cloudy water. "Actually—the issue has been heating up again. The spotted owl isn't making such a great comeback. And with the way the former administration loosened environmental restrictions . . . Oh, hello," she said to our waitress—a woman with frizzy eighties hair and too much base makeup.

"I want a burger," James Henry said, snapping his menu shut. "The grown-up kind."

The woman wrinkled her nose. "Me, I'd order the pizza. We're not supposed to let folks know, but they're the frozen kind. That's a good thing around here," she said, lowering her voice. "Chef's on a bender again."

"Pizza it is," Mom said.

When the pizza arrived, it tasted like cardboard, but at least it was good and hot. We were the only ones eating in the establishment, although there were a few guys watching football at the bar. One of them sent my mom a beer. "With compliments," the waitress said, setting it down.

"Where are you from?" James Henry asked her. "You sound Southern."

"Texas, sugar." She beamed. "The most beautiful country on God's earth."

I willed my brother not to ask how she wound up here.

"We used to live in Florida," he said. "But we live in Seattle now."

"You're a long way from home, aren't you?"

For some reason I couldn't explain, I felt homesick. I missed the lightness I used to feel on sunny days at the beach. I missed the hot sand on my toes. I missed being warm.

After lunch we headed north. Even on a misty day, the Olympic Peninsula was spectacular. Every now and then we glimpsed mountains through breaks in the fog. The dark and foreboding peaks of the Olympics rose steeply from remote river valleys that could swallow you forever.

Then there was the ocean. We twisted in our seats the moment the Pacific came into view. Clouds rolled off the water with just enough light playing through their vapor to cast the waves in pink. We stopped for a short while to watch some surfers.

"Looks fun," James Henry remarked.

"Looks cold," I said. "And . . . there are sharks."

He shrugged. "There are sharks everywhere."

"Yeah, but I attract things that bite," I said. "Remember the alligator?"

"That was scary," he admitted. "Maybe you're cursed."

"Alligator? What's this?" Mom asked. We'd never told her about that day in Florida with Dad. James Henry started to tell her the story until I made a face at him. The last thing Mom needed was to get more upset than she already was. The other day, I thought I'd seen her taking some pills. Was she on blood pressure medication now?

Turning away from the coast, we drove down a twisty road to the Hoh Rain Forest, home to giant dripping trees. Here we parked and went on a short hike. We crossed small creeks with aquatic grasses that undulated in the crystal-clear current. Some of the trees were wider than our house. James Henry raced up and down the trail, running back every few minutes to give us a preview of the next wonder that awaited us. I stared up at the canopy. Moss dangled from tree branches like old men's beards. The Hoh reminded me of those ancient primeval displays you see at natural history museums. I could imagine dinosaurs here.

On the way out, we drove past miles and miles of clear-cuts. Entire mountains had been shaved. "There has to be a better way," I said, staring at the beginnings of a new forest, the trees plotted out in identical rows, exactly the same height and width.

"It's an ugly business, the timber industry," Mom said.

I rested my cheek against the cool window and closed my eyes to the devastation. Images swirled through my mind, not just of the barren landscape but also of Aberdeen and the other logging towns we had passed through. I pictured the spotted owl, eyes glowing, swooping silently through forests older than our nation. What did it mean to lose a species, to be responsible for its demise?

Dad was gone when we got back to the house. The note he left said that he was going to San Francisco for a few days. *Book stuff. I'll call later.*

Mom disappeared into her room with the note and remained there for the rest of the weekend. "Migraine," she claimed.

On Monday during lunch, the debate team came into the library. The second I saw Neal, I felt heady and sick and lost all track of whatever Amanda was saying. Of course, I pretended like we were having the most fascinating conversation ever. Out of my peripheral vision, though, I snuck peeks at Neal and tried to hear what he was saying.

Amanda narrowed her eyes. "What's wrong with you? You're acting funny."

"Head rush," I said breathlessly. "I get them sometimes."

At that moment Neal caught my eye. He walked over to us. I froze.

"You've fallen in with bad company," he said, jerking his head toward Amanda.

She crossed her arms. "You should be so lucky, Fitz."

They were friends? Friends on a nickname basis?

"I was hoping to find you," he said to me. "Congratulations. You made the debate team."

Amanda gaped at me. "Debate? You? That's just so . . . stuffy."

The words I wanted to say got trapped in the back of my throat.

Neal laughed, unfazed. He was so freaking confident. I caught a whiff of his deodorant. He smelled like pine trees. "You still grounded, Munger?" he asked. "That must suck. Maybe your parents would let you out of the house once in a while if they thought you were doing something constructive like debate."

Amanda tossed her hair. "That is the most stupid, most idiotic—"

"When?" I croaked, finally finding my voice.

"When what?" Neal asked, perplexed.

"When can I start?"

He grinned. "This very second if you like."

Amanda gave me a sly look. "Oh. I get it. It all makes sense."

She. Wouldn't. Dare. Expose. Me. Right?

"Are you high, Munger?" Neal asked. "You're not making sense."

I bit my thumbnail. *Please.*

Amanda studied the ends of her hair. "Maybe debate *is* a good idea. I like fights."

"That's the understatement of the year. You've only been holding a grudge against me since eighth grade."

"It was the seventh grade," she said, tearing a split end in two. "And quit flattering yourself. I hardly remember that stuff."

What grudge? What stuff?

Amanda knuckled Neal in the arm. "Don't be a prick."

I wished I had the balls to tease him.

Neal glanced over at the computer terminals. He mouthed something to that guy Diego. Diego made a silly face. Neal shrugged and looked back. For some reason I got the feeling this exchange had been about me.

Amanda grabbed a book off the cart and weighed it in her hand. There was a chessboard on the cover. The pawns were blood red. In the background you could see a silver dagger. Absently, Amanda flipped through the pages. When she glanced up, she said, "You make a good point about my parents. They're being . . . unreasonable."

Neal took the book from her and set it back on the cart, facedown. "The deadline for the application was yesterday, but I'm sure Peterson will make an exception for you. Everybody else does." He smiled at me. "By the way—I read your essay. You write well."

Amanda looked amused. "You know who her father is, right?"

"Mafia?" Neal guessed. "That would be just my luck."

I laughed in spite of myself. "I wish!"

Amanda shook her head. "God, Neal. You're such a playboy!"

He threw up his hands in protest "That's not what I—"

She rolled her eyes. "Whatever. Have you read that book *Lily at Dusk*?"

"Hell, yeah. That scene where Lily takes off her— Wait!" He stared at me. "That guy's your dad? Flesh and blood?"

This was so messed up. My dad was basically making friends for me with sex.

Neal let out a long whistle. "*Lily* is going to be a legend. I hope they make it into a movie."

Amanda agreed. "How cool would it be if Tarantino directed it? Oh! Maybe I could play Lily!"

Just then the librarian peered over at us. She frowned at Neal and pointed in the direction of the computer terminal where the rest of the debate team was stationed.

He held up a finger.

This pissed her off. She started making her way around her desk.

"There's a conference at Seattle University in a few weeks," Neal said in a rush. "You both should go. It will be a crash course in debate. You'll have to miss school, of course."

"Miss school?" Amanda brightened visibly.

Dragon lady was upon us. Sleek as a panther, Neal disappeared.

"Girls," the librarian snapped. "Separate. You're distracting the other students."

No one was more distracted than I.

Neal. Neal. Neal. His name beat through me like a drum.

9

RESOLVED: THE UNITED STATES FEDERAL GOVERNMENT SHOULD SUBSTANTIALLY INCREASE ALTERNATIVE ENERGY INCENTIVES IN THE UNITED STATES.

Mr. Peterson, the debate coach, rapped his chalk against the blackboard. "Memorize. For the next nine months you will eat, sleep, and breathe these words."

Sitting at the desk to my left, Neal made a slitting motion across his throat. I shook my head as if he were an amusing child. Did he know how adorable he was?

Mr. Peterson caught my eye. "What do you think of our resolution, Miss Locke?"

"Um—I feel that it's an excellent idea? That we're going to run out of oil?"

Mr. Peterson gazed at me through his Coke-bottle glasses, which gave his eyes a fishy gleam. His expression was all too familiar to me—it was the look of disappointment. "I'm sorry to inform you that how you *feel*, Miss Locke, doesn't matter one whit when it comes to policy debate. If you want to win at this game, you have to take your personal beliefs out of the equation. It's one thing to be able to write a good argument. The question is: how capable are you of articulating an argument even if you don't believe in what you're saying?"

Amanda was scribbling frantically, her expression intense. At first I thought she was taking notes, that she was feeling as in over her head as I was. Then she turned her notebook to face me. She had drawn a picture of Mr. Peterson, a perfect caricature, from his Rudolph nose down to the hem of his too-short pants. The caption near his mouth read: *Resolved: I'm a pervert!*

I shot her a look of gratitude. She knew exactly how to cheer me up. Our new friendship was far and away the best thing that had ever happened to me. Walking down the halls of Shady Grove with Amanda and knowing that everyone was staring at us was exhilarating. Her strength radiated outward to include me. I was part of a force.

Mr. Peterson continued. "I'm going to read you an excerpt from one of our recent applications. Listen carefully.

"'Not only should juveniles be tried as adults, but we, as a society, should bring back public hangings. Watching their peers flap in the wind as a consequence of bad choices would make a strong impression on the minds of troubled youth. In the future, they would be less tempted to commit criminal acts if they saw firsthand the faces of death. Furthermore, communities could raise funds for youth at risk by charging admission to juvenile executions.'"

My face turned red. It was my essay he was reading from. Mine. A part of me wanted him to tell the class that I was the author. The larger part, the coward in me, suspected it was best to remain anonymous.

Mr. Peterson took off his glasses and wiped them with the hem of his shirt. "This is obviously tongue-in-cheek. But it works. Why?"

Neal raised his hand. "The author sounds convinced of the argument, so we believe it too. And the point the author makes about getting up close and personal with consequences is a good one. One of the problems with education right now is that kids have no fear of failing. So what if you get an F? Your teachers will still send you along to the next grade."

Mr. Peterson nodded thoughtfully. "Anyone else have anything to add?"

Amanda's hand shot up. "Public executions would make great reality TV."

Everyone laughed. Amanda stood and bowed, flourishing her hand like a queen.

My heart hammering, I bit my lip, wanting to speak up. I disagreed with Neal on the point he'd made about kids not having a fear of failing. I had a fear of failing. I feared failing all the time. But, I realized, this was probably not something a guy like Neal could understand. He'd more likely become president before he'd fail at anything.

The time to say something had passed. Mr. Peterson now walked around the room handing out permission slips for the upcoming conference at Seattle University. "I would highly encourage any new team member to make attending the conference a priority."

Amanda took off for a doctor's appointment right after class.

I was almost to my locker when a pair of hands covered my eyes. "Guess who?"

"Neal!" I laughed giddily.

He leaned against a neighboring locker, close enough that I could smell his cinnamon-flavored gum. It took me three tries to get my locker combination right. When I finally opened the door, all of my shit tumbled out.

Neal helped me pick up my books. "I'm impressed you got Amanda to do debate," he said. "She's usually not one for school activities."

"So you two have known each other for a while?"

"Mandy and I have a complicated history," he admitted.

Mandy?

"Our parents are friends. We played together as kids. Hide-and-seek. Doctor."

Doctor?

"What happened?" I asked, trying to sound like I couldn't care less.

"We went out in middle school. I broke up with her. She got pissed."

If he broke up with Amanda, how did someone like me stand a chance with him? "Why'd you end things?" I asked.

He thought about this a moment, then shrugged. "I didn't want her to dump me first. Yeah. I know. Lame. It was a long time ago. We get along fine now. We're like siblings who pretend to hate each other. But we look out for each other."

Neither of us said anything for a moment. Across the hall, one of the drinking fountains was overflowing. Lately, some kid had been plugging up the drains with gum. Neal brushed his hair out of his eyes. "I'm glad Peterson picked your essay to read today. It was brilliant. You've got a dark streak, Charlotte Locke."

"Shh." I put a finger to my lips. "Don't tell anyone."

He laughed, then said, "I have a question for you."

"Fire away."

"I noticed on your application that you're not in GATE. How come?"

My stomach knotted. What would he say if he knew about my learning disability? I faked a mischievous smile. "That's one of my darker secrets."

He grinned. "You're trouble, aren't you?"

I could tell he wanted me to be, so I shrugged like it was true.

When he knuckled me playfully under the chin, it was all I could do not to scream with joy.

Saturday morning, the end of my third week at Shady Grove, my phone buzzed. It was Amanda. Though we'd traded a few texts at school, she'd never called me before. "I'm still on house arrest," she said as casually, as if we talked on the phone every day. "But my mom wants to meet you. She wants to make sure you're not a bad influence. Plus, she thinks your dad is hot shit."

"That's disgusting," I said. "He's my dad."

"He's your *hot* dad. How about I pick you up in half an hour? You can stay at my place tonight. Just tell me where you live. FYI—if your dad's home I'm coming inside."

"He's on book tour." I laughed, feeling a little shameless. But what was I supposed to do? Amanda had accepted me so quickly in large part because she thought it was cool that my dad was a writer. I had to play him up, right? "Let me check with my mom about coming over, and I'll give you a call in a bit."

Mom was grading papers when I asked for permission. She didn't even look up. "Have a good time," she said, her words muffled by the red pen in her mouth.

"I might do drugs," I joked, just to see if she was paying attention.

"Take a sweater. It's supposed to be cold."

I studied her for a moment. Her eyes were moist and bloodshot. This entire week she'd been like one of those Stepford Wives—brittle and false. And I'd noticed that she'd been subsisting on a diet of coffee, Cheerios, and bananas.

I called Amanda back and gave her directions to our house. Then, after packing an overnight bag, I hunted down James Henry, who was in the kitchen, beating together a bunch of eggs. "What are you doing?"

"What does it look like I'm doing?"

"Cooking?"

"Duh."

"You never cook," I said.

"It's for my science fair project. We're working on it today. Want some?"

I stuck out my tongue. "You know I hate eggs. But thanks."

"Too bad," he said. "They're really good for you. You need the protein. You're getting too skinny."

Since when did my brother notice my weight? This was a little weird. Choosing to ignore his comment, I asked, "Do you think Mom is acting strange?"

"Hell, yeah. Look." He opened the refrigerator and pointed to the phone book that was sitting on top of a take-out box. "And last night I found a block of cheese in the pantry."

I shook my head.

"It's the change," he said matter-of-factly.

"You mean the move and her new job?"

"No, no, no. The *change*! She's probably going through menopause. We've been studying this in health. It makes women Mom's age act crazy for a little bit."

James Henry—resident expert on middle-aged women's reproductive health.

"She and Dad have been fighting a lot," I said.

"Parents fight. It's no big deal. Besides—Dad's not even around this week."

"That might be part of the problem," I said.

Now he looked worried. "What do you mean?"

What *did* I mean? "I'm not sure."

"Well, while you're thinking about it, would you mind taking the recycling out?"

"Okay." I grabbed the bin and shouldered my way into the garage.

Surprise, surprise. Milton Zacharias was sitting on the concrete, cutting up pictures of weird-looking mushrooms. "Hello," he said, looking up at me.

"You're doing James Henry's homework?" I asked. "I hope he paid you. Actually—you probably had to pay him. My brother *loves* homework."

"Didn't he tell you? I'm helping him with his science fair project," Milton said. "Pretty soon he'll be hunting mushrooms for fun and dragging you along with him. Your brother is amazing. He did all the graphs and charts. He's kind of a genius, isn't he?"

"He is. I'm surrounded by brainiacs."

He held up two cutouts, trying to decide between a mushroom that looked like a brain on a neck and a stark white mushroom, almost bridal in its appearance, its stalk sheathed by a delicate garter. He frowned. "There's not room for both of them on the poster."

"No contest," I said, nodding at the white mushroom. "That one. It's beautiful."

"*Amanita virosa*," he said. "Its common name is the destroying angel. It's the most deadly mushroom in the world." He handed me the other cutout. "*Morchella esculenta*," he said. "People all over the world pay good money to eat morels."

"I'd gag. That thing is nasty looking."

He studied me a moment. "I think I've just learned your fatal flaw."

"What? That I don't like mushrooms?"

He laughed. "This project is actually a study of human behavior. You just told me a lot about yourself. Beauty matters more to you than substance."

"You're kind of rude."

"I'm sorry . . . I didn't mean . . ." He stood up. "Stick around. We're making scrambled eggs and morels. You'll love them."

"Truly tempting," I said sarcastically. "But I have a better offer and I hate eggs."

Our eyes locked for a moment. Milton stared at me, not laughing this time. "Plain-looking mushrooms can be just as poisonous as the pretty ones," he finally said. "But it's the pretty ones that get people into trouble."

"Avocados," I said suddenly, to break the strange tension between us. "They're ugly, and I eat them."

A horn honked. I peered out through the garage. Wearing oversized sunglasses and a scarf over her head, Amanda looked glorious in the front seat of a cherry-red Jeep Wrangler. It was the first time I'd seen her car.

"That girl," Milton said. "I know her. She got kicked out of my school. What's she doing here?" Understanding dawned on him, and he stared at me. "Wait—that's your better offer?"

"She's my friend," I said proudly.

"If you say so." He gave me this strange look, like he couldn't possibly imagine someone as cool as Amanda wanting to be my friend.

Screw him, I thought, lifting up the lid of the trash can and slamming it down loudly to prove that I'd caught his drift. Then

I dashed inside, grabbed my overnight bag, and jogged out to Amanda's car.

Off in the distance I could see Mount Rainier, the giant volcano that dominated the landscape of western Washington on sunny days. It looked like a giant white chocolate Hershey's Kiss. It was unbelievably enormous. Amanda was telling me that you could climb to its summit. "My dad is going to take me up there next year," she said. "He knows all about mountaineering."

She was driving way too fast for the twisty roads. I clutched the roll bar for dear life. The wind was whipping my hair all around. I was trying to ignore the fact that it was cold enough for black ice to have formed on the asphalt. It killed me how at ease Amanda looked behind the wheel, one arm resting on the window, belting out the lyrics to a Reptile song.

Was Milton right? Was it crazy that Amanda and I were now friends? What was it that she saw in me? Was I simply a foil—there to make her look all the brighter?

"I'm kind of a lead foot," she said, laughing at my obvious fear of her driving. "But don't worry—I've been driving for years. My brother Keith taught me when I was thirteen. I had to fake being nervous when I took my driver's test."

I prayed she wouldn't ask me about my driving. To change the subject, I complimented her on her boyfriend's music.

"He's great, huh?" she shouted.

"Great!" I agreed.

"Who's your favorite band?" she asked.

"Radiohead."

"Really?" She glanced over at me and frowned. "We're going to have to change that pronto. They make me want to slit my wrists."

"You have to give them a chance," I said. "Radiohead takes a few listens. They're sophisticated. Subtle."

"Please." Amanda snorted. "You shouldn't have to work for music." She put on her blinker and turned down an unmarked wooded lane. Her neighborhood was called simply the Heights. "It's the *other* Clyde Hill," she said, making her fingers into quotation marks.

I looked at her blankly.

"You know—Clyde Hill? Where Bill Gates lives?"

"Sure."

She groaned. "Do I have to teach you *everything*?"

The Mungers' driveway was long and curvy and flanked by a ravine. There was a creek at the bottom. You couldn't even see the house from the road because of all the trees. When we reached the top of the driveway, my mouth dropped. The house was fantastic, with natural wood siding, huge glass windows, and a suspended metal staircase that led up to a balcony. It reminded me of an enormous tree house, the kind people pay loads of money to stay at when they go on ecotours.

"Holy shit," I muttered.

"It's been featured in *Seattle Weekly* and *Architectural Digest*," Amanda said, pressing the opener for the massive three-car garage. We parked next to a Jaguar convertible, as red and gleaming as nail polish, with an all-white leather interior.

"My mom's car." She shrugged, like Jaguars were everyday.

"Wait until you see what my dad drives. It's a Beamer with a racing engine. It's in the shop right now, while my dad's in Brazil. I could tell you what he's doing, but then I'd have to kill you."

We were in the kitchen when Amanda's mother glided in— tall, thin, stunning. Suddenly I felt self-conscious. My hair was a mess from the drive. My cheeks were windburned. I was in no condition to meet anyone's mother. She reminded me of pictures I'd seen of Carolyn Bessette-Kennedy. "Call me Katherine," she said, extending her arm and drawing out the syllables of her name. *Kath-er-ine*. Her skin was as fine as alabaster. Her fingers were marble cool. Her nails, perfectly manicured and not too long, made me think of seashells. And her wedding ring . . . well, I understood now why some people called them *rocks*.

"Amanda." She frowned. "Can you offer Charlotte some water?"

Amanda opened the refrigerator and gestured at the top shelf like a game show hostess presenting the grand prize. There were rows and rows of fancy bottles, most of the names foreign.

"Or do you prefer room temperature?" Amanda's mother asked.

Who were these people? "Uh, tap is fine?"

Katherine touched her fingers to her lips as if I'd just said something horrifying. Amanda stifled a laugh and handed me a bottle of Evian. Katherine's cell phone rang. "Excuse me," she said abruptly, and then motioned for us to leave.

"She's a real bitch," Amanda whispered as we left the room.

"Parents . . ." I waved my hand vaguely.

We passed a couple of photographs on our way upstairs.

Amanda stopped and motioned toward one. "That's my brother, Keith," she said. "He's the only person in the world who truly gets me. He works for the Peace Corps in Indonesia. Keith's bipolar, you know. Mom pestered him to death about taking his meds, so he went someplace where she couldn't bug him. It's textbook."

In the picture, Keith was standing on a beach with his hands on his hips, smiling at the camera. In spite of the dreadlocks and goatee, you could tell he was Amanda's brother. They had identical green eyes. He didn't look unstable.

"You can't imagine how much I miss him. We're like this close," Amanda said, crossing her fingers.

"My brother thinks I'm a flake," I muttered.

"I fell apart after Keith left," she said. "I was a mess. God."

"What happened?" I asked.

She shook her head, as if it were too painful to talk about. Amanda, I knew, saw a shrink. But like everything else, she made being messed up seem cool.

Amanda had her own suite of rooms. Her bedroom was simple, elegant, and done all in white like a classy big-city hotel. Her closet, on the other hand, was as lavish and spacious as a Hollywood dressing room. It was decorated with old *Wizard of Oz* memorabilia. "Some of it's from the original set," she said. "My dad knows some movie people."

She tore through her closet and piled a bunch of clothes on her bed. "For you," she said. "I don't wear them enough. They're too muted for me. But they'll be great on you."

"You've got great taste," I said, admiring the designer labels. I didn't want to know how much her castoffs had cost. What would it be like to never have to buy stuff off the discount racks?

"I have a whole philosophy on clothes," she said, holding up a pair of big gold hoops to my ears. "The right clothing can help you tap into the more hidden parts of your personality."

"These are nice," I said sincerely. "I like them a lot."

"Too bold for you," she said, putting them away.

"Isn't that the point according to your philosophy? Maybe I secretly want to be bold."

"That's not quite how it works," she said. "You're the kind of person who looks best in understated things and minimal makeup. As important as it is to experiment with your look, you also have to know what you can and can't pull off."

What, exactly, had she just said?

"Come in here." She beckoned me into the bathroom. "I've got some lotion you might like."

The bathroom was like a spa, with an open shower, a Jacuzzi tub, and all kinds of fancy shampoos and conditioners. It smelled like an aromatherapy boutique. There were about ten different kinds of lotions on her counter, most with French labels. She handed me a bottle. "This stuff is great. It really softens the hands. You should use it twice a day."

"You're giving this to me?"

"Of course," she said, smiling. "I don't need it."

"Your house is really peaceful," I said, feeling as out of place here as a black stain on a wedding dress.

"My mom had this feng shui lady arrange the furniture," she said. "It totally improves the *chi*. And twice a year we have a shaman come say a peace blessing."

Late that night, after we'd done our toenails, after we'd watched *Love Story*, after Amanda had made me over to look like the female lead of the movie—Ali MacGraw—she lifted up a corner of her mattress and retrieved a Ziploc baggie and a small silver pipe.

"Pot helps me sleep," she explained. "It gives me good dreams."

"Yeah. Me too," I said lightly. Inside, my heart was pounding. My mind searched frantically for a way out of this that would leave me with my dignity intact. Not that I wasn't curious. I was. But I was also terrified. "What about your mom?"

"She takes her Ambien at nine. She'll be out cold until morning." Without bothering to turn around or cover herself up, Amanda stripped and put on her nightgown. It was the kind of thing you saw on Victoria's Secret models.

I went into the bathroom to change. Amanda teased me when I emerged. "Modesty isn't a virtue, Char."

How could I explain myself to her? Nature got her body just right. She didn't need to hide herself.

She moved around the bedroom turning off all the lights. Then we went outside to her balcony. It was a beautiful night. The moon was just a sliver. Stars glimmered like tiny fragments of glass. It was cold too; a thin layer of frost glazed the metal railing. Someone was burning a fire nearby, and the air smelled of wood smoke.

With great concentration, Amanda packed a small clump into the pipe. I watched intently, too alert to even blink. "Here," she said, passing the pipe to me. "You're the guest. You get to go first."

"You know—I think I'll pass tonight. I'm kind of in a weird head space."

"Suit yourself. You're missing out, though. This is great bud."

I lay down on the stone balcony, wishing I had the guts to be carefree like Amanda. "My mom smoked pot," I said. This was sort of true. My mom had told me that she'd tried it once and that it had made her really paranoid. "She was a hippie. Before she got pregnant with me."

"That's so sad," Amanda said distractedly, the pipe in her mouth.

I closed my eyes and listened to the sounds of the night: the leaves rustling through the trees, the creek, a raccoon fight. I wouldn't mind being grounded every day if I got to live like Amanda.

"I could stay at your house forever," I said.

Amanda rolled her head toward me, her eyes enormous emeralds. "I can't wait to leave."

10

Seattle University—where the debate conference was being held—was just a stone's throw from Capitol Hill, the coolest neighborhood in all of Seattle. According to Amanda, fitting in here (where the locals sported full-body tattoos, multiple piercings, and sometimes whips and chains) was a real coup.

Seattle University was also the school where my mom taught.

"I'll stay out of your hair this week," she promised as she drove me to the conference. "You can pretend I don't exist if we happen to run into each other. I won't be offended."

Because of her class schedule, she had to drop me off a few hours early. "You can hang out in my office," she said. "Or wander around. Or . . . never mind."

"Never mind *what?*"

Mom concentrated on parallel parking into a space. I watched her glumly. Since the incident the night of James Henry's birthday, I hadn't tried driving once. Even the thought of it twisted my stomach up in knots.

"I was going to say that you could come to my eight o'clock. But I figured you wouldn't be interested."

I stared out the window. Students stumbled across the urban campus with coffee cups in hand. No one was socializing at this hour. "What's your lecture about?"

"*Tess of the d'Urbervilles.*"

"We read that in school last year. It was so depressing."

"Wasn't it though?" She sighed dreamily.

"I'll come," I said, unhooking my seat belt. "Maybe the guys will be cute."

She shot me a look. "Think again, jailbait. If one of them so much as looks at you, he'll be getting an F for the semester. Besides—don't you remember what happened to poor Tess?"

"Not one good thing, right?"

"Exactly!"

No doubt to make a point, she sat me next to one of her older students—a distinguished-looking black man with enormous biceps. When he reached out to shake my hand, I noticed that half of his other arm was missing. I couldn't help but stare. The skin at the end of his stump was knotty, like a hot dog.

"Somalia," he explained. "I got caught in a crossfire."

My face burned. "I'm sorry. I didn't mean to be rude."

"Don't you worry about it," he said. "It gets me sympathy from the ladies."

Mom approached the podium slowly and with confidence. She

looked around the auditorium and smiled at her students as if she were genuinely happy to see them. "Good morning, class," she said, her voice filling every corner of the auditorium. The students who had been talking went instantly mute. "What did you think of last night's reading?"

A guy in the front row raised his hand. "I didn't know milking cows could be so erotic."

The class laughed, but not in an out of hand way. My mom laughed too.

"I'm glad I didn't live back then," a girl behind me said. "I'd definitely be a *fallen* woman."

"You slut," the guy next to her teased.

"Play nice, kids," Mom said lightly. "Most of us would be considered morally bankrupt under the social mores of the Victorian age. And if we weren't, we'd be *really* horny."

Who was this woman who was cracking sex jokes like a comedian? I stared transfixed the entire lecture. So did most of her students, who obviously worshipped my mom. When the lecture was over, my new friend, the guy with the missing arm, asked, "Well, what did you think?"

"I didn't realize she was so—" My hand flopped as I searched for the words.

"Command presence," he said. "That's what your mother has. It's a rare quality, hard to pin down, but you know it when you see it."

Could you have command presence and just not know it?

I hoped so. I really hoped so.

⸴ ⸴ ⸴

The people who were running the debate conference—our coaches—were a mix of college debaters and law students. They were funny. Smart. They swore a lot. They talked so quickly it was impossible to understand them. When some brave kid in the front row asked if they could slow it down a little, they explained, "We're training your ears. This is nothing."

Then they introduced to us the concept of *spreading*—a method of making as many arguments as possible within the given time constraints of a speech. One of the guys demonstrated the technique. When words exploded from his mouth like machine-gun fire, I slunk down in my seat. I'd never seen (or heard) anything like it. A girl could get hurt around here.

I glanced around to see who else was freaked. No one else looked scared. However, I saw that the room was full of pen twirlers. I nudged Amanda. "I think we have to learn how to do that if we want to be taken seriously."

During the break, she tapped the guy in front of us. "How do you do that pen thing?"

His eyes grew wide. "Amanda Munger?"

When she looked at him blankly, he said, "I'm Eliot. Eliot Black. We had history together at Lake Washington?"

Lake Washington High, I'd learned, was possibly Seattle's toniest school, and was one of the schools that had kicked Amanda out. I'd never gotten the full story. Sometimes, with Amanda, it was better not to ask. Not that she was ashamed of her past. But she enjoyed having her secrets.

"That year was kind of a blur," she said to Eliot.

"Kids still talk about you. That time you got caught in the lab with—"

"Eliot," she interrupted. "The pen thing?"

"Oh. Right." He brushed his hair out of his eyes. "It's addicting," he warned us.

"Do all debaters flip pens?" I asked. "Is it like some kind of secret requirement?" Pen twirling. Bullshitting. Speed-talking. Debate was not at all what I'd been expecting—not that I'd known what to expect. Eliot shrugged. "Some people say it distracts the judges when the other side is speaking. I like it because it annoys my teachers." He showed us how to use our middle finger to propel our pens around our thumbs.

Amanda got it right away. She made it seem effortless.

"You're pushing too hard," she said, watching my technique.

That afternoon, when we'd all gathered after a quick lunch, we discussed the debate resolution at such length that I lost all sense of its meaning. It was like a cube drawing that suddenly shifts shape when you stare at it for too long. By the time the coaches dismissed us, I had a tower of handouts in my possession—data about everything you could imagine that might relate to energy.

There were essays on global warming and the high price of foreign oil. There were abstracts of testimony from the *Congressional Record* for and against drilling in the Arctic National Wildlife Refuge. There were articles about solar, wind, wave, nuclear, and hydroelectric power. There were studies of various government taxes and acts.

Some of the readings downplayed the oil crisis. There were

reasons to be hopeful. The world was on the brink of a new adventure. The bulk of the stuff, however, warned of an unfathomable global crisis. The world was fucked.

"Just put this evidence in your files," the coaches said.

Evidence? Files?

The other kids had come prepared. They dragged boxes of information around campus like pets. It seemed like Amanda and I were the only two people at the conference who hadn't known that at the end of the week there'd be a tournament. Why hadn't Mr. Peterson told us? Then again, Amanda and I spent so much time passing notes back and forth during debate that it was entirely possible we'd missed hearing him.

"Shoot me now," I moaned when we got back to our dorm room, collapsing on my tiny twin bed.

"We'll need ammunition," Amanda said.

"Uh—I was kidding?"

She slung her purse over her shoulder. "What I meant was that if we're going to do this debate shit, we'll need supplies. Let's go shopping."

"We're not supposed to leave campus—"

She started for the door. "Are you coming, or what?"

We walked out to Amanda's Jeep. She programmed her GPS. Then a computerized woman directed us to an office supply store just a short ways from campus. Within minutes, we'd filled our shopping cart with file boxes, folders, legal pads, scissors, tape, and pens. Amanda paid with her mom's credit card, and we loaded it all up in her car. I stood at the passenger side waiting for her to unlock the doors.

"I hate Walmart," Amanda said, gesturing at the one across the street.

"Me too. They're really big in Florida."

"I keep forgetting that you're Southern."

"I'm not," I protested. "I just lived there for a few years."

She grabbed me by the wrist. "Let's go," she said, walking in the direction of Walmart.

"Wait," I said, jogging to keep up.

"I need some makeup," she said. "They have it there. Real cheap."

"You're not making any sense. You just said you hated Walmart."

Her mouth twitched. "Ever heard of the five-finger discount program?"

I froze.

"Don't worry, Char," she said, linking her arm through mine. "It's *so* not a big deal. Walmart is one of the most corrupt places ever. There's a great documentary about the place that you should watch sometime. I do have principles. I'd *never* do this at Nordstrom's."

The store was hopping with kids and moms. In spite of the bustle and noise, I felt removed from my surroundings, like I'd stepped into some alternate dimension.

Attention Walmart Shoplifters!

Amanda picked up a packet of eye shadow and admired the shimmery colors. "I could give you a makeover tonight," she said. Out of the corner of my eye, I noticed her tucking a tube of lipstick into the pouch of her hoodie.

A sales clerk approached us. "Can I help you girls with something?"

I couldn't meet his eyes.

Amanda crossed her arms and stared him up and down. "Where are the condoms? My boyfriend is coming into town next weekend and, well . . . you know." His ears glowing like hot coals, he led us to another aisle. "Which do you recommend?" Amanda asked. "Ribbed? Or studded?"

When the guy turned and fled, Amanda cackled like a witch.

I stared at her, incredulous. "That was a ploy to get rid of him?"

"Sometimes it's like taking candy from a baby." She bumped my hip. "Hey. Earth to Charlotte! What's wrong?"

"My head hurts," I lied, furious with myself.

"Most stores budget for shoplifting," she said reassuringly. "Technically, we're helping them to keep their numbers normal. And as long as you take the cheaper things, you don't have to worry about the sensors."

What was wrong with me? Wasn't I supposed to want to do this stuff?

Amanda grabbed a *People* magazine from the newsstand. "This we buy. It makes us look legit."

A security guard was stationed by the exit. I was so nervous I nearly choked on my gum. Amanda made some inane remark to him about the weather. If he was checking her out for goods, they weren't the stolen kind.

"Is your head still bothering you?" she asked as we walked back to the car.

When I nodded, she tossed something at me.

It was a box of Excedrin. Extra strength.

She was impossible. She was magic.

Stock issues. Paradigms. Inherency. Tabula rasa.

My mind was reeling with these new debate vocabulary words and phrases. Every night that week I stayed up late trying to cram all the new information. I was mainlining coffee like it was going out of style. Next to the other kids at the conference, I was but a sapling in a rain forest. A grain of sand in the North Cascades. A pebble in the Puget Sound. And it was getting worse.

"We're going to play you some footage from last year's nationals," our coaches said on the fourth day of the conference, "so you can see how it's really done."

The two two-person teams were murderous. They jabbed their fingers like darts. They lacerated one another with their wits. They tossed facts around like grenades. And they talked so fast I had no idea what they were saying.

Something about Africa? Health care?

Fact: Debate was the art of public speaking.

Fact: I got nervous when teachers called on me in class.

Yes—I'd known both of these things when I applied for the team. But I'd talked myself into believing that if I showed up to practice, did the research, and surrounded myself with other debaters, I would learn public speaking through osmosis.

I reminded myself that there were good reasons for me to be doing debate.

Neal.

College.

My future.

Amanda was on the team.

But when the clip ended, I couldn't help but slump down in my seat.

"What's wrong?" Amanda asked. Though it looked like she was typing notes on her laptop, when I glanced at her computer screen I saw that she was cyber-shopping.

"We're doomed!" I said. "We don't even have an affirmative case yet! The tournament's two days away."

She smiled slyly, hit the WORD icon on her computer, and retrieved a document. Unbelievably, it was an affirmative case. Something about hybrid cars and tax breaks.

"Where did you get this?"

"Maybe I wrote it."

I looked at her skeptically. She rolled her eyes. "Fine. I have my resources. It doesn't matter where it came from. No one's going to care."

"That Eliot guy?" I guessed.

"He's a nice kid," she said, indirectly confirming my suspicion. "Look. It's a *mock* tournament tomorrow. It doesn't count. You're freaking me out a little. What gives? You need a little fun. Want me to call Neal? I'm sure he'd love to come hang out with us. Besides—you're obviously into him."

"I don't like . . . it's not like . . . I mean, I don't like him—"

"Like, like, like," she snapped. "You like him. He likes you."

"You think?"

She nodded emphatically.

I bit my lip. "Does that bother you?"

She squinted at something on her computer screen. "Why should I care?"

"You guys went out. Isn't there like a friends-before-guys policy?"

She snorted. "That was *eons* ago. Neal's like a little brother to me."

"He's our age," I reminded her.

"Do you have to make everything so difficult?" she asked, faking exasperation. At least—I thought she was faking it. She wasn't really annoyed. Was she?

The day before the mock tournament, the coaches farmed us off to various classrooms to work on our speaking skills. Amanda skipped out on this debacle.

"Family emergency," she explained to Claire, the girl in charge of us.

From the window next to my desk, I observed Amanda relaxing on a bench. She'd taken off her jacket and was using it as a pillow. Her hair was fanned out behind her like peacock plumage. Guys gawked at her as they walked across the quad.

And here I was stuck inside with a girl named Claire who dressed like a hippie and didn't shave her armpits. Now Claire was saying, "I used to throw up before rounds. You get used to it."

Used to what? Speaking? Barfing?

"I have this fun little exercise to help us loosen up."

For a moment I was worried she was going to make us do one of those kindergarten exercises where you shake your arms and legs.

What she had in mind was worse. She passed around a shoe box brimming with folds of paper and instructed us each to take one. "You'll have ten minutes to prepare a speech on the topic you draw."

Mine read: *Public schools should install condom dispensers in their lavatories.*

She had to be kidding me. She wanted me to talk about *sex*? In front of strangers? *Uh, I don't think so, Claire.*

Amanda's voice carried across the campus. I gazed back out the window. She was chatting away on her cell phone. Whoever she was talking to was making her laugh. Now she stood up. She glanced around. She was trying to flag someone down.

"After each speech we'll do a few minutes of oral critique."

Wait a minute. The guy walking toward Amanda—was that . . . Neal? What was he doing here? He was too advanced for conferences. Oh God! What if Amanda had said something to him about me liking him?

She wouldn't! Would she?

WOULD SHE?

"I'm starting the timer now," Claire said.

My heart pounded while the minutes ticked away. I couldn't think. I doodled a palm tree. I doodled Neal's name. Somehow my palm tree morphed into a penis. I gave it a condom. Maybe I could show condom cartoons instead of giving a stupid speech.

Something hit the window. Looking down, I saw Amanda and Neal giggling.

That did it. "It's a girl thing," I explained to Claire as I gathered up my things.

"Need a tampon?" she asked loudly. I wasn't fooling her any.

I waved good-bye over my shoulder, not bothering to turn around to see who was staring.

Stay cool, I reminded myself when Neal saw me. "You missed all the fun this week," I said. I made *fun* sound vague and mysterious and arched my eyebrow in an Amanda-like way. Amanda was trying to get me to laugh by making horns above Neal's head.

He swatted at her. "You're like a pesky mosquito, Munger."

"'Cause I make you itch so bad?" Her comebacks were always lightning-quick.

"What are you doing here?" I asked Neal.

Neal produced three tickets from his jacket. "Cloud 9, anyone?"

Amanda kissed hers like it was the winning lottery ticket.

"What's Cloud 9?" I asked.

"You've never heard of Cloud 9?" Neal asked.

"It's this amusement park just a short ways south of here," Amanda said. "It's not like Six Flags or anything, but it's still fun."

"What about the tournament?" I asked, scanning the schedule for tomorrow. "Don't we have to prepare tonight?"

"Would you quit obsessing about that stupid thing?" Amanda groaned.

"You're doomed anyway," Neal said, "with Amanda for a partner."

"I remember why I hate you now, Fitz!" She pretended to strangle him.

"Don't leave me alone with her!" Neal begged, trying to get away.

They *were* like brother and sister.

Amanda glared at me meaningfully. "C'mon, Char. The boy wants you—"

"I'll go," I practically shouted before she could incriminate me further.

"Let's make a pact," Amanda said. "We have to ride every ride at Cloud 9."

It was almost midnight. Lying on a park bench, Amanda clutched her stomach. "Make it stop." Amanda, it turned out, had a low tolerance for roller coaster rides. This was the first indicator I'd had that she wasn't invincible. Maybe. Plus, she'd stuffed herself with funnel cake and cotton candy. "Ugh." She leaned over to puke.

I grabbed her hair.

Neal jumped back to avoid being splattered. "There goes the cotton candy."

"We should get her home," I said.

Amanda flapped her hand to get our attention. "But the Vortex! We have to ride the Vortex."

"You're crazy, Munger," Neal said.

Amanda pouted. "We made a *pact*!"

"You're not really in a condition to ride anything," I said gently.

She sniffed. "Fine. You two go. I'll wait here."

"We can come back some other time," I suggested.

She waved us away, in charge even when sick. "Go!"

The Vortex was a type of Gravitron—one of those circular rooms that spins around and around and relies on centrifugal force to hold you in place. It was lit up like a Christmas tree and looked just like a flying saucer. We didn't have to worry about lines this late in the evening. The operator said he'd keep us turning a few extra minutes since we were his last ride of the night.

The lights went off. The room began to spin. We all started to scream.

"Look at me," Neal said. With great effort I moved my head. Everything was a blur. "What's the weirdest place you've ever been kissed?" he asked.

Just then the floor began to fall away. We were pinned to the wall like flies. I started to laugh, then hiccupped instead. Embarrassed, I tried to cover my mouth, but I couldn't move my hand. Neal was strong, however. Defying a force greater than gravity, he mashed his lips to mine.

Amanda was sleeping in the passenger seat of Neal's Toyota Prius. It was two in the morning. Neal had kissed me! The world felt surreal—everything was alive and breathing in this entirely new way.

The tournament, however, now less than six hours away, was a growing knot of fear in the back of my neck. Neal glanced at me in the rearview mirror. "There's a party in Belltown. There will be dancing. You want to go?"

He was asking me to choose between two impossible things: him or my future. With an ache in my heart, I shook my head. "I can't. But I really want to."

"That's what I figured. I thought I'd ask." He reached back and gave my leg a little squeeze. "I think it's cool how much you care about doing well tomorrow. You're going to be great at debate."

Amanda, who had been sleeping in the front seat, suddenly

snapped to attention. "Dancing? Did somebody say something about DANCING?"

Back at the room, she stripped out of her clothes and changed into a fresh outfit right in front of Neal. He clapped his hands to his eyes. "Do you have *any* sense of modesty?"

"Sense?" She wadded up her puke-stained shirt and tossed it in the trash, frowning as if she'd had nothing to do with its condition. "What I sense is that you're peeking, Fitz. Nakedness is the most natural state. It's people who make it weird. Besides. Need I remind you that you've already seen me naked?"

My stomach dropped. He had?

Neal uncovered his eyes. "That time we went skinny-dipping? That doesn't count!"

"It counted, all right," she said. "You were just too stupid to know it." Amanda twirled around in tight jeans, a silver blouse, stilettos, and shoulder-dusting earrings. "How do I look?"

"Like a disco queen," Neal said. "But I think it's an eighties party."

She waved her hand. "People will be too drunk to care."

Sitting on my bed, a pillow in my lap, I tried to act like I was having fun. Amanda narrowed her eyes to slits. "I can tell you're worrying about tomorrow," she said to me. "I'm telling you to stop!"

"I'm getting a migraine again," I lied. "I should sleep."

Amanda tossed me the green bottle of Excedrin. "Problem solved!"

Neal came to my defense. "The girl doesn't feel well, Mandy. Give her a break." I searched his eyes for some acknowledgment of our kiss. He squeezed my shoulder in this friendly way that could have meant anything. "Drink water," he said. "You're probably dehydrated."

"I'll talk you up," Amanda whispered to me before leaving the room.

Would Neal mention our kiss to her? Feeling like a little kid who has to stay home while the big kids get to do fun grown-up things, I waited until they disappeared into the darkness. Then I logged on to Amanda's laptop. Could I learn everything there was to know about alternative energy in the approximately four hours that remained?

Control your thoughts. He's just a guy.

He was the only guy who counted.

What's the weirdest place you've ever been kissed?

Now I had an answer.

Neal had kissed me.

Neal. Neal. Neal.

Outside, there was a distant rumble of thunder. Heat lightning lit up the campus, giving it this gothic look. Around three a.m., the wind picked up. It started to rain. The thunderclaps grew louder. The sky was now alive with electricity. I opened my window to smell the ozone. Treetops whipped around in circles as if they were possessed. Suddenly there was a deafening boom. Everything went dark. The next morning the tournament was canceled due to a citywide power outage.

I'd stayed behind for nothing.

11

The next Friday, Amanda invited Neal to see a movie with us at an art house theater downtown. I still hadn't told her about our kiss. For one thing, I suspected it was in bad form to have been making out with a boy while your friend was lying sick on a park bench. For another thing, I wasn't entirely sure if Amanda would approve. She and Neal went way back. Would she think I was good enough for a guy she'd been involved with—even if it was only a silly middle-school thing?

Since our night at Cloud 9, nothing more had happened between Neal and me. But then, we hadn't been alone together. *These things take time*, I told myself. *Be patient.*

Though I was pretty picky about the books I read, all I really wanted from a movie was for it to make me forget about my life. I was a sucker for even the god-awful ones. The movie Amanda had chosen for us to see was *Ordinary People*. It had won the Oscar for Best Picture in 1980. "It was Robert Redford's directorial debut," she told us as we waited in line for tickets.

"Redford," Neal said. "Is that guy even still alive?"

"Have you been to the Sundance Film Festival?" Amanda asked, not answering his question. "I go every year."

Neal made a face. "Sundance is for neophytes."

"It's a cool scene," Amanda said, tossing her pink mane. "Last year I met Matt Damon."

"Good for you," Neal teased. "Did you give him a blow job?"

Amanda punched him in the arm. "For your information, he complimented my hair. He said it was *incandescent*."

Trying to think of something to contribute, I said, "I like looking at the Sundance catalog."

Amanda rolled her eyes. "That thing? It's so *pretentious*."

"It's nouveau riche," Neal said.

Luckily, we were walking into the theater, where it was dark and neither of them could see my consternation. I envied how easy they were with each other and themselves. I envied how easily everything came for them. I wondered if I'd be that way if I'd grown up incredibly wealthy and in one place—without the added baggage of a learning disability. Because they assumed good things were in store for them, good things inevitably happened to them. It was a formula that I failed to grasp. Formulas were mathematical, though.

"We should sit in the back," Neal suggested, steering me to a seat. "It makes for a more panoramic experience."

"I get the aisle," Amanda said. "Because I have long legs."

"I get the middle," Neal said. "Because I'm a guy, and what guy doesn't want to be surrounded by cute chicks?"

"Hot," Amanda corrected him. "We're *hot* chicks."

Ordinary People was about a family coping with the loss of their eldest son. I thought it was a moving film—tragic but ultimately redemptive. There was no disguising my tears when the credits rolled.

Afterward we went to the coffee shop above the theater. The chairs were the old movie kind with red velvet on the seats. Amanda ordered a regular coffee and dumped in a ton of cream and sugar.

"You want some coffee with that?" Neal joked.

"Leave me alone. This is the way they drink coffee in New Orleans."

"We're a long way from New Orleans, baby."

"Maybe I've got Cajun ancestry," Amanda said, pouting a little.

"That would explain your craziness." Now it was Neal's turn to order. "I'll have a doppio," he said to the barista. "Ristretto."

"What's a doppio?" I asked.

"It's for purists," Neal said, making a face at Amanda.

"It's for dopes," Amanda quipped. "You'll hate it, Char." She ordered a coffee for me. "My treat." She fixed it the way she'd fixed hers. "You can afford the calories. Trust me. You've been looking a little gaunt lately."

Neal led us to a table by the front window. "Someone was crying," he said, elbowing me in a teasing way.

"That poor kid . . . The one who lives, I mean. Blaming

himself for his brother's death. His mom blaming him too. She was awful."

"I wanted to cry too," Amanda said, "out of boredom. That was like a *Lifetime* after-school special. Ugh."

"I thought the acting was good."

Considering this, Neal took a sip of his doppio. "The performances seemed really dated to me. But as a rule I don't like movies that try to manipulate my emotions."

"Guys always freak out when stuff makes them cry," Amanda teased. "God forbid someone might think they're gay."

Neal stared at her pointedly. "Trust me. I'm not gay."

"What a waste of time," Amanda said, pouring more cream into her coffee.

"Can you believe *Ordinary People* beat out *Raging Bull* for Best Picture that year?" Neal asked. "C'mon! We're talking about Martin Scorsese's finest work."

"I liked *Cape Fear* a lot," I said.

"Oh, Char," Amanda said, exasperated. "Really?"

"What was wrong with *Cape Fear*?"

"*Cape Fear* was Scorsese's most commercial film," Neal explained. "But I'll admit—it wasn't bad for what it was. And Juliette Lewis is a babe."

I wanted to hug him for coming to my rescue. I wanted to kill Juliette Lewis for being a babe.

"You know what?" he said, studying me. "You look like Juliette Lewis."

"I see that," Amanda agreed. "You both have really big lips."

Neal bumped my knee under the table, sending an electric

surge of hope through my body. "She's got a dark streak too."

After we'd finished our drinks, we started walking back to Amanda's Jeep. Amanda wanted to go to this bar she knew of over in Ballard. "My brother Keith worked there," she said. "They know I'm his sister. They won't check our IDs."

"Keith walked on water," Neal explained to me. "He and my brother were pals. He's just one of those people you have to like." He smiled as if remembering something particularly crazy.

How much easier would life be if you had a cool older brother to pave the way? To help you figure out what to do and say and how to act? To help you figure out who to be?

"I haven't seen Bailey in years," Amanda said. "How is he?"

"He's chasing this born-again virgin down in Eugene," Neal said, rolling his eyes.

"Why's he wasting his time?" Amanda asked.

"Bailey's not sure if she's serious or if it's all a big hoax to make him super horny. If she does cave, think how mind-blowing the sex will be after all that build-up."

Amanda snorted. "That's the dumbest thing I've ever heard."

"Or maybe she's a genius. Bailey has started talking about wedding rings."

We all grew quiet once we got into the Jeep. The top was down, and the sound of the wind made talking impossible. It was nice, though, not having to talk. Trying to keep up with Neal and Amanda was exhausting.

The bar, we discovered a short while later, had gone out of business.

"Just my luck," Amanda groaned.

"Whatever!" Neal laughed. "You're the kind of person who makes her own luck."

"That I am," she agreed.

Whatever had happened between Neal and Amanda in middle school seemed to be water under the bridge now. They were friends. Good friends. I wasn't jealous of their friendship. I wasn't. I swear I wasn't.

Amanda liked the idea of having adversaries—which meant that she was finally starting to take debate seriously. When Mr. Peterson talked, she paid attention. She took notes and raised her hand a lot.

I still hadn't made any more progress with Neal. With all of his extracurricular activities, he was super busy. But he smiled at me a lot, smiles that were loaded with hidden meaning, smiles that were meant for me and me only, smiles that kept me hoping.

One Friday afternoon in mid-October, Mr. Peterson reminded us that our first big tournament of the fall—held at Whitman College in eastern Washington—was less than a week away. "I expect all of you to devote your weekend to preparing for it," he'd said.

The next day I rode my bike over to Amanda's on the Burke-Gilman Trail. Neal and Diego were coming over to the Mungers' house as well. Diego was Neal's debate partner, and the four of us were going to pool our research. Amanda was tackling the research part of debate with surprising enthusiasm. "It's like being a detective," she'd told me.

I knew Amanda wanted to work for the FBI or the CIA someday.

As Amanda and I sat on the island counter in the kitchen, I began to feel restless. "Has Neal had many girlfriends?" I asked, chewing on my thumbnail.

Sucking on a Jolly Rancher, Amanda said, "Most of the girls he's dated have gone to private schools. They're usually the prissy type, if you know what I mean."

Most? *Most* sounded like a lot. And no, I didn't know what she meant.

"Any idiot can tell he thinks you're cute," she said.

"Cute in a good way? Or cute like a little kid?" My heart raced, waiting to hear what she'd have to say. Amanda was smart about guys—smart about everything, for that matter.

She popped another piece of candy into her mouth and bit down hard. "I'm not going to dignify that with an answer," she said. "Don't you know—the secret to getting boys to like you is to *know* they think you're hot shit?"

"It's amazing you look so great," I said. "Your diet is a mess. You think Mountain Dew is a rational meal replacement."

She chuckled at this. "I believe in the three C's: Cigarettes, caffeine, and candy."

"That's a screwy belief," I muttered. "But you're doing something right."

"I'm doing everything right," she said, hopping down from the counter to answer the door.

A moment later, Neal and Diego walked into the kitchen dragging huge crates. "Files and files of evidence," Neal explained, seeing my eyes widen with dismay. How did he have the time to do so much work and research? "I've got tons more at home. In my bedroom."

"I'll bet," I said, wrapping a lock of hair around my finger nervously.

"You should see it sometime," he said with a pointed look.

Wait—did he mean his debate evidence or his bedroom?

"We'll take the elevator up to my dad's office," Amanda said, leading us to a part of the house I'd never seen before. "He's away again on another top secret medical mission." She said this tongue in cheek, but you knew she thought that the sun rose and set on her dad.

Dr. Munger's home office was enormous, as big as the entire first floor of my house, and was fully equipped with a high-speed copier, a fax, several computers, a minibar, and a small kitchen. The perimeter was lined floor to ceiling with hardback books. In one of the corners there was a life-size human skeleton.

"It's real," Amanda informed us. "My dad uses it to scare off kids at Halloween."

"I prefer my skeletons to stay in the closet," I joked, at once pleased with myself for having actually said something witty, and creeped out because THERE WAS A CORPSE IN THE ROOM!

"I want to hear more about your skeletons," Neal said, placing a hand on my shoulder. "Who is Charlotte Locke?"

I tried not to shiver at his touch. And his question. I felt like an impostor. Deep down, I knew I was not who he wanted me to be.

The paintings on Dr. Munger's walls were of the abstract variety—the kind that usually made me feel stupid because I never understood what they meant or what feeling they were supposed to stir.

"Those look like Clyfford Stills," Neal said.

"We studied that guy in Art History, right?" Diego asked.

Amanda laughed. "They ARE Clyfford Stills. My grandfather had them commissioned."

"Yeah, right," Neal said. "Clyfford Still is one of the most famous artists of the twentieth century."

Amanda crossed her arms. "He was friends with my grandfather, okay?"

Diego stood before the painting. "Didn't we see some of his stuff on that field trip to the art museum?"

"That's right," Neal said. He turned to me. "Have you been to SAM yet?"

"Sam?" (And was I the only person in the room who hadn't heard of Clyfford Still?)

"The Seattle Art Museum." In a low voice I thought might be just for me, Neal added, "We'll have to go sometime."

Katherine looked in on us once and brightened when she saw Neal. "It's so good to see you again," she said. "You used to be such a fixture around here. Can I get you a snack?"

When Neal shook his head, Katherine smiled at me. "I'd love to get my hands on an advance copy of your father's next book. What's the status?"

Her friendliness made me nervous. I liked her better in ice queen mode.

"He just got a two-book deal with Random House," I said, hating myself for saying it because, although it was true, I'd said it to impress everyone. "His new book is due out next fall."

Amanda made shooing motions with her hands. "You can leave now, Mom."

After she left, Amanda said to Neal, "I think she wants you to be her snack. Her little cougar snack."

Neal ignored this and said, "She trusts you to be alone with boys?"

Amanda folded her hands under her chin and screwed her face into this angelic expression. "Debate *is* the kind of activity good kids do."

"If only she knew the shit that goes on at Whitman."

"What kind of shit?" I asked.

"You'll see," Neal said, nudging my foot and sending an electric current through my body.

"Count me in," I practically gasped.

"Peterson looks the other way after hours. As do we with him." Diego made a guzzling motion with his hand. "Let's just say he likes his vodka."

"I like *my* vodka," Amanda said.

We all laughed.

Once we'd finished cutting and clipping articles to add to our stock of debate evidence, Diego eyed us speculatively. "Hmm. There are four of us. We could do a practice round. Girls against boys?"

"Me say good idea," Amanda said. "And—after each person's speech, we have to drink a beer."

"If we each do two speeches that's *eight* beers!" Neal exclaimed. "You're crazy, Munger."

"No. I'm *thirsty*. Are you afraid you can't keep up?" She raised an eyebrow. "Or"—she grinned slyly—"we could play strip debate."

I didn't hear what was said next. My pulse was racing too hard. I was NOT taking my clothes off. Not with Amanda around, at any rate. I'd pale in comparison. Literally. But if I made a stink about not wanting to play, Amanda would tease me about being a prude—which was the last thing I needed Neal thinking about me if anything unprudish was ever going to happen between us.

Pretending that my phone was buzzing, I excused myself to the hall outside. When I returned, I made a show of acting ticked off. "I have to go," I said. "Something came up—my parents want me home. I guess I'll have to practice some other time. Or wing it."

"Practice speaking in front of a mirror," Neal suggested. "It helps."

Amanda waggled her pinkie. "Wing it on home, little birdie."

It was dusk when I left. The sky was slate blue and pregnant with rain. By the time I reached the Burke-Gilman Trail, it had started to pour. Breezy gusts knocked my bike around as if it were but a wind chime. The trail was an eerie place tonight: the trees were alive and cruel, lashing around as if possessed. There were a couple of ominous cracks, followed by the sound of falling branches—or, God forbid, entire trees.

A few miles from our house, I hit a bump at the wrong angle and tumbled to the ground. Though I wasn't hurt, I'd landed in an enormous puddle of mud—more of a pond, really. After I'd collected myself, I discovered that the chain on my bike was broken. I'd have to push it home.

I tried to picture what I was missing right now at Amanda's. Were they all drunk and naked? Having an orgy? On second thought, maybe I didn't want a visual. I didn't want to admit that my feelings were hurt by how glib Amanda had acted when I left.

As I neared the end of the trail, I saw a bearded man wearing a black jacket. He stared at me with a cold expression, his eyes as opaque as nickels. I increased my pace as I passed him, and made sure the bike was between us. My heart beat wildly.

He started to wave and shout. "They've got chickens for sale at Safeway!"

Was he crazy? Was he insulting me? Or was this what ax murderers said right before they killed you?

Except for the green glow of the television, our house was dark when I finally arrived. I let myself in the back door and grabbed a towel from the laundry room. Water streamed from me onto the white linoleum.

"Hello?" I called out tentatively.

When no one answered, I wandered into the den. It was empty.

The music on the television was rising to a dramatic crescendo. In spite of my bedraggled state, I was sucked into the horror movie that was playing. A teenage girl raced across a desert on a full moon night, fleeing a masked killer. She searched desperately for shelter behind squat cactus plants and sage bushes, but always just missed making herself invisible. Finally, she reached a canyon. There was no place left to run or hide. The killer's knife flashed as he lunged toward her.

The girl leaped. A coyote howled.

Icy fingers grabbed my neck from behind. I screamed. James Henry and Milton high-fived each other and fell to the floor in laughter. I tried to speak, but my teeth were chattering too hard with fear. Milton suddenly noticed my waterlogged clothes. He stood up. He expression grew serious. "What happened to you?"

I crossed my arms in case my nipples were poking out. "You—" Unable to get out the words, I just shook my head.

"Mom and Dad went to the symphony," James Henry said.

"So you called mushroom boy to entertain you? What—is he like your babysitter now?"

"Babysitter! I'm way too old—"

"It's not so funny to go around scaring people. Murder?" I sputtered. "It happens to girls. Haven't you heard of Jeffrey Dahmer? Ted Bundy? The Green River Killer?" I grabbed the remote and flicked off the TV. My hands were shaking.

James Henry muttered something about "people who need to be medicated."

Milton tried to say something, but I stopped him with a glare. "Spare me." Leaving them in the den, I retreated to the bathroom, where I filled the tub with the hottest water I could stand. It took a long time for the heat to penetrate my cold flesh.

Skimming my palm along the surface, I thought about my reason for leaving Amanda's. Had Amanda guessed that I'd lied about having to leave? Did she think I was a coward? What exactly was I afraid of? Getting naked? Or speaking in front of my friends? Public speaking wasn't just a part of debate—it *was* debate. I needed to get my act together fast if I had any hopes of doing well at Whitman.

I closed my eyes and imagined Neal's lips on mine.

Was he ever going to kiss me again?

There was a knock on the door. "Charlotte?"

"Why are you even here?" I asked Milton, not bothering to hide my irritation. "Do you and my brother have some kind of British schoolboy thing going on?"

There was a sound like muffled laughter. "I'm his mentor, remember? And we're neighbors. Your mom asked me to look in on him tonight. Plus—your brother's cool. You don't give him enough credit."

"Trust me," I said, flicking the water with my finger, "James Henry gets *plenty* of credit."

"Listen. I just wanted to see if you're okay. You don't look so hot. Not that I can see you right now," he rushed to say.

"You're saying I'm not hot?" I bit my lip.

There was a sound like a head banging against a wall. "Why don't you come watch a movie with us when you're done in there?"

"I don't think so."

"Fine." He sighed. "Have it your way. I'm sorry for scaring you. I saw a movie once about Ted Bundy. *The Deliberate Stranger?*

If you'd ever want to see it . . . Mark Harmon plays—"

I ducked my head under the water and held it there, trying to drown out the sound of his voice, the roaring in my ears, and the sudden confusion I was feeling at his kindness. "Milton," I said when I surfaced, "can we talk about this some other time?"

"Okay," he agreed. "But what exactly *are* we talking about?"

12

Neal sat next to me on the bus ride to the Whitman tournament. He was reading a book about quantum mechanics for his physics class and kept setting it down to talk about string theory and other complicated scientific matters. Every time we went over a bump, his arm jostled against mine, sending shivers up and down my spine. Too twitter-pated to talk, I kept nodding enthusiastically to keep the conversation going. Guys liked girls who were good listeners, right?

I could practically hear Amanda scoffing at this. At present, she was asleep in the seat in front of us.

I gazed absently out the window. Our bus had gotten off at the wrong Interstate exit, and we were passing through an area of defunct warehouses. Most of the windows were broken. I stared at the star-shaped holes, trying to picture the decaying interiors.

Neal waved his hand in front of me. "Earth to Charlotte. What's going on?"

Which is exactly what I was wondering but not at all what he meant.

"Oh. Um . . . what did you say?"

"I was asking how your parents get along. Was it weird for your mom to read *Lily at Dusk*? The book has some feminist critics up in arms—which I'm sure you probably know."

"I think my dad's having an affair," I blurted before I could stop myself.

Neal nodded, taking my outburst in stride. "I'm so sorry. Affairs aren't that uncommon, though. We place such a huge cultural taboo on them in America, but in other countries, like France, affairs are a way of life. In fact, I read an article once that said that affairs can actually help keep marriages fresh as long as both parties are honest."

"I might just be imagining things," I said, wanting to take back not only the confession, but the actual thought as well. I felt—disloyal. To change the subject, I asked Neal, "Where do you want to go to college?"

"I'm waiting to hear if I got into Stanford early admission," he said, adjusting his expensive-looking watch. His arm was tan, which baffled me. As far as I could tell, there was hardly any sun to be had in the Northwest. "How about you?"

Shit. He wasn't supposed to ask me this.

"I'm still narrowing down my choices," I said, picking at a hangnail. The truth was I'd been too busy with debate and my new life to give college a second thought. "I'm looking at some of the smaller liberal arts schools. Middlebury. William and Mary. Maybe Reed."

It was true that I'd looked at pictures of these schools online. But they weren't places I had a chance in hell of getting admitted to.

"Those are great schools," Neal said. "Reed is supposed to be very alternative, and Portland is a really hip town. Do you know what you want to study?"

No. I felt a squeezing pressure in my chest. I didn't know what I wanted to study. I didn't know what I wanted to do. I didn't even know how to act without embarrassing myself most of the time. And with my test scores and mediocre transcripts, none of the schools I'd mentioned to Neal were even going to be long shots.

"How about you?" I asked, deflecting Neal's attention away from me. "What do you want to be when you grow up?"

"A grown-up," he said with a straight face.

I punched his arm the way I'd seen Amanda do countless times. He made a face, like he thought the punch was somehow beneath me. Staring at my hands, I tried to think of a way to redeem myself. There was one thing . . .

"If you ever want to meet my dad—" I began.

Amanda whipped her head around. "This conversation is putting me to sleep. Let's play poker."

How much had she heard? Had she interrupted to stop me from making a fool of myself?

Neal laughed. "Okay, Mandy. Let's hear where you're going next year. Have you hired someone to do your applications?"

"Very funny. You know I'm going to Harvard. I'm a double legacy. I'll probably go somewhere international for graduate school. Maybe Oxford." She sighed as if having all of life at her fingertips was simply too exhausting to talk about any further.

We arrived at a classroom in the science building, where our first debate round was to be held. My palms began to sweat. My stomach was doing flip-flops. Although I'd just peed, I had to go again. I reminded myself of what Claire the coach had said—that she'd thrown up before rounds when she first started doing debate.

At the last minute, I decided to call home. I needed to hear my mom's voice before I faced the sharks. As luck would (not) have it, it was my dad who answered the phone.

"Debate isn't an activity for lightweights. This is the missing ingredient for you and the colleges. How are you holding up?" he said.

"I'm nervous," I admitted. "I can barely breathe."

"That's natural. Nothing worth doing is ever easy."

This wasn't exactly the reassurance I had hoped for. I'd wanted him to tell me that he was proud of me and that he knew I was up to the challenge (since I didn't know this myself). Instead, my dad wished me luck, and we hung up.

The opposing team was composed of twin Asian girls from a school in Portland, who wore matching navy blue suits, matching buns, and matching smug expressions. They kept staring at Amanda and me and whispering in another language. We were in a biology lab of some kind. Our audience—besides the judge—comprised of dead animals floating in jars of formaldehyde.

Their skin looked like it would squeak if you touched it. I felt like I owed them a good performance today.

Amanda was dressed in a formfitting lime-green dress that showed off her boobs. Our judge looked a lot like Jesus, with long hair, a long beard, and those funny leather sandals. He couldn't keep his eyes off Amanda.

"He wants you," I whispered.

"Do you think he's high?" Amanda asked.

"Jesus would never smoke pot," I said.

When we flipped for sides, Amanda and I won the coin toss and chose to argue from the negative point of view. As Twin One read her affirmative case—something about biofuels and tax credits—we "flowed" the points of her proposal onto yellow legal pads.

After this speech, Amanda rose for the first three-minute cross-examination period. Her recent interest notwithstanding, from the start I'd sensed that debate, for Amanda, wasn't going to be the most serious of endeavors. Unlike me, she didn't *need* to pad her college résumé. She got good grades without trying. And even if she got straight D's, all her parents had to do to get her into the school of her choice was donate a museum or something. Debate simply provided her with a nice escape from house arrest. I doubted Amanda would flop in an embarrassing way— that wasn't her style. She would simply make a mockery of the rest of us for caring.

This I was prepared for.

What I was not prepared for was for her to be dazzling.

Watching her interrogate Twin One was like watching a

hard-nosed lawyer in a legal thriller manipulating a murder confession out of the defense. But unlike an actor, she was working without a script. Unlike a real attorney, she had no real-life practice. She was all improvisation, but her performance was flawless. She was having fun too. She reminded me of a cat toying with its prey. Twin One now looked anything but smug. I almost felt sorry for her.

"I think that went well," Amanda whispered when she sat down.

I gaped at her. How could any one person be so freaking competent? It wasn't fair. It just wasn't fair.

As first negative speaker, my job was to present disadvantages to the affirmative's case that would explain how implementing the affirmative's plan would ultimately lead to the end of the world or nuclear war or something even worse.

But some key circuit in my brain was shorting. Though I had sheets of evidence opposing the affirmative's case in front of me, I had no idea how to synthesize the information. I couldn't think off the cuff. I couldn't seem to make my mouth form words.

"Just a second," I muttered, flipping through my papers. Glancing at the timer, I saw that I'd used one minute of my allotted eight. I sipped some water, cracked my neck, and cleared my throat—hoping that these physical actions might somehow dislodge my voice and thoughts.

Two minutes.

My arms and legs went numb. My vision blurred. My legs quivered like Jell-O.

Amanda coughed purposefully. I glanced at the timer. Three

minutes used. Five minutes left. Time would pass in a blink if I only had five minutes left to live. Now, five minutes was an eternity.

Amanda scribbled something on a Post-it note. *Argue solvency!*

More circuits were shorting. *Solvency.* That meant something, right? What?

Four minutes. WHAT DID SOLVENCY MEAN?

Another Post-it note, this one underlined twice. *SAY SOMETHING!*

"The resolution is not . . ." My voice trembled. "Solvency is a word that means—" I cleared my throat. "Biofuels are bad because . . ." I massaged my temples with my fingers.

Jesus blinked at me dispassionately.

Let me pass out, I prayed. What was that old saying? God helps those who help themselves? I closed my eyes and swayed a little, gathering up my nerve. It was time to fake a faint.

Suddenly, something was slammed in front of me. I opened my eyes. It was a script. While I'd stood there paralyzed, Amanda had written me a script on note cards, tying together the pages and pages of evidence about why biofuels were the Antichrist. Things I knew. The stuff I wanted to say.

Because of Amanda we won. In spite of me we won. Jesus awarded Amanda the highest number of speaker points. The twins refused to look me in the eye when they shook my hand. They saw me as a fraud.

I saw myself as something worse—a parasite. "I'm sorry," I said to Amanda, after it was all over, my voice cracking a little.

Amanda shrugged. "You'll get better in time. It's just nerves. No big deal."

Jesus stopped me as I was walking out the door. "It's really brave what you're doing," he said.

"What do you mean?" I asked.

He tugged his beard. "It can't be easy . . . well, you know."

What was he suggesting? That it couldn't be easy not being Amanda? That it couldn't be easy having a sudden onset of a speech impediment?

The rest of the day went more or less the same. In every round I was too nervous to talk. We made it through the tournament because Amanda kept feeding me things to say and writing out the words for me on note cards. And because she was more than good enough for both of us, we kept winning and winning and winning. With every round we won, I felt like more and more like a loser.

Mr. Peterson called a team meeting at the end of that first afternoon. He made a huge fuss over Amanda and me, and passed around our trophies for everyone to see. Neal congratulated me. "Guess you've taught Munger a thing or two," he said. "Hope it wasn't too painful."

Amanda left the room without speaking to me.

I approached Mr. Peterson afterward. "Can I talk to you a second?"

"You're talking to me now," he said in this jovial way that made me think he'd gotten an early start on his vodka.

I lowered my voice. "I'm not sure policy is my thing."

He peered at me over his glasses. "Your *thing*? Can you be a little more specific?"

"I get really stressed out," I blurted. Suddenly, the tears I'd been holding back all day burst through the dam. Unfazed, Mr. Peterson handed me a tissue. When I finally regained control, I said, "I might be more suited for something that doesn't require you to think on your feet. Like humorous interpretation or original oratory. Or maybe I could be the team manager."

Mr. Peterson smiled wryly. "Don't you think you're being a little melodramatic? You won today, after all."

"Amanda won. I'm holding her back. I don't want this to ruin our friendship."

"I hear everything around here," he said. "I know how it went for you today. I understand more than you think. It sounds to me like you didn't do your homework and that Amanda had to argue for the both of you. Debate involves work. It's not something you can just put on a college résumé and forget. I'll consider moving you *after* I see some effort."

He stopped me as I was walking out the door. "You're right about something. These debate partnership issues *can* affect friendships."

There was a party that night at the student union. The room was decorated with streamers, balloons, and Christmas lights. There was cake, fruit punch, and a platter of cubed cheese. A giant disco ball spun lights across an empty dance floor. No kid would be caught dead dancing to the boy band stuff the DJ was playing.

I felt like a trespasser and kept to the margins, where no one could see me. I hadn't earned the right to celebrate. I didn't belong here.

Amanda was gesticulating before some kids that we'd beaten earlier in the day. Whatever she was saying was cracking them up. She didn't seem concerned that I wasn't around.

When no one was looking, I slipped out a side door.

It was a strange evening. Though it was cold outside, the ground looked like it was steaming. The trees smelled sweet and earthy and made me miss being a kid. I used to love making forts, piling leaves high in a circular wall, hunching down low in the middle, spying on the neighborhood. Back then I liked being on the fringes. From a distance you could tell what was *really* going on. Now I just felt left out and confused.

One thing was all too clear to me: no amount of desire or effort was going to make me a better debater. All I could hope for was a miracle.

Hugging my arms to my chest, I watched my breath smoke the air. A few students drifted in and out of the dorms and cafeteria. No one gave me a second glance. I hoped they thought I was one of them. At the same time, the thought that in less than a year I was supposed to be heading off to college froze me more than the weather. I was so screwed.

I sat down beneath a cedar tree and closed my eyes, hoping I would just melt into the earth.

"You look like a wood sprite," a voice said—a voice that melted the chill away. Neal crouched down beside me and tapped out a cigarette from a pack of Dunhills.

"That's the kind Amanda smokes," I observed.

"I know. She gave them to me." He laughed. "She told me to quit wasting my time with the plebeian brands."

His face was just inches away from mine and almost too beautiful to take. Something about his expression made me ache. I was probably too plebeian for him as well. I peeled off a string of bark from the tree and started demolishing it with one hand. Silent tears dripped down my face.

I was glad he didn't ask me what was wrong. What would I have said? Nothing? Everything? Me?

He stubbed out his cigarette and held out his hand. "Let's get you out of here."

We walked across the commons, past the academic buildings and dorms, into a neighborhood of fraternity houses and Victorian fixer-uppers. When we turned up the walkway of one of these, Neal let go of my hand. I wiped my eyes on my sweater. Some guys were sitting on the porch, drinking hunch punch from Mason jars. One of them lifted his glass when he saw us.

"Neal," he said.

Shit. It was Jesus the judge. Praying that he wouldn't remember me, I tugged my hair out of its ponytail and shook it around my face. After handing us each a glass of punch, Jesus led us inside the house. Neal looked back at me as we clambered up the rickety stairs. "Michael was a senior at Shady Grove when I was a freshman," he explained. "Now he relives the glory days by judging high school debate tournaments. How pathetic is that?"

Michael/Jesus grinned at him from the top of the landing. "Does your girlfriend know what a fuck-face you are?"

Girlfriend? He thought I was Neal's girlfriend?

I held my breath waiting for Neal to correct him.

He didn't. Did that mean——?

Michael led us to his room. A purple lava lamp illuminated an enormous terrarium. Piled high like a stack of pancakes was the largest snake I'd ever seen. "Her name is Baby," Michael informed us. He was studying me in a way that told me that although he recognized me, he wasn't sure from where.

"A snake?" Neal shook his head. "You're demented, dude."

He flipped through Michael's CDs and popped in a Bob Marley disk. Michael retrieved a bong from under his bed. When he passed it to me, I inhaled like I'd done this a thousand times. I'd watched Amanda enough to know what to do.

Neal seemed taken aback when I coughed and coughed, like he'd expected better of me. "Pot always does this to me," I said. "I think I might have asthma."

Sometime later, maybe half an hour and two hits later, Michael took Baby out of her tank. She coiled around his arm and seemed to like it when he stroked her head. I watched with widened eyes. The pot was really starting to work. I felt numb and happy, dreamy and alert.

"You can hold her," he said, handing her over to me. "She's a python. They're not poisonous."

The width of her surprised me, as did the cool, silky texture of her skin. This was crazy. I was high as a kite and holding a snake. I couldn't stop laughing when she pooped on my wrist. I excused myself to the bathroom to wash it off.

Practice speaking in front of a mirror.

"You're very high, Charlotte Locke," I announced.

It can't be easy . . . well, you know.

"Feel yourself forming words," I said, drawling out the words.

You'll get better in time.

There was a knock on the door. It was Neal. "Everything okay in there?"

"Peachy keen," I said, opening the door and stumbling out.

Baby was now draped around Michael's neck. Her tongue flickered at his ear.

"She has a nice aura," I said. "Snakes are the bomb."

"She's really messed up," Michael said to Neal.

I wasn't sure whether he meant the snake or me. I didn't care. Time had lost all sense of meaning. Nothing mattered. Everything was A-okay. I wrapped my arms around my middle. My organs hurt from laughing so much.

Baby was back in her terrarium. It was just Neal and me in the room. I had no idea how long we'd been there. Had I fallen asleep? Was it time for another hit off the bong?

"Where'd Michael go?" I asked.

"He went to a party."

"So are we in deep dog shit with Mr. Peterson?" I asked.

He patted his cell phone. "Diego's covering for us. No worries."

He was lying on top of Michael's platform bed, fiddling with a Magic 8 Ball.

"What are you asking it?" I asked.

"If you should come up here."

"What does it say?" I tried to keep my tone casual.

The water sloshed as he shook it. "'Ask again later.' I guess that's that."

"Oh." I bit my lip.

He patted the bed. "It's a stupid piece of plastic. What are you waiting for?"

Climbing up, I banged my shin. The pot had made me clumsy. "That was dumb," I muttered.

Neal traced his fingers over the scrape. "Is this dumb?" he asked. I couldn't breathe. I couldn't blink. Every molecule in my body was on high alert. "You're a funny girl," he said. Then he was kissing me.

Within minutes we were both panting. I couldn't get enough of him. With my tongue I explored ever inch of his mouth, as he did with mine. We were sealed together as tightly as two stickers. When we finally broke apart and I tried to tell him how much I liked him, he put a finger to my lips.

Slowly, assuredly, he lifted off my shirt and unfastened the hooks of my bra. I didn't protest. Who knew it would feel so good to be naked before a boy? When I helped Neal remove his sweater I was surprised to discover that he smelled a little of BO. I didn't mind, though. It was such a human thing.

And then . . .

"Hold on a sec," Neal said. He leapt down from the bed and started riffling through drawers. "Michael's gotta have a condom here somewhere."

A condom?

Shit. We *were* moving kind of fast, but it hadn't occurred to me that we might actually have *sex*. Was this what I wanted? Now? I rubbed my brow, trying to think.

Not that I wasn't enjoying . . . *this*. But had I led Neal on?

Was I a tease? Would Neal be pissed if I said no?

"Found one!" he exclaimed triumphantly just as I was on the verge of saying something coy about saving some stuff for later.

I bit back my words as he climbed up.

Roaming each other's torsos with our hands, we kissed some more. Though Neal's build wasn't the stocky kind, his muscles were well developed from playing lacrosse. He gasped when I rubbed my hand over the rise at his crotch, which at once gave me this sense of power and made me ache even more for him. Off came our jeans. Our socks. Our underwear. Neal touched me in a slow deliberate way that made me spin.

How had he gotten so experienced? Were these things he'd learned from those prissy private school girls?

We'd moved past the point where sex was a rational decision. It was something we were hurtling toward. I didn't plan to tell Neal this was my first time. But when he entered me, I let out a cry of pain.

He pulled back. "You're a virgin?"

"It's totally no big deal," I stammered.

He studied me with red-rimmed eyes.

"It's a technicality," I whispered, pulling him close.

And then he was all the way inside me.

Luckily, his eyes were closed so he couldn't see how hard I was clenching my teeth. It hurt a ton more than I was expecting, though there was a good feeling behind it too that left me wanting more. I ground my hips against his like I'd seen actors do in movies. Neal moaned, which I took to be a sign that I was better at sex than debate.

Oddly, though we were literally joined, I'd felt closer to him when we were just making out. I sensed that he was off in some other world now, somewhere beyond my grasp.

Afterward, while he slept, I cradled his head in my arms. His hair curled around his ears like vines. He looked like some fairy-tale prince. Though a part of me wanted to get dressed—I felt hollowed-out, sore, and self-conscious about my nakedness—I wanted to savor every second with him. Waking him up, I sensed, would spoil things.

Staring at the ceiling—dotted with a tiny array of fake glow-in-the-dark stars—I contemplated what had just happened. My thoughts whirled round and round.

I sucked at debate.

Neal liked me.

Amanda was pissed at me.

Neal *liked* me.

A snake had pooped on my wrist.

Neal LIKED me.

I was no longer a virgin.

NEAL! NEAL! NEAL!

It was dark still, but you could tell it was morning now. The birds were starting to chirp. Someone struggled to start a car. The ignition failed to catch. There was another sound too, a strange rhythmic thumping. It took me a minute to realize that it was Baby, tapping her nose against the glass terrarium.

"Let's just keep this between us," Neal whispered when he finally woke up.

I studied his fingernails, massaging them with my hands. They were so smooth and pink, like tiny babies. "Even from Amanda?"

"Especially from Amanda." He rolled toward the wall.

Trying to guess what he was thinking, I said, "You're probably right. We wouldn't want her to feel left out."

"Yeah. Poor Amanda," he laughed. "If you're really worried, we could include her next time."

Next time. NEXT TIME!

I mussed up his hair. "Think again, buster. Best friends don't share *everything*."

"Too bad. I guess you'll have to be good enough for two."

Michael/Jesus knocked on the door. "Good morning, kids. Are you decent?"

We got dressed quickly and hustled back to the hotel.

Amanda sat next to me on the bus ride home. I guessed she was no longer mad about my debate performance yesterday. "I don't know why I choked like that," I said, apologizing again. "I talked to Peterson. Told him you should probably have a different partner. Told him how much I suck."

"I'm so over it, Char," she said, resting her head on my shoulder. "You know how much I adore you. Now let me sleep. I'm exhausted."

She didn't ask where I'd been the night before—which made me think that she too had been out all night. I knew that she and her boyfriend Boone had an *understanding*. But I couldn't ask her about her evening without incriminating myself—though secretly I was *dying* to incriminate myself.

13

Coach Peterson gave us the next week off for "mental rejuvenation." Though I was delighted to forget my public-speaking debut/debacle, the forced break squeezed me out of Neal's GATE-wing orbit. And since "we" were keeping "us" a secret, there was no one I could ask about what was going on with "him."

Especially not "him."

On Tuesday night I stayed up late studying. It was the end of the first quarter and I had a Chemistry final the next day. Because of all the time I'd been putting into debate and my new friends, I was nowhere near prepared.

Around midnight, my bedroom door swung open.

"I was out in the hall," my brother said, his hair all messed up from sleeping. "I saw your light. How's it going?"

"Ever hear of a thing called knocking?" I asked, trying to

hide the all-too babyish-looking chemistry flash cards that I'd had to make for myself.

He scooped up the cat—sleeping by a heat vent on the floor—and sat down at the end of my bed. "Do you want some help? I could quiz you."

"Got it covered," I said, trying to ignore the fact that he was frowning at me, and trying *really* hard to ignore the fact that my twelve-year-old brother had a better grasp of chemistry than I did.

"You haven't told me anything about your debate tournament. Was it cool?"

"Yeah," I said, dryly. "It was *cool*."

Now that I'd officially hurt his feelings, James Henry got up to leave. He paused at the door. "What's your problem, anyhow? I was just trying to be nice."

"Go back to sleep," I said with a lump in my throat.

Wednesday afternoon, on my way to Chemistry, I spotted Neal down in the regular kids' hall. "Hey, Neal!" I called, waving to get his attention, my heart racing full throttle.

He brushed past me without acknowledging my existence. But—he'd pressed a note into my hand. *The Back Forty. Now.*

The Back Forty was the lot where the regular students were supposed to park. It was unpaved and at least half a mile from the school—well out of range of Shady Grove's fat security guards. I glanced in the direction of my class and bit my lip. Not that my teacher would care or even notice if I didn't show. This was one of the perks of being in the regular classes. Our teachers bought whatever lame excuses we dished out for skipping. It was easier for them to do this than to fill out the convoluted discipline form. Hadn't Miss Gordon told us that she believed in experiential education? What was going on with Neal and me was definitely *experiential* and *educational*.

"Adios, suckers," I said to no one in particular as I walked out the double back doors. My body buzzing with excitement and nerves, I tried to think of what Amanda would tell me to do.

Just act like you've got someplace to be and a legitimate reason to be there.

Neal was waiting for me at an old Buick, leaning against the hood with his arms crossed. I could hear Amanda again. *Keep him guessing. Act a little bored.*

Though I wanted to ask him whose car this was, I studied the ends of my hair. "This better be good. I'm missing my Chemistry final."

He opened the back door, ushered me inside, and pulled off my shirt. "Consider this a bonus experiment," he breathed into my ear.

How could I argue with that?

Helium. Neon. Argon. Krypton. Xenon. Radon.

It hurt even worse the second time around.

Third time was the charm.

Oh, baby!

We always met at a different car.

Sometimes Neal would hide and make me guess his location, sending clues via text messages. If it was raining, he'd direct me to certain closets or locker rooms. *If you dare*, he always added.

I dared.

I double-dared.

I double/triple/quadruple-dared.

I never asked how he knew about these places. All that mattered was that I was the one who was with him now.

ME!

Not some prissy prep school girl.

College applications?

They could wait.

Parental drama?

Wasn't any of my business, now, was it?

Extracurricular activities?

Got it covered, Dad.

I doodled his name inside my notebooks, where no one could see.

Charlotte and Neal.

Neal and Charlotte.

Neal. Neal. Neal.

We did it in the bathroom in the library.

Amanda was shelving books just outside the thin door. I could hear her popping her bubble gum and singing along to some song by the Violent Femmes. *I take, 1, 1, 1 for my sorrow* . . .

"What if she hears?" I whispered.

"Even better!" he whispered back, driving me delirious by kissing my neck.

The secrecy *was* a thrill. But I wanted the whole world to know about us. Or at least all of Shady Grove.

"What are we?" I asked.

"We're great," he said. "Don't you think?"

"Yes," I whispered. "We're great."

I hope you know this will go down on your permanent record. . . .

Neal. Neal. Neal.

He was like a drug.

He was better than a drug.

Just say yes.

Yes.

Yes. Yes. Yes.

Hello. My name is Charlotte Locke, and I'm addicted to Neal Fitzpatrick.

So what if I wasn't in GATE? So what if my grades were slipping?

I was getting an A in life. An A-plus-plus, thank you very much.

One plus one equaled us.

Neal and me.

PART TWO
WINTER

14

It was winter in substance if not in fact. Sometime in mid-November the rain set in, moving over the landscape in great quavering sheets. If you lived in Washington, you inevitably became a student of precipitation. You learned to differentiate between a fine mist and a medium drizzle. You contemplated the great fat drops that blew in from the Pacific and that sometimes smelled of fish. You began to realize that there were subtle variations to the colors of the clouds. The sky, in fact, began to seem like a living, breathing thing. Some days the weather felt personal. Most days the weather felt Biblical.

Out here you learned how to put a positive spin on negative weather. The Saturday before Thanksgiving, all the ski resorts in the state opened. The forecasters were going nuts. "What a winter it's going to be for skiers and snowboarders!"

As usual, my brother had lucked out. Snowboarding was a go.

Every Saturday now, James Henry, Milton, and a bunch of the other brilliant kids from the Barclay School would ride the ski bus up to Stevens Pass. Here they learned, competed, and generally had a blast.

My brother—according to my brother—was a natural at snowboarding. "And you should see Milton!" he exclaimed one night at dinner. "He's unbelievable. He could probably go pro."

"Lucky him," I said.

"I'll probably be able to go pro in a few years," James Henry added.

"Lucky you."

Lucky lucky everyone.

Unfortunately for me, they didn't have lessons to help you navigate the kind of wilderness that I was braving. Debate. Shady Grove. Amanda. Neal. All I could do was stumble around blindly and hope for the best.

Hope is a four-letter word.

In November, we went to two more debate tournaments—both as hellish for me as Whitman. At my second tournament, I started to develop a stutter. At my third tournament, my hands and legs trembled in every round. But because Amanda was such a force, and because Amanda overcompensated for my incompetence, and because Amanda was so *lucky lucky lucky*, we kept winning and winning and winning.

At debate practice sessions I saw the other students shake their heads and wince when it was my turn to speak. A couple of times Mr. Peterson tried to work with me one-on-one. He'd give me a topic, say, for example, solar energy, and then he'd ask me to list its pros and cons. Simple. Easy.

Except that it was impossible.

"I do see that you're trying," he said. "But you need to relax. You need to breathe."

Amanda had no problems fighting off our blood-hungry opponents. She feasted on teams all across the northwest. The competition nicknamed her the Terminator. Her voice was her weapon, and what a weapon it was. So much of what she said was off-the-cuff bullshit. Like, for example, the time she argued that drilling for oil in the Arctic would trigger massive earthquakes that would ultimately cause the North Pole to melt, killing off Santa and Rudolph and otherwise destroying the world. And maybe Mars too, come to think of it. Who knew what she really believed about anything? But with policy debate, you had to take your own personal feelings out of the equation—while, at the same time, sounding utterly convinced of whatever point you were arguing. This was Amanda's genius.

"It's a game," Mr. Peterson reminded me. "It's just a game."

"It's a game," Neal said. "Winner takes all."

"It's a game," Amanda said. "You have to play to win."

But during the debate rounds, when the opposing team members sounded so deadly serious as they attacked point by point your every last argument, it was hard to remember this. It was hard to remember this during the cross-examination period, when you were being questioned so harshly that you began to feel like the collapse of the entire world might well be your fault if you conceded your point.

Every time we went into a round I felt dizzy with responsibility, so dizzy that I couldn't follow through with the steps I needed to take—such as arguing, such as linking together evidence, such as finding the holes in the other team's case, such as speaking in full sentences, such as breathing—to hold up the structure of the debate.

I told myself that Amanda actually came to enjoy the added challenge of having me for a partner. Making up for my flubs upped the stakes of the game and became a test of her ability to prevail against impossible odds.

Me. The impossible odd.

To compensate for my incompetence, I was now doing the lion's share of our research, filling our file boxes with brilliant evidence that I'd found on Google or in articles from *Scientific American*.

"I'm not totally worthless," I joked—feeling totally worthless.

"No way. We've got a good system going," Amanda assured me.

But at a team meeting right before the Christmas holidays, when Mr. Peterson announced that he'd be switching me to dramatic interpretation after the New Year, I realized that she'd finally said something to him about me.

Who could fault her? We both knew I was holding her back.

Truth be told, I was relieved. But why, I wondered, hadn't she said anything to me about it? Mr. Peterson went on to talk about other team changes, such as Diego wanting to switch to

Lincoln-Douglas. Then he dropped the bomb.

"Neal and Amanda will be our new policy dynamo."

So. This was why she hadn't said anything.

Mr. Peterson beamed at Neal and Amanda from behind the lectern. "I think we have a real shot at winning Nationals this year," he said.

In spite of my dismay, I made sure to be the first to congratulate them. Amanda hugged me. "Oh, Char! I was worried you'd be upset. It's nothing personal. You know that, right?"

A couple of our teammates were watching this exchange, not bothering to mask their curiosity. The only way to keep my dignity was to own up to my shortcomings. "We both knew this was coming," I said, blowing my hair out of my eyes. "You deserve a better partner. Someone who knows how to argue without tripping over her tongue."

"That's not why—"

Neal gripped my shoulders in a big-brotherly way—you'd never have guessed what we'd been doing in the backseat of his car right before this meeting. "So can we count on you to help with research?"

I forced a laugh. "Sure. If you pay me."

"We can work something out," he said, giving me a knowing wink.

Amanda was fiddling with her necklace, acting like there was some flaw in the design that she'd never noticed before. You could tell, however, that she was paying close attention to the look I was giving Neal, that she—for lack of a better phrase—smelled a rat.

As I was leaving the room, Mr. Peterson stopped me. "I know this is hard for you," he said. "Not everyone can do debate. George Bush, for example. And he still got to be president."

I didn't thank him for the encouragement. Me and George Bush. What a pair.

I made it to the bathroom before breaking down. Amanda followed me—blithely unaware that she was part of the problem. She was leaning against the sink when I came out of my stall, applying a fresh coat of ruby gloss to her mouth. Her lips were as moist as roses in the morning—unlike mine, which were perpetually chapped.

She fished a packet of Kleenex from of her purse and handed me a couple. "Blow it off, Char. Everyone knows that Peterson plays favorites. I got lucky."

Lucky.

"You could find another way to impress the colleges," she said.

I splashed cold water on my face. "Yeah. Like maybe I'll join the math bowl." I was not about to quit debate—my one ticket to the upper echelons of Shady Grove.

"I need a cigarette," she said. "Want to come outside with me?"

I snapped my fingers. "That's it. I'll start a smoking club. Then I can be president of something. That'll look good on my résumé."

"You'll probably have to start smoking first." She dabbed a lash out of her eye. "Let's go have ourselves a meeting."

She dragged me out to the woods that bordered the edge of

Shady Grove's campus. It was raining, but the trees provided shelter. We shared a slightly damp stump that made up part of an old campfire ring. The moisture brought out the crystal flecks in the rocks. Amanda lit two cigarettes, then handed one to me. "Here," she said. "Everyone's got to start somewhere."

I pretended not to notice the lipstick smear on the filter, though it kind of grossed me out. But not as much as inhaling the thing did. It was like spraying a can of grit into my lungs. Amanda cackled as I coughed and coughed. "It gets easier," she said. "Trust me."

Rain dripped down through the branches, a strangely soothing sound. I waited until I'd smoked half my cigarette before commenting on her new partnership with Neal.

"You two will be great," I said. *Fanfuckingtastic*, I didn't add.

"Char—I know," she said.

"You know you'll be great?"

She looked at me pointedly. "I *know*. I know about you and Neal."

I swallowed. "Neal didn't want me to say anything."

"It's written all over your face." She flicked her hand dismissively. "I guess you're not a virgin anymore?"

"You thought I was a virgin?"

"Duh. You were like the queen of virgins when we first met." With a stick, I began demolishing the charred remains of a log. "If there's ever stuff you want to ask me—" she offered.

The air smelled bad, like garbage. Somewhere nearby, there was a dump. Amanda pulled a Twix out of her purse and offered me half. I shook my head. I hadn't been hungry since I'd started seeing Neal. My clothes were getting baggy. In bed at night, when I traced my fingers over the contours of my body, I could feel the outline of my ribs.

A crow swooped down and landed on a nearby log. It watched us with its beady eyes, and cocked its head as if trying to understand our silence. Amanda tossed it a chunk of Twix, and it flew off with a strand of caramel dangling from its beak like a worm.

"Are you guys like boyfriend-girlfriend now?" she asked.

"Neal's never said . . . I don't know. I think so. What do you think?"

"Why does he want to keep it a secret?"

I frowned. "He says it makes things more exciting."

It was raining harder now. I had to hold my notebook over my head to stay dry.

"Hmm." Amanda fiddled with a thread that was unraveling at the hem of her miniskirt. "If you want my opinion," she finally said, "I think it's weird."

It was Sunday. Christmas was less than a week away. Miraculously, my family was all up at the same time, congregating in the kitchen. Mom was grading papers, humming Christmas carols and drinking something called kombucha that looked and tasted nasty but was supposed to be some kind of miracle cure for everything. Dad was reading the *New York Times*. He'd just gotten a new pair of glasses and was very proud of them. He made a point of cleaning them every five minutes. James Henry was making blueberry pancakes, his one cooking specialty. He only made them on very special occasions. The very special occasion this time was that he was being considered for a full scholarship for a summer school program at Columbia. We were heading to New York for Presidents' Day weekend so that James Henry could interview with the admissions committee in person.

"Can we go to MOMA when we're there?" I asked.

"We could look at some colleges," Dad suggested.

"Sounds like a blast," I muttered.

Dad poured himself another cup of coffee. "Any word on your SAT scores? You retook the test last month, right?"

I pretended to.

"Not yet. I mean, no word yet on my scores."

"Have you picked a safety school?" James Henry asked.

"I'm considering my options."

"Oh, hey—look at this." Dad handed me a section of the paper. "There's an article here about fuel cells. I thought maybe you could use it for debate."

"Uh—I'm not . . . Thanks." I pretended to glance over the article.

Hearing something in my voice, Mom glanced up from the essay she was grading. "How come you never have your friends over? I'd like to meet Amanda. And that guy you whisper about on the phone?"

"His name is Neal," James Henry said, flipping a pancake into the air.

I shot him a look. "You need more chores if you have time to eavesdrop."

"You have a boyfriend?" Dad asked.

I glared at my brother. "You have syrup on your chin. And no, he's not my boyfriend."

"I think it's nice that Charlotte has made some friends," Mom said absently, frowning over something one of her students had written.

That afternoon, on a whim, I biked over to Amanda's. No one answered when I rang. The house was so big that the Mungers seldom heard their doorbell. The door was open so I let myself in. I guessed when you were as rich as they were, you didn't have to care about theft. I found Amanda upstairs with Neal. They were sitting on the floor of her bedroom surrounded by corn chips, empty soda cans, and stacks and stacks of research. Apparently they weren't wasting any time when it came to their partnership.

"It's the holidays," I said. "You guys need to get a life."

Amanda busted up laughing.

"What's so funny?" I asked.

She took a deep breath, looked at Neal, and the two of them went into hysterics. "You had to be there," she said.

Wrapping an afghan around my shoulders, feeling excluded but not wanting to show it, I wandered out on the balcony. *Amanda's not perfect*, I reminded myself. *She can be crass. She can be mean.* But the flip side was that she was fun, unafraid, and never boring.

The ground was hard with frost. At least it wasn't raining— yet. The sky, however, was starting to look ominous. The nearly bare branch of a maple tree brushed up against this side of the Mungers' house. Had Amanda ever used this tree to sneak out? I reached out to touch a limb. If you climbed up on the railing of the balcony you could probably step out onto a branch. Once you got to the trunk it wouldn't be too hard to shimmy down. You'd have to commit, though—you'd have to really believe you could make it. Any hesitation and you'd fall.

Though I'd been MIA for at least fifteen minutes, neither Neal nor Amanda came outside to check on me. When I finally went back inside, I sat down next to Neal and leaned my head against the bed.

"Tired?" he asked.

"I haven't been sleeping well lately," I said.

"Maybe you're pregnant," Amanda said without looking up. Neal paled.

I'm not pregnant, I mouthed to him. I was on my period, as a matter of fact. Plus, we were always careful. I may have had a learning disability, but about some things I had some sense.

Closing my eyes, I allowed my mind to drift. Amanda's and Neal's voices blurred into an unintelligible murmur. I started thinking about the conversation I'd had with my dad. How furious would he be if he knew that I hadn't looked at any college applications in over a month? Or if he found out that I was getting a C in both Math and Chemistry? (I was going to have to forge my mom's signature on the next report card.)

Every now and then I'd catch a glimmer of a debate discussion Neal and Amanda were having: *oil spills, electric cars, tidal energy, nuclear war.* But I couldn't hold on to the words long enough to comprehend their meaning, so I just let them wash over me without trying to understand. I was spiraling off into a galaxy far, far away.

Until I heard this:

"There's that rave over Presidents' Day weekend. We could do it then."

I opened my eyes and blinked.

Neal and Amanda were sitting very close, their knees practically touching.

It's nothing, I assured myself. They're old friends.

"I'll talk to my brother," Neal said. "I know he can get us some."

I cleared my throat. "Get what?"

Neal raised an eyebrow at me. "She's back!"

Amanda wrinkled her nose. "We're talking about Ecstasy. Are you in? Oh. Wait. You're out of town on Presidents' Day weekend. Too bad."

Best friends don't share everything.

Jingle bells. Batman smells. Robin laid an egg. . . .

Christmas came. I ate too much. Most of my presents were of the practical variety. A new calculator. A vocabulary workbook. A day planner. Cash.

Bah, humbug.

On the day before New Year's Eve, Mom was downstairs in the kitchen trying to arrange take-out Thai food into something that resembled a home-cooked meal. Amanda and Neal were due to arrive any minute. Outside, I could hear James Henry practicing tricks on the new skateboard he'd gotten for Christmas. Milton was outside too, coaching him. Apparently, mushroom boy was also an expert skateboarder.

Dad was locked in his study, having some big-deal conversation with Meeghan. They were talking about a title change for the new book, he'd explained, though none of us had asked for an explanation.

I was getting dressed, which meant that I'd emptied half my closet into a heap on the bed. On the one hand, I wanted to look sexy. On the other hand, I didn't want anyone to think I was *trying* to look sexy.

All of a sudden I noticed flashing lights bouncing off the mirror above my dresser. Glancing out my window, I saw that Amanda had arrived . . . with a police car in tow. James Henry skated past them a couple of times. Milton stared blatantly.

I fired off a text to Neal. *What gives?*

Neal: *Speeding ticket. Who are those kids on the skateboards?*

Me: *I have no idea. Stay clear of them.*

I settled on a pair of ripped jeans and a black shirt that emphasized my new thinness. When the doorbell rang, I hurried to get there before anyone else. Who knew what my parents might say if I left them unsupervised?

"I'm above the law," Amanda shrieked, bounding into our house like it was her own. Neal, James Henry, and Milton followed her in.

"You must be Amanda," Mom exclaimed, cocking her head slightly as if trying to understand Amanda's hair. She'd just re-dyed it to a shade of pink that was as neon as an *Open* sign.

"You missed quite a show," Neal said. He had, I noted with a mixture of pleasure and revulsion, brought along a copy of my dad's book. "Amanda told that cop she had a bladder infection and was about to wet her pants. The dude actually bought it. Pretty girls get away with so much."

Milton raised an eyebrow at me. *Pretty girls?*

I rolled my eyes. *Neal is just stating the obvious.*

I was pleased to see that Neal had traded his usual jeans/T-shirt ensemble for a blue oxford shirt and khakis. My dad—when he emerged from the study—was obviously impressed with his Ivy League appearance. "Call me Julian," he said, pumping Neal's hand.

I was the only one who saw my mom frown. She'd worked hard for her doctorate and wanted everyone to call her Dr. Locke, probably her children included. Recovering quickly, she gave Neal a warm smile. "I'm Margot." She gestured at the cheese, crackers, and nuts she'd set out on the coffee table. "Help yourself to anything."

I willed James Henry not to say anything about Neal being my boyfriend, though I wanted the whole world to know what we were—myself included. Thankfully, my brother was wrapped up in some conversation with Amanda. She was telling him all about this famous skateboarder she'd once dated.

"You look familiar," Neal said to Milton. "Do you play lacrosse for Barclay?"

"I used to," Milton said, taking a seat on the couch. "I quit."

"Did I hear someone say something about Barclay?" Amanda asked, drifting over to us.

"Guilty," Milton said. "I go there."

"Do I know you?" she asked, tilting her chin to one side.

"It would seem that you don't," Milton said dryly.

"I went to Barclay for a while," Amanda said, adjusting her bra strap. "But the teachers stifled my creativity, and I had to get out of there."

"That's interesting," Milton said, peeling the shell off a peanut. "A lot of artists and writers have gone to Barclay."

"Omigod!" Amanda snapped her fingers. "Now I remember. You're the guy who started the mushroom-hunting club."

"I'm its seventh member," James Henry proudly.

"Milton's my brother's mentor at Barclay," I muttered. "He lives nearby."

Neal gave Milton this *you've-got-to-be-shitting-me* look. "Mushrooms?"

"We have a Web site if you're interested," Milton said, oblivious to the fact that he was being mocked. "There's a link to it on Barclay's home page."

"Let me get this straight," Neal began. "You quit lacrosse for *mushrooms?*"

"No." Milton gave him a hard stare. "I quit lacrosse because I'm not very good at lacrosse, and it wasn't much fun after a while."

Amanda looked amused. "And mushrooms are fun?"

"Yes. They are. They're also important." Milton picked up a *National Geographic* from the coffee table and began thumbing through it, obviously trying to end this conversation.

Mom walked over and cleared her throat. "Whenever you're ready, we can move into the dining room. Dinner is served."

I was grateful for the interruption. Things were getting weirdly tense.

James Henry dimmed the lights and turned on the stereo. A tango started playing a second later. After we started eating, Amanda was the first to speak. "This is delicious, Mrs. Locke. You'll have to give me the recipe."

"My recipes are top secret," Mom said.

I shot her a look. *Really*.

"I'm good with secrets," Amanda said. "I have to be. My dad has a very high level of security clearance."

"Is your dad a secret agent man?" Milton asked.

Amanda narrowed her eyes. "My dad works for the CDC. I'd tell you more, but then I'd have to kill you."

"Don't tell me, then."

For some reason, Milton's dry rebuff made me smile to myself. "Amanda wants to be a spy someday," I said, to fill the awkward pause.

"You'd probably have to change your hair," James Henry said. "To blend."

"Ha." Neal looked at Amanda with amusement. "Call me crazy, but you're not the kind of girl who's ever going to blend."

"Crazy," Amanda said, helping herself to another spring roll. "But I'll take the compliment."

Milton gave me another funny look. I shook my head. No doubt he was thinking that I'd somehow hoodwinked Neal and Amanda into being my friends. Maybe I had. So what? Now I just had to figure out how to keep them.

Neal, who was sitting across the table from me, turned to my dad. "I loved your book. I couldn't put it down."

I could feel his leg jouncing under the table. Being around my dad was making him fidgety. I understood. Hooking my foot with his, I smiled reassuringly. Milton wiggled his eyebrows at me in a mocking way. Shit. I'd hooked the wrong foot.

"Thanks," Dad said to Neal. "*Lily at Dusk* has been a surprising hit with people your age."

Neal set his copy on the table. "Would you mind signing this for me?"

"Not at all." Dad dabbed his mouth with his napkin. "Charlotte tells me you're headed for Stanford. That's impressive. Do you know what you want to study?"

"Dad!" I interrupted. "That's kind of a personal question."

Amanda came to my dad's defense. "He's just trying to think about what to say when he signs the book. Right, Julian?"

He smiled at her. "Exactly."

Was it my imagination, or had Mom just narrowed her eyes at Amanda?

Neal shrugged sheepishly. "Actually—I want to be a writer. I'll probably major in journalism. I've written a couple of stories for Shady Grove's literary magazine. I'm the editor."

"It takes a long time to make a living as a writer," Dad said gravely. "And journalism's a tough business these days. Are you prepared to grit it out for years?"

"My parents have some really good connections at the *New York Times*."

"Knowing the right people makes all the difference," Amanda said.

Dad beamed at Amanda. She was speaking his language. "That's one of the cardinal rules of life."

Mom cleared her throat. "Amanda—what are your plans before you become a spy?"

Neal answered for her. "Amanda's a double legacy at Harvard."

"It's true," she said. "But I'm thinking of taking a year off when I graduate."

"Really?" Mom took a sip of her wine. "What would you do for that time?"

"Don't tell us if you're going to have to kill us," Milton joked.

"I'm not sure," Amanda said. "I might try to do an internship at the White House. I'm very interested in politics. Or—I might backpack across Europe. I want to see the world before I commit to a career."

"I lived in Austria the summer before I started graduate school," Dad said, "with some buddies from college. We had a blast." He smiled to himself and shook his head, as if remembering some particularly hilarious debauchery.

Mom stood up and began clearing the table.

"I'm not finished!" James Henry protested when she grabbed his plate.

"Can I give you a hand?" Milton asked, rising from his seat.

After dinner, we moved into the den for coffee, ice cream, and fortune cookies. James Henry put on an old episode of *The Simpsons*. "Are we really watching this?" Amanda whispered to me.

Overhearing, Milton said, "*The Simpsons* is genius."

"It's not bad for a cartoon," Neal remarked amicably.

Amanda bit into her cookie, glanced at her fortune, and laughed.

"Let's hear it, Girl Wonder," Neal said.

She smirked. "'What's yours is mine, and what's mine is mine.'"

Milton nodded sagely. "That about sums it up."

Amanda ignored him. "What does yours say?" she asked Neal.

"'Now is the time to go ahead and pursue that love interest.'"

"You can't argue with the ancient Chinese!" Amanda exclaimed triumphantly.

"No," Neal said, studying her in an odd way. "I guess you can't."

Milton made this *you've-got-to-be-kidding-me* face. I scowled at him. Seriously—what was the guy's problem tonight?

"'A golden egg of opportunity falls into your lap this month,'" James Henry read.

My mom sighed. "I sure hope it doesn't break. Egg stains are a royal pain." She broke open her cookie and frowned. "There's nothing in mine!"

"'You look pretty,'" Dad said.

My mom seemed at once taken aback and pleased. "Why thank you."

"It's my fortune," Dad corrected her. "Not that you don't look pretty."

"You're beautiful, Mom," James Henry said loyally.

"And Julian *does* look pretty," Amanda joked.

Though Mom smiled at this, the corners of her mouth were tight.

"Read us yours, Milton," my brother said.

"'Help! I'm being held prisoner in a Chinese bakery!'"

Everyone laughed, but somehow this got James Henry talking about a project he was working on for social studies about Communism and torture—which was a total mood killer.

Amanda leaned back and stretched. "Neal—I hate to be a party pooper, but we should leave soon if we're going to get any work done tonight. We've got a big tournament coming up the first weekend in January," she explained to my parents. "In Southern California."

"Charlotte didn't mention anything—" Mom began.

Before I could stop her, Amanda said, "It's just for policy debate."

I bit into my fortune cookie to buy myself time. It got really quiet, and I grew aware of how loudly I was chewing. "Oh, didn't I tell you? I've switched to dramatic interpretation."

"Our coach was the one who suggested it," Amanda chimed.

"Charlotte's very talented," Neal—reading the situation—rushed to say. "Her writing is great."

Milton looked at me. "What kind of stuff do you write?"

"She wrote a hilarious essay for her debate application," Neal said.

I gave him a grateful smile.

"It was pretty good," Amanda agreed. Then she grabbed her purse. "Neal—we really do have to go."

Ever so slightly, Milton shook his head.

At the front door, Dad handed Neal his business card. "If you want to show me any of your writing, I'd be happy to take a look. It sounds like you're taking the right steps to get ahead."

"Thank you."

It was a grizzly evening. The trees lashed madly in the wind. Clouds billowed like jellyfish. Chilled, I wrapped my arms around my body.

"They're smart kids," Dad observed as they got into the car. Was he wondering what they saw in me? Did he suspect, as I secretly suspected myself, that they were way out of my league? That I was the butt of their jokes?

"You never told us your fortune," Milton said.

I'd stuffed the slip of paper into my pocket without reading it. Moving underneath the porch light, I read the words aloud. "'The world may be your oyster, but it doesn't mean you'll get its pearl.'

"Tell me something I don't know," I muttered.

Mom rested her hands on my shoulders. "Oh, honey—you're my pearl."

Closing my eyes, I leaned back and surrendered myself to her warmth—little suspecting this would be the last time that simple comfort would be enough.

15

Amanda pulled off the cover to her hot tub. Steam rose into the frigid air. I was wearing a red bikini from middle school that I'd bought on a whim and hadn't worn since my sudden onslaught of boobs because it was so revealing. Surprisingly, it still fit. It was late night toward the end of January.

Amanda unwrapped her towel and stepped buck naked into the hot tub. The girl couldn't get enough of her own body. "What happens if your parents come out here?" I asked. "Won't you be embarrassed?"

"They know how I look." She shrugged, lowering herself until she was neck deep. "They changed my diapers when I was a baby. Besides. They're not weird about modesty. Unlike *some* people."

I stepped into the hot tub and slid down to my shoulders.

"So. How are things with boy wonder?" she asked.

"I'm sick of the secrecy," I said, hating myself for revealing my insecurities to Amanda, but desperately in need of her advice. "I'm thinking of saying something to him about it. What do you think?"

"Neal's a complex guy," she said, tracing circles over the surface of the water. "I don't know that he'd want to place limits on a relationship by defining it. You should give him some space," she added. "Guys like it when they have to work for your attention."

"How much more space does he need?" I cried. "It's not like I'm following him around or anything."

"You wear your heart on your sleeve," Amanda said, snapping the water with her finger. "Don't you know that about yourself? If Neal so much as looks your way, you light up like a Christmas tree."

Was she right? Was I somehow too . . . adoring? I glanced off into the darkness so she wouldn't see the hurt in my eyes.

Amanda sighed.

"What?" I asked.

"I miss Boone. Long-distance relationships suck."

"Guys everywhere check you out," I said, trying to sound nonchalant and failing miserably. "I know you've had some flings at the tournaments. How come you don't ever give those guys a chance?"

"High school guys?" She faked a gag. "Besides—Peterson says it makes me more intimidating that I'm getting a reputation for being such a heartbreaker. I'm taking one for the team!"

"Amanda Munger," I said sarcastically. "Team player extraordinaire."

She fixed me a pointed glare. "I carried us. In every single round. In case you've forgotten."

I dunked beneath the water and held my breath, giving myself a moment to think.

"You did it to win," I said when I resurfaced. "It had nothing to do with being part of a team."

New York, New York. The Big Apple. The City That Never Sleeps. From the moment we landed, all I wanted to do was sleep.

My head pounded. My body ached. I felt hot, then cold, and then hot again. Because I wanted to enjoy the trip, I didn't say a word to my parents about being sick.

On our first full day, we went to MOMA. I stood a long time in front of the van Gogh painting *The Starry Night*, studying its whorls and waves. Docents—mostly tall, elegant women in pearls—moved in and out of the gallery. The slow click of their heels made me think of water dripping in a cave. They fielded question after question about van Gogh's insanity.

Squinting at the painting, I tried to feel a glimmer of his craziness. But what I saw instead was his fervor for the natural world. The painting was so alive—the town and the landscape and the atmosphere all mingled together into something animated and breathing. Everything about it, every last detail belonged there. Every brushstroke had a purpose.

I started to feel dizzy and stumbled backward to sit down on a bench.

"What's wrong, honey?" Mom asked, coming to my side.

"I don't know," I said as a single tear dripped down my face.

She felt my forehead. "Jesus, Charlotte. You're burning up."

She ushered me out and hailed a cab on Fifty-third Street. Then she sent me back to the hotel.

New York, New York. Bright lights, big city.

I missed the gourmet dinners. I missed the Broadway shows. I missed everything except for the extra mints that the woman from housekeeping gave me. They were stale.

To pass the time when I wasn't sleeping, I worked on memorizing a selection from *The Glass Menagerie*. Dramatic interpretation, the kind of debate I was now supposed to be concentrating on, involved me reading—with inflection—a published piece of literature for seven to ten minutes. If you wanted to win at dramatic interpretation (DI, it was called), you had to ape the personalities of losers and freaks (well-adjusted characters being too boring to merit the attention of the judges). Here lay the problem—at least from my point of view: if I did too good a job portraying my characters, people might start to associate me with them.

I didn't suck at DI. But I wasn't very good. I didn't *want* to be very good.

At least the other performances were usually interesting enough to hold my attention. And no one ever asked me if I had a speech impediment, which counted for a lot.

New York, New York. City of dreams.

Obviously, we didn't go on any drives to colleges. The last thing anyone wanted was to be holed up in a poorly ventilated space with me.

Not that it mattered. What could a college trip possibly mean to a person who'd failed to turn in a single application? The deadlines had come and gone, without me.

In a way, I was proud of myself for refusing to waste time and energy on something that wasn't going to amount to anything. I knew there'd be hell to pay once my parents found out. My mom would blame herself. My dad would blame me (and my mom). James Henry would be embarrassed about the fact of our being related (like he already was). What could my family do, though? At the very least, I'd bought myself a few months of freedom. Three. Maybe four if I was lucky. For the moment, I could breathe. As for the rest of my life—wasn't it mine to ruin?

James Henry aced his interview at Columbia. No one expected anything less.

Then, on our last day in New York, Mom got to meet Meeghan. They went out to tea. She'd been very quiet since that meeting. Distracted.

"What's she like?" I finally asked on the plane ride home when my dad got up to go to the restroom. "Agenty?" I wiped my nose with a tissue. How could one person produce so much snot?

"Young." Mom stared out the window. "Competent. Brilliant."

"Is she pretty?"

"Very."

New York, New York. The city so nice they named it twice.

Though I hated to admit it, Mr. Peterson had been right to pair Neal and Amanda as partners. They were like dancers the way they sensed each other's needs without having to use words. Neal was an excellent speaker, articulating his point of view in calm, measured tones. As a listener, you instinctively believed what he was saying because he conveyed great trustworthiness. He was the perfect counter to Amanda.

She always made the closing statements. Watching her give that final speech was not unlike watching a tigress close in on its prey. Weight on her toes, eyes locked with the judges', she'd pound her fist into her palm to underscore the fault lines in the opposing side's arguments, arguments that were often more rational and better researched than her own. Yet every time, she sealed the deal. She was so convinced of her superiority, she convinced the judges too. She convinced everyone.

In late February, on the way back from a tournament in Eugene, Oregon, we stopped for lunch at an IHOP. While the rest of the team swarmed the booths inside, Neal, Amanda, and I took over the patio.

Amanda quickly brought the conversation around to her new favorite topic: Ecstasy. "The rave was the best time *ever*," she said for like the hundredth time since Presidents' Day weekend. "It's such a bummer you were in New York."

"We danced all night," Neal said. "I usually hate dancing."

"X really opened me up," she said, taking a sip of ice water. "You can't imagine how good it feels. It's not addictive or anything. It just makes you really happy, you know, kind of slows things down and speeds them up."

I nodded like I understood. *Happy.*

Amanda glanced at Neal. "Remember how we shared brain waves?"

"How could I forget?" he said, smiling a little.

Amanda's phone rang. She made a face. "Boone," she mouthed, and scurried out.

"They're having problems," Neal said.

"I'm sure they'll work it out," I said.

Neal shrugged. "I think it's over."

My heart began to hammer. I felt like there was a bird trapped in my rib cage. Neal cared about me. I was positive. A guy couldn't fake being turned on. But I was dying for him to solidify our relationship. Like maybe call me his girlfriend. Or change his Facebook status to *in a relationship*.

I concentrated on drowning my fries in a pool of ketchup. Neal leaned in close. Our foreheads almost bumped. In spite of myself, I looked up. His eyes were as cool and deep as glaciers. *You own me*, I thought. Surely everyone could see this thing burning between us.

He placed his hand over mine, flooding me with relief. It was still there. What we had. Unfortunately, right then Amanda returned and plopped herself down. Neal let go of my hand. I made a face and nudged her foot, hinting at her to scram.

"What?" she asked. "Why'd you just kick me? Are you trying to tell me something, Char?"

My face turned red. I mumbled something about having a leg twitch.

"Maybe you're getting Tourette's," Amanda said, helping herself to some of my fries.

"Be nice," Neal said, giving Amanda a hard look.

The bus started up, and the rest of the team filed quickly out of the IHOP.

Mr. Peterson beckoned to Amanda, who rolled her eyes. "He probably wants to strategize."

Standing behind Neal, staring at the nape of his neck, I realized that it was imperative that he know I was as game as Amanda when it came to trying certain things. I leaned forward and whispered into his ear. "I did some thinking when I was in New York. I want to be open to new experiences. Mind-expanding experiences. You know what I'm saying?"

16

My mom lay under a mound of covers, a pillow drawn over her eyes. This was her second migraine this week. I scanned the room. Mom's side, strewn with books, student papers, coffee cups, coins, and brochures for trips to exotic locations (that she never took), needed a good tidying. On the other hand, Dad's half was as spotless as the hotel suites he now frequented. Once again, he was out of town. Surprise.

This time, I hadn't bothered to ask why. I knew.

I knelt beside Mom. "Is it cool with you if I spend the night at Amanda's?"

"Of course," she murmured, spacey from painkillers.

"I don't have to go," I said, half hoping she'd ask me to stay.

"I could use the quiet."

Is Dad having an affair?

Silence.

With Meeghan?

Silence.

"Do you need anything?" I asked. "Water? Drugs? An ice pack?"

Ask me to stay.

"Have fun tonight, kiddo."

My eyes stung with guilt. She was going to let me deceive her.

Two squirrels started up a game of chase in a maple tree outside. Their feet clattered briefly on the bark. As gently as I could, I shut my mom's windows and closed her curtains. Then I left.

Moments later, we were driving. Or rather, Amanda was driving and belting out the lyrics to "The Killing Moon," an old Echo & the Bunnymen song. Lately she'd been fancying herself as something of a rock diva. She reminded me of Pink, though she'd be pissed if I told her this. Amanda thought Pink was a hack.

"Where are we going?" I shouted as we passed the turnoff to her house.

"The mall," she said, cutting down the volume. "We need costumes for tonight. The rave is a masquerade. BTW—I've invented a friend for us. Her name is Melody. My mom thinks we're spending the night at her house and that you two are helping me to prep for the Berkeley tournament."

"Your poor mom," I said. "You're evil. You know that, right?"

She grinned. "That's why you love me so much!"

To avoid a weather-induced traffic jam, Amanda exited the freeway and took the back roads into Bellevue. Some of the puddles we splashed through were as deep as ponds.

"Are you nervous about Berkeley?" I asked.

"I don't get nervous," she said, rapping her knuckles against the window. "Besides, Neal and I are beyond ready."

Her lips twitched with a mysterious smile.

Though the garages at the Bellevue Square Mall were mobbed with Saturday shoppers, we had no problems parking since Amanda left her Jeep with the valet. Wandering through Nordstrom's, we tried on sunglasses and earrings, tested lotions and eye shadow, and grabbed at the free samples the store models were offering. As we walked through the juniors' department, I saw that prom dresses were already on display even though the dance was months away. My hands reached out as if possessed to touch the luxurious fabrics.

Amanda tugged my sleeve. "Let's try some on!" She pulled out a strapless magenta number and pressed it to her body. "Yeah?"

"It's cute," I agreed. "You could probably buy a car for what it costs."

"Not anything I'd drive. Here," she said, pulling out a plain gray dress. "This looks like you."

"Thanks a lot," I said. "It's boring."

"Remember—you said it. Not me."

I took a step back. "What are you saying?"

"Geez. Lighten up! You're no fun today."

A saleslady unlocked a huge dressing room for us to share.

Amanda quickly stripped down to her lacy thong and flapped her boobs in my face.

"Freak," I said, disgusted with myself for playing right into her game. "You should go to prom naked."

Amanda thought the first dress made her hips look too big. The second one washed her out. The third one was the strapless magenta gown. She sucked in her stomach while I zipped her up. Letting out her breath, she gasped, "Oh my God!"

The dress hit halfway down her shins—tea length. It made her skin shimmer.

"Wow!" I said.

She clapped her hands to her cheeks. "I have to get this."

"You don't even know if you're going to prom," I reminded her.

"I'll wear it tonight," she said, sucking on a strand of hair, "I'll be a prom queen. My mom's wedding headpiece can be my tiara."

She danced down the hall to the three-way mirror. "It's way cute from the back!"

Just to see how bad it would look, just to see how insulted I should be, while Amanda was gone I locked the door, undressed, and slipped the gray dress over my head.

What I saw when I turned to face the mirror astonished me. The dress skimmed my frame without being tight, fluttered just about at my knees, and the spaghetti straps deemphasized the broadness of my shoulders. The color matched my eyes almost perfectly. I looked beautiful, not in a loud, dazzling way, but in the quiet way of the moon.

Amanda rapped on the door. When I opened it, she looked shocked. "Jesus, Char. You look—"

"It's four hundred ninety-nine dollars," I said.

"Too bad," she said. "It's worth every penny."

"What if you bought it?" I suggested. "We could return it tomorrow."

She frowned. "No. You have to be something totally different than me. We don't want people thinking we're twins."

"I don't think that people are going to think—"

"Besides," she interrupted, "Nordstrom's is way too classy a place to cheat."

When I walked out to the mirror, the saleslady gushed, "That dress was made for you."

"My friend can't afford it," Amanda said. "She's just trying it on for fun."

The clerk furrowed her brow. I couldn't tell if it was because she felt sorry for me, or if she was pissed that I'd wasted her time.

I was still fuming when we headed out to the thoroughfare of the mall. It wasn't fair that Amanda always got to be the center of attention. It wasn't fair that she would outshine me tonight as usual simply because she had the money to do so.

"What's wrong?" she asked, readjusting the dress bag she was now carrying.

"I'm hungry," I said quickly.

"Thank God! You seriously need to eat. You looked gaunt in that dress."

"I've lost like five pounds. It's not a national emergency."

We ordered slices of pizza and Cokes and took them over to the fountain to eat, where it was bright because of the skylights. The water echoing off the cement structures muffled the din of the mall activity and made it sound as if you were hearing everything from a great distance. Ignoring the signs that said PLEASE DO NOT THROW COINS INTO THE FOUNTAIN, Amanda tossed a quarter into the water.

"Aren't you going to tell me your wish?" I asked sarcastically.

"That's bad luck. You wouldn't approve anyway." She smiled to herself.

Lucky lucky lucky.

She bit into her pizza and watched it lovingly as she pulled it away from her mouth, using her fingers to sever a runaway strand. "This is heaven. Why did you let me get it? I have to throw it away if I want to fit into my dress." She stood up and walked off to find a trash can, leaving me to wonder why she hadn't offered it to me if she was really so concerned about my weight loss. I was actually still quite hungry.

While she was gone, I watched a couple of goth girls striding through the mall like they owned it. Their steel-tipped combat boots clicked the floor in unison. Ornate crucifixes dangled from their necks. They were noticeably out of place at Bellevue Square, and I wondered if they'd come here to feed off the reactions of the other shoppers.

They gave me an idea.

When Amanda came back, she was beaming. "I just remembered. We have a Tin Man costume up in the attic. The school put on a production of *The Wizard of Oz* when Keith was a senior. I could paint your face silver. You could wear gray tights."

The Tin Man? The trusty Tin Man? Stiff? Rusty? In need of lubrication? Could anything be less sexy?

Just then, a frazzled woman walked by. She was literally dripping shopping bags. Two young children—obviously hers—trailed in her wake. One of them tripped and landed on her mother's Prada heel. The woman spun around abruptly, her nostrils flaring like a horse's. "Do you need me to *show* you how to be good?" she asked.

The kids went mute. Their eyes were like puddles as they tried not to cry.

"Actually," I said, turning slowly back toward Amanda, "I've decided you're right. We should be different tonight. I'm going to be a dominatrix."

17

Neal's brother Bailey lived on the sixth floor of an apartment building over by the University of Washington. Though he was a student there, he was out of town this particular weekend, chasing his born-again virgin girlfriend, Mindy. Bailey had given Neal the keys to his apartment and some other stuff that I was trying hard not to think about. Neal was carrying this "other stuff" in a film canister in his pocket.

"Bailey must be so frustrated," Amanda said.

Neal was rooting through the pantry for snacks. "They have these rules. Blow jobs are okay as long as she doesn't have to swallow. It doesn't count as sex if he only goes partway in. I seriously think he might propose to her this weekend. Ugh."

There was a picture of Mindy on the refrigerator. I leaned in closer to look. She was wearing a pink sorority sweatshirt, had long ash-blond hair, and was holding a pumpkin to her chest. Nothing in her expression suggested a manipulative nature. But then, she was older than me. Who knew what life had taught her to do?

Neal found a box of Ritz crackers and tossed one of the bags to us. They were so stale they didn't crunch. Amanda took one bite and spat hers out in the sink.

I cleared my throat. "What made her decide to become a born-again virgin?"

"Bailey's cute," Amanda said, as if I hadn't spoken. "When does he get back?" Without taking his eyes off of her, Neal took a long swig from his beer. Amanda laughed. "I know what you're thinking. But you've got it all wrong. I *feel* for Bailey. All that frustration could give him an early heart attack. If I could help in any way—"

"You're such a harlot," Neal said dryly.

Unable to think of anything witty to add, I wandered into the den.

It was dark except for the glow of a purple aquarium. Water burbled rhythmically out of the filter. Tiny striped fish drifted through the portholes of a miniature shipwreck. A couple of bottom-feeders rested on the turquoise sediment, gills heaving, their whiskers splayed out to the side. I found a shaker of fish food and spanked out a few flakes. The fish darted to the top of the tank and mouthed up the specks in seconds.

My face was hot and flushed. I pressed my forehead to the cool glass, closed my eyes, and tried to imagine myself underwater, my body shrunken to miniature size, my hair floating upward like kelp. Anxiety pulsed through my body like fire. Was I ready for this night? I was envious of the fish, for their immaculate little world. They were safe. Protected. Admired just for existing.

From the kitchen, I heard Amanda say something to Neal about blue balls. "You don't know what you're talking about!" Neal laughed.

Across the room, there was a small fishbowl sitting on top of a bookcase. I walked over to look. Its sole occupant was a stunning steel blue fish with long fins that billowed around its body like a million gossamer threads.

"That's Brutus," Neal said, coming into the room with Amanda.

"Poor guy," I remarked. "He's all alone."

"Brutus is a Siamese fighting fish. They're very territorial. If you were to put him in the aquarium with the other fish, he'd go ballistic."

"Et tu, Brute?" Amanda asked. To me she explained, "That's from *Julius Caesar*. It's what Caesar says when he realizes that he's been betrayed—"

"I know the play," I said coldly. "I'm not illiterate."

Neal tapped on the glass. Brutus got huffy and puffed out his gills.

Amanda sat on the couch and started flipping through a magazine. "Hey, Char," she said. "There's an article here about learning disabilities."

"Why would she care about that?" Neal asked.

"Hasn't Charlotte ever told you why she's not in GATE?"

My face grew very hot. "Shouldn't we be getting dressed?"

"What's the rush?" Amanda said. "The rave won't start before midnight."

Just then the intercom rang. Saved by the bell. Diego had arrived, along with this other kid from the team, Tyler Hyatt, a sophomore whose parents had forced him to do debate. Though he'd won a lot of awards, he usually hyperventilated before rounds and had to breathe into a brown paper bag to calm down. Tyler and I seldom talked, but I'd always felt a certain kinship with him. He'd come dressed as Darth Vader, which I found a strange costume choice for a person with a history of breathing problems.

Diego was Elvis (or an Elvis impersonator). When he walked through the door he pointed at Amanda, did a couple of hip thrusts, and crooned "Love Me Tender" into his fist.

Amanda laughed. "You wish. Too bad you ain't nothin' but a hound dog."

Neal was leaning over a cutting board. I watched him from the other side of the kitchen island, but he was too engrossed to see me. Using an X-Acto knife, he divided up a thin strip of segmented paper that looked like a tapeworm. No one noticed when I excused myself to the bathroom.

Sitting on the toilet, I buried my head in my hands. My skin prickled. *This is what you want*, I reminded myself. After all, had I not told Neal I was ready?

Ten minutes later, Amanda banged on the door. "I have our stuff. We can get ready now."

I didn't say anything.

She knocked again. "Char? Are you okay?"

I opened the door a crack. "I think I might have a fever."

She elbowed her way in and pressed the back of her left hand to my forehead. "You're cool as a cucumber. Look," she said, rolling back her tongue. Underneath lay a tiny white square. In her right hand she held a beer cap that contained another square. "For you," she said. Sensing my apprehension, she added, "Don't worry. It's only half a hit."

I cleared my throat. "Is it Ecstasy or acid?"

"Acid. Neal says it's better. More intense."

"Are you just doing half?"

"No."

"Then why am I just doing half?"

"I don't know. Maybe Neal thinks you can't handle a whole hit."

I lifted my chin. "I think I want the full experience."

She shrugged and trudged back to the kitchen, returning a minute later with an entire square. Without saying a word or taking my eyes off her, I dabbed it under my tongue.

Amanda's dress was even more amazing outside the store. The fabric was cool to the touch and oh-so luxurious. The hem was exquisitely fine. The skirt was heavy in a wonderful way, with the weight of opulence. "It's perfect," she sighed when I zipped her up.

She allowed me to do her makeup, something I was fairly good at, thanks to the fact that when he was younger, James Henry sometimes allowed me to dress him as a girl (we pretended he was my little sister). It took me forty-five minutes to tease Amanda's hair into an Audrey Hepburn updo. If she walked under a magnet she would've been lifted off the floor with all the bobby pins I used. But my work was impeccable. You couldn't see a single piece of metal. To make sure her hair stayed in place, I sprayed on half a bottle of Aqua Net. Amanda could dance as hard as she wanted tonight without fear of a single hair moving. She was stunning.

Lucky lucky lucky.

"Your mom would be proud," I said. "You look very—" I tried to think of something to say that would annoy her just a little. "Virginal."

"Whoa," she said, waving a hand in front of her face. "So that's what a tracer is."

"I don't feel anything yet."

She opened the door to the bathroom. "I'm going to talk to the guys."

After she left, I donned fishnet stockings, bloodred stilettos, a thigh-high miniskirt, a black leather corset, and a studded collar —all of which I'd found at a store across the street from Bellevue Square called the Dragon's Lair. The costume used up all my Christmas money, though the sales clerk assured me not to worry. "You can't put a price on transformation!" To lessen the sting of the cost, she'd given me a discount on a whip.

Next, I ratted my hair into a black halo, rimmed my eyes with dark eyeliner, and applied ruby lipstick (the shade was called Vampire Bride).

I was dismayed when I stood back from the mirror to admire my transformation. My costume was just that—a costume. I didn't look shocking. I didn't look different.

There I was. Myself. Plain old Charlotte Locke.

Boring. Mediocre. Average.

I walked out to the kitchen. The remaining squares of acid were scattered across the kitchen counter like bits of confetti. I still wasn't feeling anything.

My friends were gathered around the TV, watching an old rerun of *The Love Boat*. Charo was the special guest star. No one was paying any attention to me.

Finally, Neal looked up. "Wow. You look . . . interesting."

Diego whistled.

Amanda eyed me up and down. "That skirt is dangerously short. Careful."

Was there some greater meaning to her warning?

"The acid isn't working," I muttered.

"It takes a while to kick in," Neal said.

I stood by the side of the couch, waiting for him to make room for me. When he didn't, I sat down on the armrest beside him. He was now in costume too, though I wasn't sure what he was supposed to be. He was wearing a wife-beater shirt, wristbands, baggy jeans, a mullet wig, and a baseball cap advertising chainsaws. On his arm he'd painted several tattoos, one of which said *I Love Pamela Lee*. Sensing my confusion, he said, "I'm trailer-park trash. Can't you tell?"

I lashed my whip.

A horn blew. The Love Boat slipped away from the landing. Passengers swarmed the upper deck, throwing streamers out over the railing. Their shouts and laughter blurred together like the sound of a great crashing wave.

"All aboard," Amanda said.

Neal saluted her. "Aye, aye, Captain!"

We were riding the elevator. Bouncing on my toes, I tried to push us down faster. "It's not working," I said through clenched teeth.

"Relax," Neal said. "If you don't chill out you're going to have a bad trip."

Have a bad trip, have a bad trip, HAVE A BAD TRIIIIIIIIP!

Covering my ears, I ducked to avoid the words. They were coming at me fast, like balls out of a pitching machine. Everyone was staring. I discovered I could hear their thoughts. "I am NOT uptight!" I tried to scream. But the letters slid around my tongue like marbles.

The elevator opened to the front lobby. As I stepped out, the room dissolved. I fell to my knees and buried my face in my hands.

"Charlotte!" Neal said sharply. "Look at me. *Look* at me!"

Peeking through my fingers, I saw his pupils. They were as black and still as the ponds in Florida where the gators lived. "Quit trying to control the trip. That's what's making you wig out."

I stared down at my hands. They were smeared with lipstick. Or . . . was it blood? Slowly, I curled my fingers into a fist. The veins in my wrists popped out in 3-D. I looked back at Neal and cocked my head to the side, studying him. *Was it really Neal?*

His pupils sprang out at me suddenly, as if released from a

jack-in-the-box. I leaned over and vomited into a palm plant.

"This is crazy," Amanda said.

"You okay there, Vader?" Diego asked.

Tyler was crawling around on the floor, trying to grab up fistfuls of carpet. He pointed at Neal. "I'm sick of you!"

"Better take away his light saber," Amanda muttered.

"They'll be okay once we're outside," Diego said. He was always so calm. "The fresh air will help. We can walk to the rave."

"Does that sound nice, Charlotte?" Neal asked in this soothing voice, as if I were a toddler. "Some nice fresh air?"

All I needed now was a pacifier.

The rave was a giant circus—only it was the audience who was the main act. Lasers flashed like gunfire. Music thrummed loud and wild. The bass shook the walls and floor and ricocheted through my body like a runaway pinball. For the first time in my life I *understood* music. I *was* the music.

But it was too much for a mere mortal to take, like lightning and earthquakes and tornados all at once. I was going to split apart. And it would be nuclear.

Neal and Amanda waved their arms, whipped their heads, and stomped in time to the beat. They were exquisite. Primordial. Prehistoric. All of us—we were beasts.

Tyler—who knew where he was? Lost to the night as well.

"Where's Vader?" Diego asked.

Amanda shrugged. "Survival of the fittest, man!"

Diego stood behind me. His hands rested on my shoulders.

"I'm keeping you upright!" he said when I glared at him over my shoulder.

"Why can't you be Neal?" I whimpered, but the words came out all garbled.

The crowd was growing. The walls bulged to accommodate.

Diego pressed his stomach into my back. His arms came around my waist. I could feel him—his thing—hard against my butt. He started grinding it against me. As soon as I could, I untangled myself and bolted for the bathroom. The line was wrapped around the door. Several of the stalls had OUT OF ORDER signs. A girl dressed as a fairy darted past us all and puked into the garbage.

I pushed my way outside. I was a tiger. Panting.

"Watch it!" a gnome shouted as I elbowed him in the head.

Once free of the otherworldly throngs, I stumbled around the corner of the warehouse and ducked into an alley. It was refreshingly dark. Cool. Empty. The walls pulsed with music. I kept expecting them to burst, and for the crowd to roll out over me like a tsunami. I upended an old crate, sat down, and stuck my head between my knees.

There was this loud ringing inside my ears. *The bell tolls for thee*, I thought, remembering the John Donne poem my father often quoted.

When I finally sat up eons later, I noticed a gaggle of people clustered around a side entrance. They were smoking cigarettes. Laughing. Guzzling water and alcohol from bottles. One of them was a DJ I recognized as a kind of local celebrity. He was making out with some groupie girl. From where I sat, no one could see me. I inched my crate closer.

Jesus.

The girl making out with the DJ? She wasn't exactly girlish. The curly hair. The tilt of her chin.

Hi, Mom.

The Catholic schoolgirl uniform was one of mine. Who knew that migraines could turn around so fast?

Shit. Shit. Shit. Shit. Shit.

Somehow I found my friends. Or they found me. What mattered was that we were all together again. They took me back to Bailey's apartment. "You're tripping," Amanda said. "This isn't real, Char. Snap out of it."

I started to cry.

She led me to the bathroom and instructed me to wash up. When I splashed my face, I breathed in some water and started to gasp and choke. Then I was vomiting, and Amanda was holding my head, stroking my hair, and telling me it was going to be okay.

How could I have doubted her?

She was my friend. My best friend. I was beyond lucky to have her.

Lucky lucky lucky.

When she flushed the toilet, I noticed that the particles swirling away formed strange geometric designs. I leaned closer to get a better look. My head dropped down into a dark sucking tunnel, a tunnel with no light or exit, only black empty space, terror, and a nasty urine smell. A black hole to end all black holes.

✦ ✦ ✦

Charo was trying to tell me the Love Boat was sinking.

"You need to get into one of the lifeboats," she said. I begged her to sing the Chiquita Banana song. "You're not listening!" she snapped.

I shrugged. "It's just a stupid show. It's not even *on* anymore. It's not real."

She studied me with pity. "You're not real," she said, rolling her R's.

"What do you mean?" I asked.

She smiled sadly.

"Tell me what you mean!" I shouted.

Isaac the bartender walked up. "Is this girl bothering you?"

Charo crossed her arms and stared beyond the railing, pouting. "I am sick of trying to help the passengers. They are such children."

He readjusted the crocheted poncho that was falling off her shoulders and helped her climb into one of the rafts. "You can't take it personally," he said. "Not everyone wants to be saved."

"I was just fooling around!" I pleaded, but they were already gone.

Scanning the deck, I saw that it was now deserted.

"Come back," I whispered. Water started lapping overboard. The ship sank some more. Then, with a great creaking moan, it heaved and tilted forward. I clung to the railing. The horizon was jagged with black waves.

"Please come back!" I screamed, but my voice was lost to the ocean.

✐ ✐ ✐

When I came to, I was clutching the headboard of Bailey's bed. I was thirstier than I'd ever been. I walked into the kitchen and poured myself a glass of water, trying not to notice all the commotion in the air; the tracers, the dancing particles, the shifts of light and color. Someone had left the sliding-glass door to the balcony open. As I made to shut it, I remembered something I'd read once, about how people on airplanes near doors would be sucked out—seat and all—if ever a door blew open mid-flight.

Passengers in an exit row may be asked to assist during an emergency.

I waited. No one came to my aid. There was no sign of my friends.

I'd been abandoned.

Abandoned.

ABANDONED!

People were disposable. Like trash.

I'm trailer-park trash. Can't you tell?

One could be disposed of. It was all a matter of who you knew. It was a game. All of it. I was a pawn. Not a player.

I sat down on the couch and sank into the cushions. At first I trembled with cold. Then I grew hot. I was burning. Inflamed. My core was hot. Hard. Like one of those fire logs. If I didn't do something fast I was going to combust.

There was a noise. I heard it the way you hear a fly.

A steady annoying stream of bubbles.

The fish were staring at me. Laughing at me. Baring their teeth like piranhas. They smelled my vulnerability. My naiveté. My sweetness. They hungered for it the way you hunger for something you think you can't possess. But they would try. They meant me harm. They would harm me if I didn't hurt them first.

They were malevolent.

One of them, an angel fish, waved her fin at me. She puckered her lips. "Come here, sugar," she said in a low, throaty voice.

I tiptoed closer. "Yes?" I whispered.

"You lost," she said. "You were never even a player."

"What did I lose?"

"You know." She snickered. "You never even had a chance."

"What are you talking about?" I screamed.

She blew some bubbles at me. "I don't have time for losers!" Then she darted away.

Fueled with a strength that wasn't quite human, I lunged for the aquarium. I lifted it skyward, arms fully extended, electrical cords dangling around my neck like snakes. Then I tipped my palms.

Water cascaded out along with everything else. The glass exploded as it landed. Fish hit the floor with a sickly thwack and flopped off to various corners. My feet disappeared in a warm tide of water. A ribbon of blood ran down my ankle.

As the room grew strangely silent, I realized the ringing in my ears had stopped. The game was over. I'd done my work. I was the victor. Finally.

Crying with relief, I stumbled back into Bailey's bedroom, where I shut myself into his closet. Burrowing deep into a pile of laundry, I made myself into a ball and closed my eyes tight. I was shrinking. Shedding. I was going back, way back. I was in a tunnel again, only this time I was going in a safe direction. Now I was in a cave. A warm red cave. A womb. I was . . . unborn.

18

I woke up wet, cramped, and utterly disoriented.

What was that horrible smell? And why the fuck was I in a closet?

As I readjusted my position—a shoe was digging into my back—the memory of the night came back to me in a rush. Waves of shame broke over me. Though it seemed a sensible idea to stay in the closet forever, I slowly slid back the door to the closet.

Two people lay slumbering in bed. Neal and Amanda.

Amanda was on her side, sheets falling off her hips, the butterfly tattoo in the small of her back exposed. Neal slept on his stomach, head turned toward Amanda, his left hand grazing her neck. Amanda's prom queen dress, tossed carelessly into a corner, had landed in such a way that it resembled a squat, headless child.

Bile rose in my throat.

Trembling, I backed into the closet, right into the arms of an old coat. My fingers clutched the sleeves for comfort. The wool was scratchy and smelled of mothballs. My clothes were soaked. I smelled like vomit. I needed a hot bath and a toothbrush. I needed water. I was a bottomless pit of need.

It was all I could do to not scream. The two people who mattered the most had betrayed me. Something deep inside my chest cracked open.

No crying. Not now.

I grabbed my overnight bag from the corner and headed for the bathroom, trying to avoid the sight of the den.

The toilet flushed. A moment later, Tyler walked out of the bathroom, rubbing his hands on his T-shirt to dry them. He stared at me. "What the hell happened last night?"

I shook my head numbly.

"You went on a rampage," he said with a tone of disbelief.

I didn't blink.

"You killed the fish."

"That really happened?" I whispered.

"You're so fucked," he said, his voice almost reverent.

Inside the bathroom, I stripped off my dominatrix clothes and stuffed them into the bottom of the wastebasket. The sink turned rock gray as I scrubbed off my makeup. I found some toothpaste under the counter, brushed my teeth with my fingers, and scoured my hair with a bar of soap.

The door to the bedroom was still shut when I emerged. Good. I had no desire to see Amanda and Neal—like, ever. I needed to get out of here fast. I was scared. Scared for myself. Scared *of* myself.

I caught a glimpse of Tyler and Diego trying to clean up the mess I'd made. Though I wanted to help them, my body recoiled when I began to move in their direction. Instead, I quietly left the apartment.

Once outside, I leaned against the bricks and closed my eyes. That it was sunny seemed a particularly cruel joke. My head throbbed. My entire body ached. I was a zombie. When I opened my eyes, I realized that I wasn't in the nicest of neighborhoods.

The air smelled faintly of garbage. The children playing had wary, tough expressions, as if they were used to looking over their shoulders and scattering at the sound of trouble. Two guys across the street were leaning against the hood of a beat-up brown car. They stared at me in a hungry way. I strode off as if I had someplace to be and knew exactly where that was.

After a few blocks, I came to a McDonald's. I bought myself a Coke and some fries and slid into a booth. Two little Hispanic girls in the booth in front of me—dressed identically in pink Sunday frocks—kept squirming around to stare. Rubbing at my face, I worried that I might not have removed all the makeup. I'd been too wigged out earlier to look at my reflection.

Eventually I gave up on eating and considered my options.

Fact: I had to get home.

Fact: I had no money left, no credit card, no checks, no cell phone.

Fact: I couldn't call my mom. No way.

Mom. Oh God! Had that been real last night? What I'd seen? I pressed my fingers to my temples. No. I couldn't deal with that right now. I shook my head to erase the image.

Who else did I know in Seattle with a car?

I bit my lip. Could I? Did I dare?

I found a phone book and flipped to the Z's. Luckily, *Zacharias* wasn't that common of a name.

"Hello?" Milton said, picking up the phone.

"Milton— it's Charlotte." My voice was raw and hoarse. "James Henry's sister?"

"Oh. Um. Hello." There was a long silence.

"I didn't know who else to call," I said. "It's not an emergency. But kind of."

"What's going on? "

"It's . . . well . . . I need a ride."

"Are you okay?"

"I'm fine," I said too loudly.

"You don't sound fine. Where are you?"

By force of will, I gained enough control of myself to give him my location.

"Please don't tell anyone about this," I added.

"I'll be right—"

I cut off my phone. Then I went outside to pace, trying not to care that everyone was staring. A long line of cars snaked around the McDonald's drive-through. The street bustled with shoppers out to make the most of a rare sunny day.

Miraculously, Milton arrived within twenty minutes. I didn't want to know how fast he'd driven. "You look like hell," he said as I got into the car.

"You have a real way with girls," I said, turning my head toward the window.

"You reek," he continued obliviously.

I interrupted. "Stop."

Something in my voice got his attention. "I was just try-ing . . ." he said. "Sorry."

"I know. It doesn't matter."

Out of the corner of my eye, I caught Milton glancing at me, his brow furrowed with fake concern for my well-being, the not-entirely-unpleasant smell of whatever wheaty cereal he'd had for breakfast emanating from his breath. Though I tried to ignore him, it was all too much.

Finally I snapped. "What? What's the problem?"

"Excuse me?"

"Why are you staring?"

He made this clicking noise with his tongue. "You seem edgy."

"Yeah? Here's a thought: Feeling like a specimen in a petri dish sure doesn't help."

We rode in silence for a while, me trying not to retch at the smell of myself, Milton thinking God-only-knew-what about me. As we crossed Lake Washington, whitecaps slammed against the side of the floating bridge. It was a windy day. There were a lot of boats out on the water. To the east you could see the Cascades rising above the landscape like giant teeth. To the south you could see Mount Rainier. It looked extra clean today. Whitewashed. It must have snowed up there recently.

"You're shaking," Milton remarked. "Are you cold?"

"No."

He turned on the heater, then reached into the backseat. "Here," he said, handing me his jacket.

When I started to protest, he said, "I wasn't asking. Put it on. You're freezing."

A few minutes later, Milton popped a disk into his stereo. To my amazement, "How to Disappear Completely," one of my all-time favorite Radiohead songs, began streaming from the speakers.

I grabbed Milton's CD case and started flipping through his stuff. He owned every Radiohead album ever recorded . . . and some bootlegs I'd never heard of. I shook my head. Unbelievable.

"What?" he asked.

"You like Radiohead," I said dumbly.

"That's an understatement," he said. "Is there any other band?"

"No."

"I could burn you some stuff," he suggested.

"I'm good. No thanks."

He frowned.

"It's not you," I said. "Thanks for picking me up."

"Do you want to talk about what happened last night?"

"You can drop me off here," I said. We were just a few doors down from my house. "I don't want anyone to see . . ." My voice trailed off. See what, exactly?

"I'm not the enemy," he said.

Already out of the car, I spun around. "You were right."

He looked blank. "Huh?"

"About me. About my fatal flaw."

He started to protest. "I was just teasing you about that shit."

"No," I said. "It's true. I prefer beauty to substance."

Our eyes locked. In the icy light of late afternoon, his gray eyes looked brook clear. Something sorrowful caught in my throat. I waved him off as he tried to come after me, and turned around before he could see my tears.

"Not a word," I said, my voice just a hint of a whisper.

I spent the afternoon in bed staring at the ceiling, unable to nap or to focus on the take-home test that was due tomorrow for Chemistry. There wasn't much chance that I'd be getting any better than a C anyway. What did grades matter when you were getting an F in life? It was a lot to absorb—what had happened last night. What had happened to me. What I had done.

Was I a crazy person? Was I?

Suddenly I remembered something. I'd overlooked one of them—the fish. Brutus. The beautiful killer who'd been given his own special bowl. It's what saved him in the end.

Et tu, Brute?

Brutus. The Amanda fish.

Lucky lucky lucky.

Late in the afternoon, my brother came into my room, landline in hand. "It's Amanda," he said, his finger pressed to the mute button. "Did you guys have a fight?"

"Tell her I'm in the shower. Or napping. Better yet, tell her I'm dead."

"But you're not."

"Do it!" I snapped, shoving the phone back at him.

"She's in the shower," he mumbled. "Okay . . . Bye." He hung up. "She sounded pissed," he told me. "She wants you to call her back pronto."

"It's time for Amanda to quit getting everything she wants."

He gave me a strange look, but let it go.

"Don't bother Mom," he said a few moments later. "She's taken one of her pills. She said to cook hot dogs for dinner."

"Don't tell her anything, okay?"

"What were you doing last night?"

I laughed harshly. "Ruining my life."

James Henry moved to the foot of my bed and tried to interest the cat in a game of swat. Steerforth batted his hand a few times, got bored of missing, and retreated to a patch of sunlight, where he began grooming his prominent belly. The man who lived across the street from us was pruning his fruit trees. There was something mesmerizing about the rhythmic clipping of his shears. I didn't know his name. Except for Milton and his mother, we didn't really know any of our neighbors.

Resting my chin on my knees, I studied my toenails. The pedicure Amanda had given me the weekend before was starting to chip. I scraped off the remaining enamel.

"You're still here," I said to James Henry.

"What—?" He hesitated.

"Use your words," I said.

"Did someone . . . do something to you?" he blurted.

"Ha. That's a good one. You might be a comedian, bro!"

To take away the sting of the words, I pulled him to me in a hug. "Was Mom here last night?" I asked.

"She went out," he said. "Why?"

"No reason."

On Monday morning, I waited for the final warning bell to ring before entering the double metal doors of Shady Grove. The halls thinned rapidly as students hurried to their homerooms. The pungent scent of meat loaf seeped through the vents like a poisonous gas. At this godforsaken hour, the few kids who were talking among themselves at their lockers spoke in raspy, sleep-deprived voices.

Though I tried not to make eye contact with anyone, I could tell I was being stared at. I didn't want to guess just how many conversations were about me at this moment.

A crowd was gathered by my locker.

There was a dead guppy taped to the dial—no doubt one of the fish I'd killed. My hands shook as I ripped it down. Everyone booed when I threw it in the trash.

"Fish killer!" someone shouted.

Mid-morning, while I was retrieving my books for Algebra, Amanda approached my locker. She kept checking over her shoulder to make sure nobody we knew was watching. It was as if I were now infected with a disfiguring and contagious disease. With bravado, I straightened my shoulders and tried to remember how to breathe. When I turned around, Amanda said, "You better have something to say for yourself."

"How was the rest of the rave?" I asked.

"What?"

"Did you and Neal share brain waves again?"

Her eyes flashed like broken glass. "Do you know how much damage you did to that apartment?"

A group of Spartanettes—the girls who danced for Shady Grove and who were even more popular than the cheerleaders— drifted by. A couple of them glanced at me with wide eyes. Amanda tried to act like it was merely coincidence that she was standing next to me.

"You left me," I said though clenched teeth.

"This isn't my fault, Char. What you did—you did that all by yourself."

"I suppose it's my fault that you slept with Neal?"

"Oh." She bit her lip. "So you know about that?"

"Are you two like girlfriend-boyfriend now?" I asked, mimicking what she'd asked me just a few months ago.

"I'm not sure," she said. "It's not like we were entirely grounded in reality either."

"Did it not"—I made my fingers into quotation marks— "'mean anything'?" Had they been loud? Had I heard them while in the closet and just not realized? Did she make Neal pant? Did he think about me at all? Just how good was she, anyhow?

"I'm so sorry," she said.

"Sorry? Or just sorry you got caught?"

"Char—" Amanda adjusted her book bag. She was wearing glasses today instead of her usual contacts. They magnified her green eyes and brought out amber flecks that reminded me of the gilded pages of the old books in my dad's study. "Don't worry about the damage, okay? I can cover the cost. Just so you know—Neal feels really bad about everything."

I whacked my forehead with my fist. "Oh! So that's why I haven't heard from him!"

A teacher poked her head out of a classroom. "Girls. You're tardy. If you don't light a fire immediately, I'm giving you both detention."

"It's not looking too good for you around here," Amanda whispered. "What are you going to do? Transfer?"

"I don't think that's any of your business."

She shook her head slightly. Then, with a small wave, she turned and clomped off in her wooden clogs. The sound echoed eerily off the walls of the empty corridor like something out of an old war movie.

Without looking back, I walked off in the other direction, out the back doors of the school, past the faculty parking lot, past the GATE lot, past the athletic fields, down to the back forty, the parking lot where Neal had made me guess which cars he was hiding in. I wondered what games Neal would play with Amanda. What games would she play with him?

Winner takes all.

Sitting down to smoke a cigarette, I braced my back against the wheel of a car. It was raining, but I didn't care. I was done caring about anything. Caring only got you hurt. The air smelled like mud. Mud and motor oil. Absently, I picked at the gravel, plinking rocks in the direction of my feet.

"Where there's smoke there are smokes," a high-pitched male voice said.

The body it belonged to appeared a moment later. I didn't

recognize the kid, although at a school as large as Shady Grove, that didn't really mean anything. The goatee he stroked did little to hide the purple acne that clotted his face. He peered down at me through orange John Lennon glasses. "Think I might bum one of those?" he asked, jerking his head toward the cigarettes.

I held out the pack of Dunhills. "Have at them. I'm quitting."

He examined the box. "This is a fancy-pants brand." Nevertheless, he tucked the box into the pouch of his hemp pullover, ripped off the filter of his cigarette, and smoked the remainder as if it were a joint. "Hey—don't I know you?"

"I don't think so."

He flicked the butt away carelessly, scattering tiny orange embers into my hair. Cackling at my displeasure, he squatted down beside me. "Yeah. I know you. You're that bat-shit crazy girl. The fish killer." My face flushed red. I scrambled to my feet. "Where are you going?" he asked. "I was just playing with you."

I walked away quickly, my arms folded across my chest, lips mashed together to keep from crying.

"Here, kitty, kitty," he said, cracking up with laughter. "Here, fish killer."

I reached down, grabbed a fistful of pebbles, and held them up warningly.

"You really are a freak!" he shouted.

But he left me alone after that.

There was an art-house movie theater about a mile from Shady Grove. I scrounged for some change at the bottom of my backpack and came up with enough money to buy myself a ticket to the noon showing of *Deliverance*. I didn't really care what I saw. I was just glad to sit in the darkness and know that the three other people in the theater—a woman with an oxygen tank, her obese companion of indeterminate gender, and the man in the front row with the shiny bald head—didn't know the first thing about me.

The movie was violent, sick, and scary.

It matched my mood perfectly.

Afterward I walked the five miles back to our house, replaying scenes from the movie in my head to distract myself from my sorry life. The weather had turned nasty. The wind picked up. Branches and pinecones were flying like whirlybirds. I had to hold my skirt down with my hands to keep it from flying up in my face. Cars roared past without seeming to care that they were splashing small lakes on me.

It took me a long time to reach home. As I shuffled up the driveway, I saw James Henry sitting on the lowest step, seemingly oblivious to the rain. His hair was plastered to his forehead. He looked small. Fragile.

"You better get inside," he said, his voice oddly flat. "Mom and Dad are waiting."

My stomach sank. I ran through the possibilities.

Milton had called.

Amanda had called.

Neal had called.

I licked my lips and swallowed. "How bad is it?"

James Henry's shoulders started to heave. "They're getting a divorce."

PART THREE

SPRING

19

"It's not your fault," Dad said about the divorce—which hadn't occurred to me until he said it. Later on in the week, he sent some movers over to collect his stuff. They worked quickly and efficiently, finishing the job of breaking up our family in a matter of hours. Dad informed us he'd be going to Mexico for a few weeks to decompress. "I'll be in touch as soon as I'm back," he said. "We'll do something fun."

Fun was for other folks.

Mom bought a pack of cigarettes the day Dad moved out. At first they made her cough. Now she was sucking them down as if they were vitamins. She was also watching a lot of reality TV. She was particularly addicted to that monster fish show.

Could her students tell that something was amiss? That thing she had—command presence—could you lose it? Or was the essence of command presence that you exuded it most when the chips were down?

I wondered what our neighbors thought of us. The woman next door sometimes stared with curiosity and sympathy. She brought my mom a casserole one afternoon. After she left, Mom tossed it into the trash. "It's not like someone died."

"We just need some time to process," my brother said. "Right?"

"We're fine," she said automatically.

I contemplated asking her if she'd been making out with any celebrity DJs lately. But there was only so much truth a person could handle at a time. And I sensed that whatever might or might not have happened between her and the DJ, the divorce wasn't all that simple. Something had been wrong with my parents for a long time.

Mom hadn't noticed that I was missing school.

Most days I pretended I was going. I got up, got dressed, and then headed off in the direction of the bus stop. She didn't ask why I no longer wanted her to give me rides. I think she appreciated my self-reliance.

When I was sure no one was watching, I ducked into the woods that bordered our subdivision. The creek ran high and fast from all the recent rainfall. This time of year, there weren't any salmon. Low-hanging branches trapped garbage, clothing, and old auto parts. There was a waterfall not too far away. This was my favorite spot.

Sometimes I read. I was working my way through *Jane Eyre*

(a book my mom insisted I read before I turned eighteen). "You'll learn a lot about men," she'd said. I didn't know about that. I liked Jane, however. Her life was no bowl of cherries either. Her school was so gross that half the students died from disease and neglect. Then there was the guy she loved. Rochester. Now, he was a piece of work. Secretly married to this madwoman he kept locked up in his attic. He loved Jane back, though. That counted for something. That counted for a lot.

Amanda would have liked this place. She would have talked me into sliding down the waterfall. It was pathetic how badly I wanted her to stop by or call—if not to apologize then at least to make sure I was doing okay.

But she didn't call. Not once.

Staring at the rain dripping through the trees, I tried desperately to absent myself from thought and feeling. I pretended I was just another one of the shadows. At some point, invisibility became the goal.

Neal sent me just one text. *I'm sorry.* I didn't write back. I realized I didn't know Neal. I'd never known Neal. The guy I loved didn't exist.

In my dream, someone was singing, "I wear my sunglasses at night . . . I wear my sunglasses on rainy days . . . I wear my sunglasses to sleep . . . I wear my . . ."

Realizing that what I was hearing was real, I opened my eyes. Milton stood above me with an amused expression. I sat up quickly and glanced at my watch. It was almost eleven a.m.

"Your brother said I'd find you here."

"My brother should mind his own business," I said quietly.

"He's worried about you," Milton said, kneeling down next to me in this cautious way, like I was an animal that might bite. "He says you haven't gone to school this week, but you're not sick. I wanted to see if you're okay. You seemed pretty messed up that day I gave you a ride."

"That day was . . . that day." I pressed my fingers to my temples.

"I heard about your parents."

"I'm fine."

"So you're hanging out here just for fun?" He gestured around at the woods. A squirrel scolded us from a nearby tree. "I'm not saying this place isn't nice. . . . I'm all for nature. Camping. Hiking. Snowboarding. You should give snowboarding a chance, by the way. I could teach—"

"I could ask you the same thing," I interrupted quickly. "About not being at school. I didn't know Barclay was on the half-day plan. Or is it that you smart kids are so fragile, you need more downtime than the rest of us morons?"

"I had a dentist's appointment," he explained.

Teeth were safe. I could work with teeth. "Any cavities?" I asked.

"None. I take care of my mouth." He grinned widely, showing off his pearly whites. I noticed that a front tooth was slightly chipped. Otherwise, they were perfect.

"That's important. For eating," I clarified, not wanting him to get the wrong idea.

"All the better to eat you with," he said, making this snapping motion at my throat. His lashes, I noticed, were long, thick, and wet with rain.

Teeth were not safe.

I scooted away. "You're too late," I said. "I've already met the big bad wolf."

"That guy from dinner?" His face darkened. "What happened?"

I rolled my eyes. "It's a little more complicated than that. Wolves travel in packs."

"Your friend Amanda?" he guessed, staring thoughtfully at the creek.

"Ex-friend," I corrected him.

He shook his head. "I've always had a bad feeling about that girl."

We sat in silence for a few minutes, me embarrassed at having revealed so much, Milton seemingly at ease. The creek roared in the background. Over the last few days I'd watched it steadily rise. The forecasters were predicting statewide flooding. We were having what they called a Pineapple Express.

Milton cleared his throat. "Most animal attacks are worse when you try to run."

It was time for a new subject—one that wasn't me.

"How does James Henry seem?" I asked. "He's not really talking about stuff."

"Wonder where he gets that from?"

"You're a real riot," I said.

"James Henry and your dad are pretty tight, huh?"

"They're a lot a like. Two peas in a pod. A couple of geniuses."

"Who are you like?" he asked, throwing a stone in the water.

"No one."

"You say that like it's a bad thing."

Though the forest was dark and dreary, there were hints of spring. The air smelled astringent with new growth. Ferns unfurled their necks like swans. In the boggier areas, you could see yellow stalks of skunk cabbage pressing up through the mud. Light beamed through the clouds at a brighter wattage than before. I stood up and walked over to the creek. A log had fallen across it in a recent storm. Slowly, I climbed onto the wood and eased my way across to the island on the other side. Once I was safely on the ground, I turned around to look for Milton.

He was standing, studying the log dubiously. "You expect me to cross this thing?"

"Do whatever you like," I said, wanting him to follow me but not wanting him to think I cared what he did.

There was a burn area up ahead. I made my way toward it. For the moment, the clouds had parted. A ray of light illuminated the particles of mist that hung in the air. A lone alder tree stood just off to the center. Though its bark was tinged with black, it had somehow survived the fire. It had low, thick branches. Grabbling hold, I swung up.

Milton made it across the creek and was now crouched down beside a nurse log, prodding around at the ground. A moment later he wandered over to me, cupping something in his hands. "Mushrooms," he said in answer to the questioning look I gave him. He held them up for me to see.

"Aren't those . . . what did you call them? You said they were good to eat?"

"One of them is a black morel. It's edible and choice."

"So what's the other one? They look identical."

"You wouldn't want to mistake them," he said. "This one is a *Verpa*—otherwise known as the false morel. It might taste good, but it would make you sick." He handed them up to me, his arm accidently brushing my knee.

Stupidly, my stomach lurched. I gave my head a quick shake. Milton was the last person on the planet I needed to like. Why was he wasting his time talking to me?

Though they looked slimy, the mushrooms felt dry and cool to the touch. They smelled sweet, earthy, and ancient in a good way, like stones. Milton pointed out a couple of key differences in their heads and stalks, things you'd never notice at first glance. The black morel had pits and ridges, whereas the false morel was crinkled and wavy. The black morel was hollow, whereas the false morel was fibrous.

"It takes a while to learn to distinguish the differences." Milton said. "Even pros make mistakes. With mushrooms in general, I mean. Morels are pretty easy to identify, though."

"How do you know all this shit?"

"I don't," he said. "I know a few things, I guess. My dad is the real expert. When I was a kid he would take me on all these field trips. Back then I'd lie to my friends about where we were going. It seemed like such a dorky hobby. It *is* kind of dorky. But I loved it. I still do. It's like Easter egg hunting, only better because you get to do it all year round."

I smiled at this. "All the same, it seems best not to eat them. Why chance it?"

He looked horrified. "They have feelings!" he hissed, shielding the mushrooms from me. "You've got the wrong attitude," he said. "With most mushrooms, you're not going to get into big trouble. And the payoff . . . Just promise me you'll try them sometime. Or, I could—"

"I'll do no such thing!" I said, crossing my arms.

"They're so simple to prepare. You just cook them up with eggs and butter."

I shook my head. "I hate eggs."

He cocked his chin to one side and squinted at me. "Has anyone ever told you that you're a real nut job?"

"Has anyone ever told you that you're rude?" I retorted.

"Yeah. You." He grinned at me. I grinned back. I was, I realized, having fun. Milton was easy to talk to. I wondered if the girls at his school had crushes on him. In this chummy I'm-just-one-of-the-guys voice, I asked him if he had a girlfriend.

"Not anymore," he said.

"What happened?"

"She . . . uh . . . went to play for the other team."

"You mean . . ."

"Girls," he coughed. "She likes girls."

I clapped my hand to my mouth. "You turned her!"

He shook his head sadly. "My reputation is ruined for life."

"Whatever."

"There's this other girl . . ." he began.

"What's the problem?" I asked, my voice not as chummy before.

"She's hung up on an idiot."

"At least she's not hung up on another girl," I said.

He laughed. "Nice."

"What's she like?" I asked, not wanting to know, but unable to control myself. "The girl you like, I mean."

Thinking about her, he smiled. "She's kind of a handful, but in a good way. Sarcastic. Smart. Real."

"Well, I'm sure it will all work out for the best," I said, trying to keep the bitterness from my voice. *Lucky lucky lucky.* "Are you ever going to tell her how you feel?"

He picked up a stick and started digging a circle around the cap of a mushroom that was just barely pressing its way out of the ground. "I find it kind of interesting that you're interrogating me about my love life when you're giving nothing away about yourself."

I shrugged. "If you don't get close to people, they won't let you down."

He jabbed his stick into the ground. "That stinks."

"Reality stinks," I snapped. To kill this conversation, I jumped down from my tree. Much to my humiliation, when I landed, I lost my balance and fell on my butt. It hurt too. My eyes smarted with tears. To his credit, Milton didn't laugh.

"You okay?" he asked, holding out a hand.

I contemplated it a moment, observing his large knuckles, strong fingers, and the deep grooves in his palm. A fortune-teller would have fun with his hands, though you didn't have to be psychic to know that Milton was destined for a successful and happy life. She was a lucky girl, whoever she was.

Lucky lucky lucky.

"Got it," I said, refusing his help. Standing, I brushed off my jeans and started making my way to the other side of the creek. Once I got back to my place by the waterfall, I sat down and pretended to read *Jane Eyre*. Milton just stood there watching me.

"They're probably missing you right about now," I said, hinting for him to leave. "At that fancy-pants school of yours."

"You're going to have to quit hiding out here at some point," he said.

"Thanks for the mushroom talk," I said, without lifting my eyes from the page.

"Whatever it is . . . whatever happened to you . . ."

"It's really none of your business!" I snapped, this time looking up.

Milton had this funny smile on his face, the kind of smile you get when someone has just hurt your feelings but you're trying not to let on.

"I didn't mean to sound harsh," I said. "It's just—"

"I'll give you a ride over to school," he said, jerking his head in the direction of the road. "If, when we get there, you don't want to stay, I'll take you home. I promise."

20

"You're a good driver," I told Milton. "Amanda was terrifying."

"She's terrifying, all right," he said, braking for a pedestrian in the crosswalk. "And what's with that hair? It reminds me of Pepto-Bismol."

"It probably tastes way worse," I said, "with all those chemicals she uses to get it that color."

Milton made a face. "Luckily I haven't eaten lunch yet, because that thought really makes me want to puke."

"Please don't," I laughed. "I'm a sympathy puker."

We passed a student driver car. Milton glanced over at me. "James Henry says you don't drive. What's up with that?"

"It's complicated." Then, because he'd seemed genuinely interested, I answered honestly. "It was always my dad who was teaching me. He places this really high value on achievement and success. I guess I always felt like he was just waiting for me to mess up. With driving. With everything."

Milton pulled into an empty parking lot.

"What are you doing?" I asked.

He grinned. "This car has a super-smooth clutch."

"Your point?" I asked, chewing on my thumbnail.

"I don't think you should write off driving just yet." I hesitated for a moment. "What do you have to lose?" he asked gently.

"Okay." I took a deep breath. "Give me the damn keys."

We traded places. I started the car. We lurched forward. I could tell by the way Milton was hanging on to the window that I was worse than he'd been expecting. After a couple of laps around the lot, he said, "That's probably all my car can take for today."

"You mean—that's all *you* can take for the day." I pressed down hard on the accelerator just to see what he would do. "Yee haw!"

"Stop!"

"What's the magic word?"

"Please?"

"Say *uncle*."

"Uncle!" he cried.

Laughing, I brought the car to a stop. "That was fun."

"We'll do it again sometime. But now we should get you to school."

I got out of the car and walked back to the passenger side. He got out too. "So we're really doing this?" I asked.

"You're really doing this."

A few minutes later, we pulled up to the curb in front of Shady Grove. He smiled at me. He needed a haircut. I wanted to brush his hair out of his eyes. "Just remember," he said. "You're better than they are. Even if they can't see it."

I gave him a grateful hug and then headed inside.

As I'd suspected, people stared at me as I walked down the hall. They whispered—loud enough for me to hear.

There's that girl.

Weirdo!

Think she'll pull a Columbine?

I held my head high, as if their words had no power to hurt me. Inside, though, I was screaming. But I could do this. What's more—I wanted to. Finally, someone was on my side. Milton. What a difference this made.

My third day back to school, I heard over the morning announcements that Neal and Amanda had qualified for Nationals. The announcer failed to mention the important stuff. Like whether or not Neal and Amanda were getting serious about each other. Like whether or not they missed me.

I tried to tell myself that it just didn't matter. But it *did* matter. Two people whom I had trusted with everything had betrayed me in every way. I suspected that the memory of this time in my life was always going to sting a little. I wouldn't trust anyone who tried to tell me otherwise.

Ironically, what saved me from utter social annihilation was the fact that I was not in GATE. Down in the regular wings, no one really knew me. The ones who'd noticed me in the past thought I was something of an enigma—this quiet girl who'd somehow been tapped to be Girl Wonder's chief lady-in-waiting.

As for the GATE kids, when I saw them (which was less and less frequently now), I discovered that being regarded as something of a loose cannon had its perks. For the most part, people gave me a wide berth. I was *the fish killer*. Who knew what I might do if pushed?

There were no more dead guppies taped to my locker. None of the things that played out in teen movies happened to me. I wasn't slammed into lockers. No one duct taped any part of my anatomy. My head was spared the toilet bowl treatment (a.k.a. a swirly).

The rumors eventually fell away, and I went back to being a nobody. There was a certain peace, however, that went along with being just one of the masses. In the regular classes, I was removed from the insanity of constantly striving for something I couldn't even name.

Sometimes, in Chemistry, I caught Mimi looking at me in this questioning sort of way. I knew that if I apologized to her she'd probably take me back as a friend. Mimi was a rescuer. But I'd already been "saved" once this year. It was time for me to save myself.

To quit the debate team, I had to see the guidance counselor about signing some release forms. I wasn't thrilled about this. She was my nemesis, after all—the gatekeeper who'd kept me from GATE. But when her secretary ushered me into her office, I saw that it was a different woman behind the desk.

She stood when I walked in, and held out her hand. "I'm Alice," she said, smiling warmly. She was young, pretty, and fashionably dressed. "How can I help you today?"

I explained that I wanted to quit debate.

She glanced over my transcript. "I don't see anything here about your college plans."

"I didn't turn in my applications," I said, staring out her window at the rain.

She gestured at a chair. "Why don't you take a seat?"

"You don't have to stress about it," I said, rolling my eyes.

"Oh, but I do." She smiled. "It's my job. Humor me a minute and allow me to feel like I'm earning my paycheck. Going to college is a big decision. Not going is an even bigger one. I'd like to hear your thoughts."

"My thoughts," I repeated.

"Your test scores are okay. Your grades look pretty good. A couple of C's. Not too bad."

"I'm not going to get into a top-tier school," I said, lifting my chin and daring her with my eyes to contradict me. "No Ivy Leagues for me. At this point, I'm probably not even second tier."

"No. You're not," she said matter-of-factly, not bothering to sugarcoat the truth, which actually made me like her more. "Is that a priority?"

"It is for my parents," I said.

"Why do you think that is?" she asked.

"They want me to be a success."

"A success. I see." She pursed her lips. "I went to a state school for college. I got my master's at another state school. I've got a job that I happen to love. But I didn't get into Harvard. I didn't even get into the University of Washington. Would you say I'm a failure?"

"No. But you're not . . ." My voice trailed off.

"I'm not what?"

"Not me," I said, finally sitting down.

"You know," she said, "parents don't always know what's best for their kids."

"They want me to be happy," I said.

"I'm sure they do. The question is—do they want you to be happy on your terms or their terms?" She waited a moment. Then, leaning forward, her eyes fixed on mine, she asked, "What do you want for yourself?"

Staring down at my hands, I studied the pattern of my veins. I'd never really noticed how *blue* they were—the color blue that ice on lakes turns right before it melts. "I don't know," I finally said. A tear slid down my cheek. "Maybe that's the problem."

Without making a fuss, Alice handed me a box of tissues. "It takes courage to admit that you don't know what you want. At least now you know where to start.

"Why do you want to quit the debate team?" she asked.

I answered quickly without thinking. "Because I hate it. And the people suck."

She raised an eyebrow. "It sounds like you *do* know what you want." She signed the release form and handed it back to me. "From what I've seen, there's a very particular personality type that excels at speech."

"Not mine," I muttered.

She drummed her nails on her desk, her expression thoughtful. "Hmm—I'm thinking . . . Have you heard of the Evergreen State College?"

I shook my head.

"It's a college down in Olympia." She rustled through her files a moment, then handed me a packet. On the cover was a picture of a tower rising above a bunch of trees. "It's a good place for kids who feel that they don't exactly fit inside the margins. And—they have rolling admissions. There's still time for you to get in for fall."

"It looks pretty," I said, thumbing through the information.

"It's beautiful. I should know." She motioned at the wall behind her, where there was a diploma from Evergreen.

"I'll think about it," I said, pushing back my chair.

21

From the school library, I checked out this annoying book called *Surviving Your Parents' Divorce*. The gist of the manual was that the most important thing was to "keep the channels of honest communication open."

Late nights were the hardest time for me. I craved sleep but couldn't shut off my brain. There was so much to think about. It was going to be a long time before I felt normal. It was going to take a while before I figured out what *normal* even was.

One morning, a few hours before dawn, I grew so agitated that I had to leave the house. It was an easy jump from my window down to the ground. Wearing a dark hooded sweatshirt, I wandered through the neighborhood like a ghost. The movement stilled my thoughts. When walking wasn't enough, I started to run. I ran to the point where the only thing I could hear was the sound of my breath. It was a strangely comforting sound—the sound of me.

As I returned to the house, I observed my mom watching me from the back porch. I grabbed an afghan from the back of our couch and went out there to face her. "I wasn't doing anything wrong," I said. "Just—running. I couldn't sleep."

"It's a pity you don't smoke," she said.

"Mom!"

"I was kidding," she said. "Where's your sense of humor?"

"I quit," I finally said. "Smoking causes cancer, don't you know?"

"Tell me you're joking."

"About me quitting or about the cancer?"

She gazed skyward, as if appealing to a higher power.

I grinned. It was good to see a glimmer of her old self, even if she was a mess. She was wearing a satin bathrobe my dad had given her for Christmas several years ago. It was starting to pill, and the color, once a pale blue, had faded to a dingy gray. One of her curls had broken free of her bun, drawing attention to the contours of her neck. She looked vulnerable. Exposed. Still, in spite of the dark circles under her eyes, in spite of the defeated slump to her shoulders, she seemed more okay than she'd been in weeks.

Command presence. She hadn't lost it yet.

On the far side of her chair sat a vase of roses, barely visible in the darkness. I wouldn't have noticed them except for the fact that Mom was fiddling with a bud. Cupping its base with her hand, she lifted it gently above the others, only to let it slide back down again. She repeated this motion over and over.

"Who are those from?" I asked, unable to keep the suspicion out of my voice.

"Would you believe me if I told you I sent them to myself?"

"Mom?" It was now or never. "You didn't happen to go to a rave recently? With . . . some music guy?" She sucked in hard on a cigarette. "Are those from *him*?"

She shook her head, but not in denial. "His name is Ewan. He's a graduate student at Seattle U. He works as a DJ on the weekends."

I started to speak, but she held up her hand.

"I wasn't . . . thinking very clearly for a while. After I learned—" She paused and studied me, as if assessing my mental fortitude. A minute later she said, "Your father is having an affair with Meeghan."

The rain was turning our backyard, which wasn't banked right, into a small pond. The flowerpots—relics from the previous tenants—were spilling water like fountains.

"I've suspected for a while," I said. "About Dad. But I didn't know what you knew. And with your blood pressure and all, I wasn't sure if I should say anything."

"Oh dear. Have you been worrying about that?" She reached out and patted my knee. "It's higher than it should be, but it's not that bad. As for the affair—I've known for a while too. But just because you know something doesn't mean that you believe it."

"I'm sorry," I said.

"Me too." She readjusted her robe, wrapping it tight around her body.

"So are you . . . seeing . . . this guy?" I blurted.

She smiled. "He has a crush on me. But . . . no. It was a one-time thing. I guess I just wanted to see if I still had it. At my age—"

"TMI!" I shrieked, no doubt rousing the neighborhood.

"Wait a minute," she said, turning to look at me. "You were at that rave?"

"Long story," I muttered.

"Do you want to tell me this long story?" she asked.

"Someday," I said. "Not now."

"I see." She brought a rose out of the vase and dabbed it at the air as if it were a dart. Deftly, she lobbed it over the railing. It landed in the backyard with a small splash. "I think I've maybe left you alone too much," she said. "Your life is a mystery to me."

I snorted. "That makes two of us. My life is a mystery to *me*!"

"How was the run?"

"Hard. But I liked it. I liked it a lot. It made me hungry, though." My appetite was back in full force. I was going to have to eat an early breakfast.

She smiled to herself. "I used to run track. In high school."

"You never told me that."

"It feels like a lifetime ago. I was pretty good at it, though. Until I got shin splints."

We sat in silence a while, just listening to the rain.

Finally, I sighed and held out my hand. "Give me one of those."

"Just what kind of mother do you think I am?" she said.

"Not a cigarette! A flower. I want to see if I can make that pot."

Mollified, she moved the vase so that it was positioned between us.

One by one, we took turns. I had a hard time factoring in the wind that had suddenly kicked up. Half of my roses didn't make it. Mom, however, possessed a keener knowledge of the laws of physics. Only one of her roses fell short of its mark.

I was sorting the recycling and breaking down boxes when James Henry wandered out into the garage to practice his drums. Lately he'd been working on a series of hard angry solos. Maybe now was as good a time as any to talk to him about our parents.

"So," I said, not really sure how to proceed, "divorce sure stinks."

"Fifty percent of marriages end in divorce," he said, taking a seat. "It's a crapshoot."

"That doesn't make it any easier," I said, frowning at a bloated milk carton. I shuddered to think what kind of bacteria was breeding inside.

"Dad says he and Mom grew in different directions."

Yeah—Dad grew in the asshole direction. Why couldn't James Henry see it?

"If he wants the truth, your brother will ask," Mom had said. "In the meantime, just try to be supportive."

My brother flipped a drumstick into the air and caught it behind his back. "Why do you hate him so much? You never talk to him when he calls."

I walked over to the driveway so that James Henry couldn't read my emotions. "I don't . . . hate Dad," I said, choosing my words very carefully. "It's just hard to talk to him." This wasn't exactly a lie.

"It's okay to feel confused," he said, his voice suspiciously nice.

Looking up, I saw that he was smirking. "Stay out of my shit!" I shouted.

"You need to *own up to your anger*," he said, quoting from chapter two of *Surviving Your Parents' Divorce*.

I started to lunge for him, but just then my phone buzzed.

For some reason that defied logic, ever since that day in the woods, Milton had been sending me texts. They were usually bizarre mushroom quotes or facts, like the current one, which said: *Life is too short to stuff a mushroom.*

"Who's it from?" James Henry asked.

"It's no one," I said, shoving my phone into my pocket.

"Then why is your face so red?"

"Allergies," I muttered, leaving the garage.

Though Milton's texts baffled me in their randomness, what was even more baffling was that he was sending me texts in the first place. Hadn't his aim in the woods that day been to urge me to go back to school?

Well—I was back.

It wasn't like he needed more friends. I'd underestimated Milton. Though he was a quirky guy, he was also popular. According to James Henry, everyone liked him. But I didn't need James Henry to tell me this. Not anymore. I saw for myself

Milton was a good guy. He was comfortable with himself. For this reason, he would always be liked wherever he went.

I was the last person on the planet Milton would ever *like* like. He'd seen me at my very worst, exuding the stink of vomit, sweat, and chemicals—to say nothing of my inner rawness. Besides— he'd admitted point-blank that he had feelings for someone. (In my mind I called her BB—short for *beautiful bitch*. I could see her all too clearly. In addition to being beautiful, BB would be studious and smart. She'd have a classic sense of style—though not so classic that you wouldn't notice her discreet but stunning figure. Without being bookish, she'd be well-read. She'd love Radiohead, and with her family connections, she'd have Thom Yorke's number on speed dial. I seriously hated BB.)

So. The only rational explanation for Milton's texts was that he was trying to take me on as his new mentee. He wanted to help me. Which meant that I needed to let him off the hook. I needed to help myself.

Climbing the stairs to my room, I texted him back.

Me: *You don't have to check up on me anymore. I'm fine.*

Milton: *Wanna snowboard this weekend?*

Me: *Things good with the girl?*

Milton: *Just say yes.*

Me: *Have u asked her out yet?*

Milton: *Did u seriously just ask me that?*

Me: *She said no?*

Milton: *U R a sadist.*

Before he signed off, he sent me a picture of one of his favorite mushrooms, complete with its Latin name, *Cortinarius violaceus.* A rare purple mushroom, it was beautiful in a frail, otherworldly way. Though I wouldn't admit this to Milton, I was starting to think mushrooms were pretty cool. They flourished without light, after all. If only we humans were so lucky.

22

For several weeks I'd purposefully and deliberately avoided Neal. This wasn't too hard since we inhabited completely different spheres. I still thought about him a lot, and realized we had some unfinished business between us. And so, one final time, I climbed the stairs to the GATE wing.

It didn't take too long to find him. He was hanging out in the lounge, reading a tattered copy of *The Metamorphosis*.

"Charlotte," he said when he saw me. He scrambled to his feet.

He was wearing a short-sleeved shirt and his arms were tan. I wondered where he'd gone for spring break. I had a sudden image of him and Amanda lying on a beach somewhere down in Baja, debating the merits of foreign policy and various high-end tequilas. His hair was different—short and bleached. He was wearing these funky eyeglasses and dark, skinny pants.

Amanda had left her mark on him.

My palms started to sweat. Though I no longer desired him, it was still nerve-racking to be in the presence of a person who'd left you to hang. But then, Neal had always made me nervous. I'd never felt good enough for him, so I could never be myself.

He kept glancing down the hall in a keyed-up way. I wondered if he was on something.

I've known Amanda a long time, he'd said. *I didn't want her to dump me first*, he'd said. Neal had always preferred Amanda. I'd just been too blind to see it.

Poor Neal. I felt a sudden wave of pity for him. He knew exactly who Amanda was and what she could and would do if put to the test. Yet he'd gone back for more.

Though he was as handsome as ever, something had changed. Looking at him, I felt the way you did when you go back to a place from childhood and discover that it's a lot smaller than you remembered.

He fidgeted with his watch. "I've been meaning to call."

"That's not why—" I took a deep breath. "How much do I owe for the damage?"

"Charlotte—" He wiped his brow. "It's been dealt with. It doesn't matter."

"It matters to me," I said.

"I think it was around five hundred bucks. But it's not—"

"Thanks," I said. "It might be a while before I can get you the money."

"What will you do?" he asked.

"Rob a bank?" I smiled to show him I was kidding. "I'll get a job, of course."

He looked taken aback. "Really? What kind?" Neal's parents, I remembered, didn't want him to work until he finished college.

"I might want to work for a veterinarian. Or maybe an animal shelter."

It seemed fitting to work with animals. A way to atone for the fish. Not that what I'd done—in the grand scheme of things— had been as terrible as all that. People eat fish every day. Though, come to think of it, maybe I'd become a vegetarian too.

"Why would you do that?" he asked.

"I have a passion for living things." As I said the words, I realized that they were true.

"Charlotte," Neal said as I started to walk away. "I'm sorry you got hurt."

I turned around. His agonized expression broke my heart all over again.

"Good luck at Nationals," I said. "And Neal . . . good luck."

23

It was the third week of April. James Henry and I were sitting on the front porch waiting for Dad to pick us up for a "fun family day in the snow" at Mount Baker—the only ski area in the state still open this late in the season. A fun family day minus our mom.

Though I begged her to let me skip this outing, she'd remained firm. "I know you're angry. But you still have to go. Like it or not, he is your dad."

I didn't thank her for reminding me.

"I'm not snowboarding," I warned. "Or skiing."

"No one says you to have to enjoy yourself. You can do homework. Or meditate."

Dad was late. Surprise! Apparently, all the decompressing he'd done in Mexico had made him lackadaisical about things like being considerate.

James Henry glanced at his watch. "He needs to hurry if I'm going to get first tracks."

"First tracks?"

"You know—when you go down a run before anyone else? It's . . . orgasmic."

"Orgasmic?" I raised an eyebrow.

"Do I really have to explain? It's a word that means—"

"Whoa." I raised my hand. "Stop right there. I'm just surprised to learn that your education is so . . ." I cleared my throat. "Advanced."

"There's a lot of stuff I know," he said, looking suddenly unsure of this fact.

"Slow it down a little, okay?"

He rolled his eyes. "What—you're like this font of wisdom all of a sudden?"

"Maybe."

Just then, Dad pulled up and honked. As I climbed into the backseat, he said, "You're going off to college in just a few short months. There's no excuse for not driving."

"Okay." I met his eyes in the rearview mirror and called his bluff. "Want me to drive?"

"Hmm." He drummed his hands on the wheel. "I didn't mean today. The conditions are going to be extra challenging on the mountain roads. You're not ready. But soon."

Right. He didn't want me touching his Audi. He just wanted me to feel bad about not wanting to. Perhaps this made him feel better about himself. Who knew? Who knew what his problem was? It wasn't me. In his own way, my dad did love me—as much as he could love anyone. I was beginning to think that maybe I knew more about love than he did. Love. No amount of fancy education could help you make sense of it.

While my dad and brother went off in search of "killer face shots," I sat at a table in the day lodge, drinking coffee and working on my latest math assignment. People stared at my open textbook on their way to the restrooms, clucking their tongues and eyeing me skeptically. Their expressions told me it was a shame, an insult, even, to forsake the wonderland outside for something as dull as mathematical proofs.

I heartily agreed. But I was making a stand. I had to show my father— What exactly *did* I have to show my father?

Clearing a hole in the fogged-up windows, I observed the ski runs outside—the long curving groomers, the bumpy mogul fields, and up toward the top of the ski area, the powder chutes and open glades. Strange clouds that looked like flying saucers loomed on the horizon. I overheard a ski patrol guy say that the clouds meant there was high wind in the atmosphere, and that the weather was going to turn ugly in a day or so.

Around noon, my dad and James Henry came trudging up the stairs. I waved them over to my table. Wordlessly, they stripped off their outer garments and spread them near the fireplace to dry. From their tense expressions, I gathered that the "killer face shots" had maybe been a little *too* killer.

Dad handed us each some cash. "Get yourselves something nutritious."

Ravenous, I grabbed a cheese and tomato sandwich, an apple,

and a hot chocolate with extra whipped cream, and took my place at the end of a long line. The three girls in front of me were discussing the pros and cons of various tooth-whitening techniques. So that they wouldn't think I was eavesdropping, I scanned the crowded room, pretending I was looking for somebody, or, even better, that somebody was looking for me.

Then I saw James Henry, standing in front of the soda case, and surrounded on either side by two guys. Both towered over him by at least a foot. One of the guys was wearing a baggy jacket that said *Bite Me* on the back. The other one's jacket said *Piss off*.

From James Henry's stance—still, stiff, his arms crossed protectively—and the loud cruel laughter of the boys, I could tell that whatever was going on was not a touchy-feely let's-be-pals sort of thing.

Damn.

I stood rooted for a moment, agonizing over whether or not to get involved. I didn't want my brother to hate me for interfering. On the other hand . . . I knew exactly how it felt when the ones you loved left you to hang. I started to make my way over, but right then the boys wandered off, their attention diverted by a hot girl in a silver snowsuit.

James Henry remained where he was. Frozen.

Suddenly there was a commotion. There'd been a collision of some kind.

I turned around and rose on my toes to see what was going on. My brother's two tormentors now dripped chili and soda and were sputtering angrily. And right in the thick of it, trying to help them clean up and apologizing profusely for toppling his food tray, was Milton Zacharias.

"I'll pay for the dry cleaning," I heard him say.

He *sounded* sincere. Was the collision merely a coincidence? Karma?

Then, for the most fleeting of seconds, I saw Milton struggle to gain control of a twitch at the corners of his mouth. Among other complicated emotions that I didn't want to think about, gratitude surged through me.

Good work there, mushroom man.

The girl in the silver snowsuit stood off to the side of the wreckage, eyeing with disgust a small splotch of red that had landed on her shoulder—she the lone casualty of justice. She perked right up, though, when Milton offered her a couple of napkins. Fluttered her eyelashes a little.

C'mon! How obvious could you get?

Rolling my eyes, I tried to tell myself that my stomach was suddenly hurting because I was hungry and not . . . NO. I was not going there. I wasn't even going to think about it.

What the hell was Milton doing here, anyhow?

When he'd texted me yesterday, he'd mentioned some big test that he had to study for over the weekend. I hadn't told him about us coming to Baker today. There hadn't seemed to be any point.

"Charlotte?"

Oh God. Now Milton was standing right in front of me. The girl had trailed him a short ways. She watched us for a moment (me standing silent and awkward—Milton sweaty and just a little stinky in that sexy guy way), nodded to herself, and then walked off quietly without saying good-bye. I shook my head. The girl made no sense.

"Hi," I finally croaked to Milton. "What you just did back there—"

"Total dork maneuver," he said. "What can I say? I'm a klutz."

"No." I shook my head firmly. "I know what I saw. Thank you."

"'Nuff said." He looked almost bashful. "It was nothing."

"Thanks for nothing, then."

He smiled. I smiled back.

"Hey," I asked, "aren't you supposed to be studying for a test?"

"Last-minute change," he said, his expression sheepish, almost impatient.

With the force of an icy blast, it dawned on me. "Oh. I get it. *She's* here," I said, making my voice sound light and playful.

I started to ask if they'd come together, but right then my brother appeared bearing an enormous tray of food, his appetite seemingly unaffected by his recent hazing. He smacked Milton in the arm. "Zacharias! You got my text! I was afraid I sent it too late. It's awesome you came. You're eating with us, right?"

"Uh, bro?" I coughed. "I think Milton might be here *with* somebody."

James Henry looked from Milton to me, his brow furrowed with confusion. "Huh? But I thought—"

"Where are we sitting?" Milton asked loudly, giving my brother a very pointed stare.

James Henry started to laugh. "Sorry, man. Didn't mean to cramp your style."

"You guys are freaks," I muttered, shaking my head as I strolled back to our table.

"You haven't said anything yet?" I heard James Henry whisper.

I sped off so I wouldn't have to hear Milton's answer. There was comfort sometimes in not knowing the truth. Then there were the truths you wished you didn't know.

Dad was on his cell phone when we sat down. He waved, mouthed, "Just a second," and walked off to talk someplace more secluded.

Without saying a word, James Henry gave Milton all his fries, and I handed over half of my sandwich. That we didn't question why Milton was without food today was perhaps acknowledgment enough of what had happened to my brother.

"Why aren't you out there on the mountain?" Milton asked me. "You're missing the fun."

"Are you kidding?" I thumped my math book. "This is where the fun is at."

"Hey!" James Henry snapped his fingers. "I have an idea! Milton. Why don't *you* give Charlotte a snowboarding lesson?"

I set my sandwich down mid-bite. When I looked up, I saw that Milton's head was buried in his hands. His neck was bright red. He wasn't saying anything.

Shit. He knew.

Yes, my crush on him—I would admit it now . . . I *liked* Milton—was no doubt disgustingly obvious and making him very uncomfortable. What the hell was my brother thinking?

Frowning at a stain on my jeans, I mumbled, "I've got tons of studying—"

"I'd love to," Milton said simultaneously.

Frantically, I scrubbed at the stain. Was it warm or cold water that you were supposed to use for mustard? It seemed imperative that I remember this fact—even though I didn't like these jeans all that much.

"But what about *her*?" I asked. "Don't you want to—?"

"It's not a big deal," he said, running his fingers through his hair. "She's—kind of oblivious."

James Henry snorted loudly and coughed out a piece of hamburger.

They were still laughing when Dad rejoined us. "What I'd miss?" he asked, scanning our faces in search of the joke.

"Nothing," my brother said. "We were just goofing off."

I stared at Dad pointedly. "Actually—you've missed a lot, Dad. But that's not something I think I can really explain to you."

My brother was oblivious to my real meaning. My father looked confused and (I hoped) maybe a little hurt. Milton wasn't oblivious or confused. He looked almost proud of me. I was proud of myself. I'd spoken the truth. There *was* a lot my dad had missed. There was a lot he was *going* to miss. He was smart in the obvious ways. But not about the things that mattered.

Half an hour later, I found myself riding a ski lift to the top of a beginner run, a rental snowboard dangling from one of my legs. Our chair swayed back and forth in the wind. Every time we crossed through a support tower, it made a loud clicking sound. I clutched the armrest tightly—not that holding on to it would do me any good if we suddenly plummeted to the ground.

"Relax," Milton said. "The only way you're going to fall off this thing is if you decide to jump. Which would be a bad idea, by the way. You're not going to get hurt today. Your brother would kill me if I let something happen to you."

I pretended to look around. "Uh—which brother is this? Where's he been all my life?"

He laughed. "I know this is going to come as a shocker, but people *do* say nice things about you sometimes."

The chair was a two-seater, and small. There wasn't any room between us. Milton's left leg was pressed tight against my right one. Through my jeans and his puffy snow pants, I could feel the warmth of his body and the hard lean muscles of his quadriceps. The gum he was smacking smelled like licorice—which made me wonder what *he* would taste like. I gave my head a quick shake and acted like the only thing on my mind was the view.

It was stunning up here. Against the glistening snow, the dark outlines of the mountain ridges appeared all the more jagged. The sun could be seen as a pale orb through a filter of clouds. Plastered with white, the trees looked like creatures out of a fantasy novel.

"Why so serious?" Milton asked. "What's going on in that brain of yours?"

"Stuff," I said.

"What kind of stuff?" he asked.

Um . . . you?

Stalling for time, I removed a glove, blew into it to warm it, and put it back on. "Lots of things," I finally said. "Like the fact that I'm graduating from high school next month and have no clue what to do with my life."

"You're not supposed to have those things figured out yet. No one does."

"I bet you know *exactly* what you want to do."

"I have an idea," he admitted.

"But of course," I sighed. "Everyone else in my world seems to know."

He shook his head. "You're wrong there. Most of my friends—they don't know. Or if they know what they want to do, they want it for the wrong reasons, like for money or power. Or worse, because they think it will get them laid."

"So what's your brilliant plan?" I asked, readjusting my scarf.

"You really want to know? It's definitely *not cool*."

"Spill it."

"I want to study the medicinal properties of fungus."

"Not cool?" I exclaimed. "What are you talking about? Mushrooms are sexy."

"Be nice." He pushed back his sunglasses. "I'm baring my soul here."

"Go on. You're doing great."

He eyed me skeptically, but continued anyway. "When I was young, everyone used to pick on me because I was so small. The same kind of shit that happens to James Henry. And I—well, I pretended that mushrooms were my friends." He coughed. "Magical friends. Like wizards."

"Magical friends?" I raised an eyebrow. "Wizards?"

He shot me a look.

"Right." I made my face look very serious. "Wizards."

He ignored this. "If you look at it one way, mushrooms really *are* magical. They have tons of medicinal properties. There's so much research to be done. Lifesaving research. There's this professor at the University of Washington who studies this kind of thing? He said he'd be my thesis adviser if I go there. He wrote this killer book on slime molds," Milton added.

"Think I could get an autographed copy?"

"Slime molds are very misunderstood," he said haughtily.

"I'm sorry." I laughed. "You might not want to mention slime molds to lady love." Milton frowned at this. I held up my hands. "I'm just trying to help you."

Changing the subject, he said, "It's hard to believe it's the middle of spring. There's a storm coming."

"How do you know?"

"Can't you smell it?" He sniffed the air.

High above us, skiers and snowboarders dropped into fingerlike chutes and disappeared into clouds of snow, whooping it up like children, some of them probably children for real. A lone skier crashed on a steep mogul run, tumbling twenty feet before he came to a stop, losing bits of clothing in the process.

"That's called a yard sale," Milton said. "We'll work you up to that." He nudged me gently with his shoulder, sending a jolt through my body.

It was time for a reality check. My voice all buddy-buddy, I said, "It's cool that you want to give me a lesson today. And I'm all for you baring your soul. But one of these days you're going to have to make your move with what's-her-name. What *is* her name, by the way?"

"Uh," he said, acting uncomfortable. "How about we talk about your love life?"

"Because I don't have one," I said, trying to joke but not succeeding. "I'm living vicariously through you, don't you know?"

Milton cleared his throat. "Do you ever talk to Neal?"

"Funny you should ask," I said. "I saw him the other day."

He shook his head. "You should stay away from that guy."

"I'm over him. Don't worry."

A sign instructed us to gather loose objects, raise the safety bar, and lift the tips of our skis or snowboards. The off-ramp loomed like a death sentence. It was all happening so quickly. "Hold on to me," Milton said, pulling me to my feet.

"Wait! I'm not ready!"

"Too late." He chuckled sadistically. "Enjoy the ride!"

Within seconds, I lost my balance and slid to the bottom of the ramp on my belly.

"Nice form," Milton said, coming to a stop beside me and spraying a wave of snow on my boots. "Are you hurt?"

"I think I bruised a boob," I mumbled.

"I'm not laughing," he said, laughing. He held out a hand and helped me up. He didn't let go right away. His voice suddenly serious, he asked, "What you said about Neal a moment ago? You're done with him?"

I opened my mouth to say yes, but instead I sneezed, spraying snot everywhere.

Milton wiped his face on his jacket. "No really. I love it when girls spit on me."

"You want to know what Neal said to me once?" I asked.

"Do I?"

"Probably not. But I'm going to tell you anyway. When I told him my suspicions about my dad, he told me he'd read somewhere that affairs help keep marriages fresh."

"That's what he said to cheer you up?" Milton's mouth dropped. "That's crap. I'm so sorry. What an ass. The only people who say things like that are people who want to make themselves feel better about having affairs."

"It's really hard to be around my dad right now," I mumbled. "Especially after everything that happened to me this year. I feel so bad for my mom."

"Your mom seems pretty tough," Milton said. "Like you."

I made a fist and mock-threatened him. "You better believe I'm tough!"

Five minutes later I was staring down a cliff, feeling anything but tough.

"It's *not* a cliff," Milton said. "This is the bunny slope. You can do this, Char Char." If it hadn't been for the fact of my terror, his frustration would have been amusing. "Look, once you make a couple of turns, you'll be fine." He demonstrated, cutting graceful swerves partway down the cliff. Then he waved at me to follow.

A shudder ran through me, and I had to sit down. Tears leaked out of my eyes, leaving trails of warmth on my frozen cheeks.

At the same time that I was crying, I was acutely aware of my surroundings, the color of the sky, the clean smell of the snow, the rhythmic kick of Milton's boots as he climbed back toward me.

I wiped my eyes on my sleeve. "I'm not a total head case. I'm not."

He crouched beside me and patted my shoulder awkwardly. "Yeah, you are. Since the day we met. But for crying? Nah. Everybody gets scared. Don't go spreading this around, but I'm pretty sure I wet my pants the first time my dad brought me up here."

I half sniffled, half laughed. "I think we're safe in that department."

He reached for my hand. "Get up." All business, he pounded his fists together. "I'm going to get you off this mountain. But you have to trust me, okay?"

Trust. That word. I forced myself to nod.

He pointed diagonally across the run. "We're going to traverse that way. You stay right behind me. If you feel like you're getting out of control, go ahead and fall into the slope. Whatever you do, DON'T LOOK DOWN!"

I zeroed in on the back of Milton's jacket as I followed him across the hill. There was a patch on one of his shoulders. I wondered about the rip it was hiding, at the story behind the damage. Imagining the possibilities, I bounced across the run, ignoring the indignant cries of the snowboarders and skiers who had to dodge me.

"Nice job," Milton said, when I joined him on the far side. "All we have to do is go back the other way. Think you can handle that?"

I sniffed for an answer, my dignity completely vanquished.

After zigzagging across the slope several times, I peeked down in spite of Milton's warning. The exposure didn't bother me so much this time. In the final third of the run, I grew brave and tried a few turns. Though I fell often, the landing was marshmallow soft.

Finally, my muscles quaking, my pulse racing, I glided across level ground.

Milton slapped my hand when I fell to a stop beside him. "You did it."

"What are we waiting for?" I asked. "Let's do that again."

Milton laughed. "Okay, Girl Wonder. Whatever you say."

"What did you just call me?"

"Girl Wonder? Is that a problem?"

I grinned. "No problem at all. It's just perfect."

The lifts were closing. I'd snowboarded for three straight hours. Now we were walking—okay, I was limping—back to the rental shop to return my gear.

Milton was carrying my snowboard, which I probably should have felt guilty about, since it wasn't very feminist to let a guy carry your things. But seeing as how my entire body was buzzing with muscle fatigue, I was just grateful. And flying high. Too high. The fall was going to hurt.

Milton likes someone, I reminded myself. *Not you.*

After we dropped off my snowboarding gear, we walked back toward the day lodge to meet up with James Henry and my dad. The temperature was plummeting. Our breaths steamed the air.

"It's about to turn ugly up here," Milton remarked. "I don't like the look of the sky."

"I had fun today," I said, not paying attention to the weather. "You're a really good teacher."

"I think you could use another lesson," he said, stopping at a bench to loosen his boots. "Maybe next weekend? If Baker is still open?"

"Wait a minute—another lesson? Are you saying that I suck?"

He straightened up and gave me a long, hard look. Then he shoved my hat over my eyes. "You're really impossible."

I pulled my hat off and ran my fingers through my hair, trying to unknot the mess of tangles. For some reason, I felt like I needed to give him something. "So I've rethought things," I said haltingly. "I guess . . . I guess I'd be willing to try morels sometime."

"For real?" he asked. His eyes were as clear as water and fixed right on me.

"No eggs," I added. "I draw the line at eggs."

"I think we can probably handle that."

There was an awkward pause after this. Milton kicked at the snow. "So—you've probably figured it out by now, huh?"

"Figured what out?"

He eyed my scarf longingly, like he might want to strangle me with it. "Your brother said I might have to spell it out for you."

"My brother?" I yelped. "You've been talking to him? About me?" James Henry was *so* dead.

"Yeah. The things he said—" Milton shook his head. "He's pretty insightful."

"Oh really?" I was fuming now. "And what does Mr. Pretty Insightful have to say?"

"Charlotte—" Milton placed his hands on my shoulders.

He was laughing, though. Laughing at me. But also—there was something else. Something that made my heart throb. A couple of snowflakes landed on his eyelashes. I swallowed. I could barely breathe.

"Don't you get it?" he asked. He wasn't laughing anymore.

I swallowed. "I don't think—"

And then I was incapable of thought, because he grabbed me, or I grabbed him, and our mouths converged, and he tasted of licorice, snow, and the wind, and he kissed me urgently but oh so softly, in a way that warmed me up and sent shivers down my spine, and I was spinning and flying and melting all at once, and I was so happy that I hardly cared when my brother cleared his throat and asked if I was going to be ready to leave anytime soon or did Milton and I need to get a room?

24

We were about half an hour from home, nearing the city of Everett. It was kind of raining, kind of snowing. The air smelled like the ocean.

Suddenly James Henry inhaled sharply. "Stop. Stop the car."

"What?" Dad asked. "Are you sick? Try not to get the seats—"

"I'm not going to puke!" my brother shouted. "Just—pull over, would you?"

Dad moved the Audi onto the shoulder of I-5. James Henry hopped out and ran around to the back to check the trunk. A moment later he banged his fist on the roof. "My snowboard. I left it back at the mountain."

Dad and I got out of the Audi. Cars rumbled past, splashing water on our shins.

"What should we do?" James Henry asked, his eyes large and wet.

Dad clucked his tongue. "Hope no one had any plans for later."

"I'm sorry," my brother said. "I was distracted by . . ."

"We don't need to know the whys," I said quickly. Dad certainly didn't need to know about Milton. "Let's just go back and find it."

Wordlessly, we climbed back in the car. Dad turned around at the next exit and we headed back toward Mount Baker.

The weather deteriorated more and more the closer we got to the mountain. We passed dozens of frozen fields rapidly disappearing under a blanket of white. The thick fat snowflakes reminded me of Communion wafers. The half-standing stalks of corn looked like a thousand frozen pistons. Cows packed together near the fence lines, huddling close for warmth. They cast us doleful stares, as if blaming us for their misery.

I was glad I wasn't driving.

My phone buzzed with a text message from Milton.

Dinner 2morrow? Morels?

Was I ready to lay my heart on the line again? Did I dare?

My phoned buzzed again.

Don't overthink this. Just say yes.

I took a deep breath. I punched in a reply. I hit send. It was out of my hands now.

"Any college news?" Dad asked out of the blue. "Seems like you should be hearing from some places about now."

Stalling for time, I cleared my throat and coughed. Well. It wasn't like there was going to be a good time to let him down. "I've figured out where I want to go," I said. "You know that school down in Olympia? Evergreen?"

"The hippie place?" Dad's voice rose hysterically.

"You should be thrilled. It's . . . affordable. And close."

"What, exactly, will this so-called bargain prepare you to do with your life? Wait tables? Work retail? Make espresso?"

"Kids do that stuff when they're trying to figure things out," my brother offered.

Dad ignored him.

We were paralleling the course of the Nooksack River. The river, coffee brown and running high, burbled like a witch's cauldron.

"Dad." I bit my lip. "Wake up. As you yourself love to tell me—I'm not Ivy League material. I've finally made my peace with this fact, and you should do the same. Just because I'm not going to a big-name school doesn't mean I'm going to get a crappy education. It doesn't mean I'm destined to be a big fat failure."

"Or even a skinny little failure," James Henry chimed in.

Dad swerved to avoid a branch. "I think this is maybe a conversation for another time. I need to concentrate on the road."

"You asked. There's nothing else to say. But you'd better get used to the idea of Evergreen. Because that's where I'm going." Slowly, I exhaled. I was shaking. But I was okay. I'd said what I'd needed to say.

"Have you even gotten in?" Dad asked coldly.

"Not yet. But I have a good feeling about it. And if I don't get in now, I'll go to a community college and then transfer. People do that. They do it all the time."

James Henry shifted around to stare at me.

What? I mouthed.

He grinned and gave me the thumbs-up.

It was dark by the time we got back to Mount Baker. Dad waited at the car while James Henry and I went to retrieve his snowboard. The resort—a day area—had cleared out completely. The snow was falling so hard that it had completely erased all evidence of the day's activity. The silence was both nice and a little creepy. We found the snowboard leaning against the lodge right where my brother had left it. Blanketed with snow, it made for a lone, ghostly form.

"That's where I saw you and Milton," James Henry pointed out. "It's going to be a long time before I get that visual out of my mind."

I tossed a snowball at him. "I'm not sure whether I should kill you or thank you."

"Oh, you don't want to kill me," he said. "I'm pretty useful."

"I guess I owe you one."

"Dude wouldn't shut up about you," he said, shaking his head. "I had to do something."

The weather was growing stranger by the second. The snow had morphed into this pelting ice that stung your face when it hit. It hissed upon impacting the ground.

Dad looked grim as we approached the Audi. He showed us how the entire exterior of the car was being covered with an icy glaze. "Bad news. We're having an honest to goodness ice storm. We need to get out of here pronto."

The mood was tense as we wound our way down the hairpin turns. In spite of Dad's turtlelike pace, the Audi fishtailed several times. The sky was dark and wet. It was hard to see much of anything.

From out of nowhere, a large branch appeared on the road. Dad hit the brakes. The wheels locked up. We went into a skid. The car was out of control. We were all just passengers now.

Time slowed.

I noticed that it was snowing again. I noticed that the needles of the evergreens were like tiny pinnacles of ice. I noticed the striations in the tree in front of us. Then everything went black as the air bags exploded.

"Everyone okay?" Dad shouted.

"Okay," James Henry said, his voice very small.

"Okay," I said, feeling very far away from my voice.

Steam rose from the hood of the Audi. There was a strange burning smell. My teeth chattered, partly from cold, mostly from shock. A short ways off, the river rushed over rocks and logs, a steady constant sound that slowed my racing pulse.

We got out of the Audi to look at the damage.

The ground was a sheet of ice. The entire front of the car was crunched around a giant hemlock. I traced my fingers over the scarred indentations of the tree. They came away sticky with sap.

"My car . . ." Dad kept saying.

"Is it still drivable?" I asked.

"I don't know. I don't know if the engine's okay. "

As he walked around to look at the other side, he slipped on the ice, hitting the ground with a sickening crunch. Then he let out a blood-curdling scream.

"Dad!" James Henry shouted.

Utterly removed from my body, too paralyzed to move, I just listened to the click clicking of the freezing rain, a sound that reminded me of falling dominoes.

"Charlotte!"

"Right." My heart going a mile a minute, I sprang into action. I gingerly scrambled over to my dad and knelt down beside him. His face was contorted with pain; he looked more animal than human.

"It's . . . my . . . hip," he gasped. "Call for—"

His eyes rolled back and his face went blank.

Simultaneously, James Henry and I grabbed for our cell phones. Neither had any reception. "This is my fault," my brother whispered. "I'm the reason we came back."

"Quiet," I hissed. "I need to think."

For all the urgency of the situation, I somehow managed to notice the beauty of the night. The world was so peaceful draped in white. The air smelled super clean.

Focus, I thought.

I pressed my hands to my temples, trying to remember what little I knew about first aid. We'd done a unit on it once in Tallahassee—in the seventh grade.

I looked at Dad. His chest was rising up and down. He was breathing. That was something. I grabbed his wrist to feel for a pulse. It took me a minute to find it. When I finally did, I thought it seemed too fast and wobbly.

Stay calm. You have to stay calm.

"Okay," I said, trying to catch my breath. "Nobody's coming to get us and the temperature is dropping. He's not going to last long out here. Let's get him into the backseat."

James Henry looked at me sharply. "Then what? We don't even know if the car is drivable. And—"

"And what?"

"You can't really drive," he whispered. "You haven't even tried in months."

"That's not true," I said. "Milton let me drive his car. I still know the basics. I'm just not smooth. But we'll be going downhill. That will help."

"What do you know about driving on ice?"

"Nothing," I snapped. "But do you have a better idea?"

He shook his head.

Together we dragged our dad to the backseat. He slid easily over the ice. Getting him into the car proved a more difficult feat. I crawled inside and grabbed him under the arms. James Henry supported him around the hips. It was a good thing, probably, that Dad was passed out. Lifting a two-hundred-pound man was no easy job. I pulled and pulled while James Henry lifted. Somehow, miraculously, we got him in.

As I slid into the driver's seat, I said a quick prayer. *Please.* Then, with a deep breath, I turned the key in the ignition. The car started. Thank God. But when I put it into reverse, the wheels squealed loudly—spinning in place.

We were stuck.

"Let's see if we can dig out the wheels," I said. "We can use your snowboard like a shovel."

We got out. We dug.

I tried to reverse the car again.

It budged a couple of inches. Then, same thing. The tires spun in place. I stared out at the darkness, shivering. "I don't know what to do."

James Henry's eyes grew wide with fear. Neither of us said anything.

Was this the end of the road for our dad? With the temperature dropping by the second, and our clothes wet from the day, the night could prove deadly for us all.

James Henry snapped his fingers. "Traction. We need traction."

"Huh?"

"Help me," he said, jumping out of the car.

He searched around a moment then started tearing off branches from trees and bushes. These he piled behind the tires. "The wheels can grip on to this stuff," he said. "Much better than they can to the snow."

Together we worked to create a mini ramp.

One more time, I got behind the wheel and started the car. James Henry waited outside to direct me.

Please, I prayed again. *Please.*

The car rolled backward. James Henry waved me on. Somehow I reversed onto the road without lurching. "Nice job," my brother said, hopping back into the car. I found the sweet spot and shifted into first gear. We were on our way.

The road was even more treacherous than I'd imagined—as twisted as a coiled snake and every bit as deadly. Though I didn't look, I felt the airiness of each drop-off we slid past. The trees—weighted down by snow—leaned over the road, creating a weird tunnel-like effect. Icy clumps plummeted from their branches and hit the hood. The fragments skittered off as slippery as mercury beads.

I was scared. As scared as I'd ever been of public speaking. As scared as I'd been on my acid trip. This time, though, the dangers were real. And I couldn't hide in a closet. I prayed another car would appear. But this was a dead-end road and nobody had any business with the ski resort this time of night.

In spite of the defrost being on high, the car kept fogging up. Hunched over the wheel, my knuckles white, I navigated through one shrinking circle of clear glass. James Henry tried to help out by wiping the windshield down with his sleeve.

Dad drifted in and out of consciousness. He was moaning a lot. I shook my head. This was crazy—me doing this when I barely knew how to drive. It was all so very surreal. Acid had nothing on a real-life crisis. No doubt I would have found the situation comical . . . if it hadn't been so deadly serious.

The wipers began to ice up. They scraped over the glass with a strange shuddering sound and failed to remove any moisture. But even if I wanted to, I couldn't stop the Audi now. The hill was just too steep and slick. My eyes burned from staring at the snow-blanketed windshield. I would kill us all before the night was through.

"I have an idea," James Henry said suddenly.

He dug around in the backseat and retrieved the ice scraper. Next, he unfastened his seat belt, rolled down his window, and climbed up on the ledge of the door.

"What are you doing?" I shouted. "I don't need you dead!"

"Just keep the car from crashing, okay? If you start to slide, remember that you're supposed to turn the wheel in the direction of the skid."

"How would you know that?"

"It just came to me. Remember—I read your driver's handbook."

I gave him a quick glance. With one hand holding the roof for balance, he leaned out over the windshield to scrape the ice. He looked like some crazy snow elf. But for the moment, his method seemed to be working.

My arms shook from the effort of steering the Audi. Sweat pooled beneath my armpits. I was reaching some kind of exhaustion point. To keep myself going, I conjured up an imaginary stadium full of people.

"Go, Charlotte," they shouted. "You can do this!"

Off to the left, the Nooksack River flashed silver in the darkness. I could hear the water rolling over stones and logs, a powerful but steady sound. I pretended it was the roar of the crowd.

It had stopped snowing. The clouds were starting to break. There were even a few stars dappling the night sky like tiny drops of spilled paint. The silhouettes of the mountains, so deep and dark, were like black holes with their utter absence of light.

Black holes. I knew something about black holes. Amanda.

Neal. Debate. Acid. Senior year. Shady Grove. My dad. I was the biggest black hole of them all. Or I had been, at least, because that's how I'd seen myself. That's how I'd seen myself before Milton came along that day in the woods. Sometimes it takes another person to help you see yourself. Sometimes it takes a mushroom boy.

According to Albert Einstein's general theory of relativity, a black hole is a region of space from which nothing, including light, can escape. Albert Einstein. A brilliant mathematician. The world's most beloved genius. But Einstein was wrong about one thing. You *could* escape a black hole. It wasn't easy. It defied the laws of gravity. It defied the laws of mathematics. But it was possible. Just barely. I was the proof.

James Henry scraped. I steered. Somehow, the miles passed.

Dad was fully conscious now and swearing with great gusto. My brother rapped on the windshield. "I see lights! There's a tavern up ahead."

Someone waved to me from the finish line. If I squinted just right, I could see that she looked exactly like me.

EPILOGUE

Some notes from my senior year:

1) It takes a long time for a broken hip to heal.
2) Nothing hurts worse than a broken heart.
3) The body has an amazing capacity to mend itself.
4) Most adults fear public speaking more than death.
5) Milton Zacharias is a damn good cook and kisser.
6) Morels (sautéed in garlic and butter) taste like sunshine.
7) My brother is one cool kid—even if he is a genius.
8) *The Sexy Victorians* is coming soon to bookstores everywhere.
9) Evergreen State College gives evaluations—not grades.
10) Some people get to glide through life.
11) No one is truly invincible.
12) Hot-pink hair is *so* last year.

ACKNOWLEDGMENTS

This book exists because of the many people who have loved and encouraged me over the years.

Sara Crowe—thank you for taking a chance on me and for being the best super-agent lady in the world. In the very best of ways, you are a true "girl wonder." To Emily Schultz—thank you for your friendship, your brilliance, and for understanding Charlotte even better than I understood her myself. The Disney-Hyperion team has been tireless in their devotion to this book. Thank you especially Catherine Onder, for always being so graceful, intelligent, and professional.

Thank you Susan Cheever, Bob Shacochis, George Packer, and the late Lucy Grealy for taking me seriously when I was a graduate student at the Bennington Writing Seminars.

The Olympia Trail Runners, Route 16 Running & Walking, and Girls Night Running gave my mind and body a much-needed outlet, while the great women of Catherine Place helped to tutor my soul.

Brian and Dayna Martin have both been tremendous spiritual mentors, as have their amazing children (one of whom prayed very hard at the tender age of six that his auntie's book would be published).

For reading early drafts and for their friendship, I am deeply indebted to Dj Knight, Laura Klasner, Meg Bommarito, Michele Perrin Roberts, Lisabeth Kirk, Shannon Aguilar Carson, Jaimie Shaver Smith, Holly Knowles, Stacey Schulte, and Stephen Duncan. A special thanks to Terry, Kay, and Susie Pruit. You will always be family in my heart.

Thank you to all my extraordinary writing sisters, especially Lindsey Leavitt, Kristen Tracy, Peggy Payne, Audrey Young Crissman, Suzanne Young, and Lisa Schroeder.

For pulling me through the darkest and toughest hours of 2009/2010, a loud shout-out goes to Brenda Nipp, Kim Mosher, Kim Webb, Lindsay Bullis, Erin Walker, Rachel Boyd, Amelia Tockston, and most especially to my uncle Harry Branch, the best guard dog a girl could ever have.

Two people deserve an entire book of homage. My brother David Martin (a.k.a. "slasher" for his editing style) helped me to find my voice and my writing form, taught me about this little thing called "plot," and helped me turn a glimmer of an idea into an entire book. It's your turn now to cross the finish line, bro. Louise Parsons was the one who first urged me to write for teenagers. Her friendship has been one of the greatest sustaining forces of my life—as has her jewelry! Who knew guardian angels came with such kick-ass fashion sense and thick Southern accents?

Lastly, I would like to thank the strangers who took me at my word in the early days of my writing career and assured me that I would make it if I followed my dream. There is no doubt in my mind that the single greatest gift you can give another person is to believe in them.